Restoration Heights

A Novel

by MJ Stringer

RESTORATION HEIGHTS
First edition. December 28, 2024.
Copyright © 2024 All Rights Reserved.
MJ Stringer
Pure At Heart Romance

This is a work of fiction. Similarities to real people, places, or events are entirely coincidental. No part of this publication may be copied, reproduced, in any format, by any means, electronic or otherwise, without prior consent from the copyright owner and publisher of this book.

For my sons, who have brought purpose, love, joy and strength into my life.

Chapter 1

*I*t began as a way to get out of the house, take a break from the children, clear her head and relax. Katherine had frequently driven by Tiramisu, a quaint Italian restaurant in an upscale strip center, on the way to her daughter's gymnastics class. From the parking lot she could glimpse bright paintings of pasta dishes, wine glasses and funny Italian characters. The crystal chandeliers hung above tables covered in red linens topped with candles in Chianti bottles, wax dripping down the sides like icing. She imagined the cozy restaurant was owned by an Italian family that still used recipes passed down from generations. She had suggested to Nathan that they go together on their next date night. But, realizing a date night was not in Nathan's near future plans, she decided she'd just go without him.

Katherine announced she was taking Thursday night off for herself. It was so nice to get out of the house, just sit for a couple of hours, drink a glass of wine, eat a meal that was still warm. She enjoyed catching up with her girlfriends from school and hearing about their jobs and the exotic places they'd recently visited. For those two hours, she wasn't just "Mom". She could relax without being interrupted every five minutes.

One icy Thursday in January, Katherine's plan to meet Stacie, her college roommate, at Tiramisu fell through. She didn't want to give up her night off- she needed those two hours to unwind and reclaim a little piece of herself. Katherine felt extremely self conscious when she was first seated by herself at the small, corner table. She dreaded the other diners eyeing her with pity, but she quickly realized they were too engrossed in their own conversations to be concerned about her lack of a dinner companion. After a glass of wine, she found herself enjoying being a spectator to the hustle of the servers and taking in the diverse array of diners- some engaged in lively conversation and laughter, others engrossed in their phones or concentrating on twirling their pasta. At the end of the evening, Katherine felt more relaxed than she had in a long time.

Slowly Katherine's weekly night out became something else altogether. She realized she could be whoever she wanted in those short hours. No one at Tiramisu knew she felt like a failure as a wife and sometimes as a mother. That her house was sometimes so cluttered it looked as if she had twelve children instead of two. Or that most days were spent in old t-shirts and yoga pants that she sometimes even wore to bed.

On her weekly visit to Tiramisu she wore her nicest clothes, put on a full face of make-up, curled her hair, even dabbed on a little Chanel. On her second visit she decided to request the same waitress and was pleased to be sat at the same table in the corner next to the window. Her waitress, Sharon, was nice and friendly but not overly chatty, which was perfect. Katherine was left to read her novel in peace or sit quietly, observing the room, entertaining herself with little stories about the other diners- imagining couples on either horrid blind dates or romantic anniversaries. Or horrid anniversaries and romantic first dates.

Occasionally her table would be occupied and she would insist on waiting at the bar. She got to know the bartender, Nick, who would greet her by name and begin pouring her a glass of Pinot Grigio as she settled into the leather bar chair. He was an older gentleman and he reminded her a little bit of her father. She always felt comfortable chit chatting with him about the weather or the latest news.

Katherine's routine continued for almost two months until one late February evening; after she was seated at her table, Sharon did not come to take her order. In her place was a young man with wavy dark blonde hair and stunning green eyes. When Katherine inquired about her usual server, he politely told her that Sharon no longer worked there, that his name was Jonathan, and he would be taking care of her tonight.

At first Katherine was a little annoyed. She didn't really like the idea of being waited on by a male. She just wanted to relax and have the comfortable feeling of reliable Sharon, who already knew she liked extra olive oil with her bruschetta, that she always ordered the cheesecake for dessert, and a box for the half she didn't finish. She did not want to be constantly distracted by Jonathan's tanned muscular arm as he refilled her water glass or deal with the fluttery feeling in her stomach as he looked intently at her while he recited the nightly specials. But by the end of the evening and after a glass of wine, she felt her guard come down. Especially after he placed a piece of raspberry cheesecake in front of her and declared it was on him for putting up with his novice service.

"That really isn't necessary. I thought you did wonderfully," she found herself telling him with a smile.

"Well, thanks. I hope you'll ask for my table the next time you come in." He returned her smile, revealing a perfect set of white teeth.

"I will," she assured him and left a generous tip.

That evening as she drove home she couldn't stop smiling. She knew it was ridiculous, but she had loved the feeling of being on the receiving end of attention from a good-looking man. Well, to be honest, a boy. At least he looked like he was barely out of high school.

She couldn't recall the last time Nathan had made her feel genuinely interesting or attractive. Sometimes he barely even looked at her as they ate their dinner. That is when he actually made it home on time. He constantly had that distracted look that meant his head was still at the office. And she was usually too busy fussing over the children anyway.

Once dinner was over, she had the task of getting the children ready for bed. Get them upstairs and into the bath, which usually ended in a battle with Madison because she didn't want to wash her hair. Or Keenan might run around for several minutes, refusing to get into the tub at all. Then after making sure they brushed their teeth, she laid out their clothes for the next day while the children chose the books for their bedtime stories. By the time she made it through the second book, she was so tired she wanted to go to sleep herself.

But she couldn't go to sleep. She had to go back downstairs and deal with the dinner dishes. Then prepare the children's sack lunches for the following day. By this time, she was usually completely exhausted. Even if Nathan had been interested in having a meaningful conversation with her, or if he tried to entice her to go up to their room for something more meaningful, would she even want to?

She recalled the days when Nathan would help her with the children's bedtime routine. Sometimes they would do it together, or he would take Keenan into their bathroom while she took care of Madison in the children's bath. Then they would all pile on Nathan and Katherine's bed and read stories, talk, tickle and laugh. It had been so long since Nathan had been involved in much of anything other than sitting at the dinner table with them. As soon as dinner was over he quickly retired to his office or the living room, leaving Katherine to tend to the children alone.

The first time Katherine had mentioned to Nathan that she really missed him spending that time with them, he promised he would make it a priority on the weekends. When he began working on the Stonehaven house, he said that he really needed to devote as much time as possible to the project until it was completed. And then he started the Johnson project and declared that it was going to consume all of his waking hours. After that Katherine stopped asking.

The following Thursday Katherine found herself taking her time with her hair and make-up a little longer than usual. She had chosen to wear one of her favorite black cashmere sweaters with a low neckline, a hound's-tooth skirt and her knee length caramel boots.

She walked through the living room where Keenan and Madison were perched on the couch watching Veggie Tales, gave them both a kiss, and then made her way to Nathan's office. He was staring at his computer, his brow furrowed, his hair a rumpled mess.

"Hey, I'm taking off," she said from the doorway.

"Ok. Have fun," Nathan said in monotone.

"They need to be in bed by 8:30," Katherine reminded him.

"I know. I got it down, babe," he replied with irritation.

She waited a few more beats to see if he'd even look up at her, but he continued to stare at the monitor. She sighed, grabbed her purse and keys and headed out the door.

Chapter 2

Spring had come early to Austin, as was usually the case. It was barely the beginning of March when the first warm front came through. Lauren had watched the forecast earlier in the week and was delighted to see that the high would reach the mid 70's on Saturday. She and James had not been to the park in several weeks, so she made it a priority to work it into their already busy day. They both slept in until nine and then Lauren made blueberry pancakes and bacon for breakfast while James watched cartoons. After taking their time eating and cleaning the kitchen, they set out to run errands.

James needed new tennis shoes and pants. His size 6's were already beginning to look like high-waters and almost every pair had a hole in both of the knees. Plus he had been begging for the new Skechers that had "springs" in the heels which James was sure would give him the ability to jump as high as Shaquille O'Neal.

As Lauren watched James spring around the shoe store in his new bright blue and yellow tennis shoes, she found herself marveling at how quickly he was growing up. It seemed that the past six years had gone by so quickly she could barely recall when James had stopped being a toddler. He no longer had the soft chubbiness of baby fat, and his voice and mannerisms now took on the qualities of the maturity of a young boy.

Even though James' baby years contained some of the most precious times of her life, she was always grateful that those days were behind her. She had never imagined how difficult being a single mother could be, especially of a newborn. Her mother had come down from Dallas and moved in with Lauren for the first two months after James was born. If it were not for that, Lauren was sure she would have never survived the difficult days and nights of caring for a newborn on her own.

Lauren had been scared and exhausted, and even though she had read several books on caring for an infant she still felt like she had no idea what she was doing. Her mother showed her how to bathe and diaper him; advised her to heat up his bottles in a pan of warm water as opposed to using the microwave. She taught Lauren how to wrap him securely in a blanket before setting him in the crib for his naps. She also spent many nights cuddling and rocking James when he was fussy and refusing to sleep, so that Lauren could get some extra rest.

When Lauren's maternity leave from her job as a third grade teacher came to an end, her sister-in-law Katherine offered to care for James while Lauren was at work. Lauren had been very fond of Katherine when her brother first introduced them, and she was thrilled when Nathan announced they were getting married. However, it wasn't until after James was born that they really connected, having the common bond of motherhood. The two became sisters and best friends, taking turns babysitting for one another, going out for girl's nights, and confiding in one another about everything. Since Katherine had already quit her job after her and Nathan's daughter was born, she was more than happy to help Lauren by watching James during the school week. Her sister-in-law also appreciated earning a little extra spending money since Nathan constantly had them on a tight budget.

"Mom! Can we go to see Madison and Keenan now?" James' voice broke into her reverie.

"Yes, let's get going." Lauren took James' little hand in hers and they left the store, James springing happily along next to her.

Lauren drove the short drive to Nathan and Katherine's house, which was in a well-established suburb with oak tree lined streets and houses built in the 1950's. The light blue two-story Victorian had been remodeled with a hint of contemporary design that Nathan boasted was his specialty. The yard was impeccable with flower beds filled with Hydrangeas, Blue Hyacinth, and Pink Autumn Sage. That was Katherine's specialty.

Katherine greeted them at the door with potholders on her hands. She was always making some type of casserole.

"Hi!" Katherine smiled, drawing her friend and sister-in-law into a hug. She gave James' head a little pat with the paisley covered potholder. "I hope you're hungry, James."

"Oh, I'm always hungry!" James exclaimed with a huge smile.

After enjoying Katherine's homemade chicken enchiladas, the kids ran around the backyard while Lauren and Katherine relaxed on the patio in comfy lounge chairs and caught up.

"Since when does he work on Saturdays?" Lauren asked about her brother after Katherine lamented that Nathan had been at the office since earlier that morning.

"Since the past couple of months. He's pretty stressed out about the Johnson's house," Katherine said with a sigh. The Johnson's house plans had become a nightmare for Nathan. The wife was constantly changing her mind on minor details and the husband pretty much let her run the show. With all of the changes and the time delays it was looking as if he would barely make a profit.

"He told me about it. It sounds awful," Lauren said recalling the conversation she had with her brother last week when he had stopped by to help her assemble the new bookcase she had bought. He had been so preoccupied he had barely even talked to Lauren as he concentrated on bolting the shelves into place. When she questioned him, he had grunted out a few sentences about how the Johnson house was causing him to work overtime and something about Katherine spending money quicker than he could earn it.

Lauren hated seeing her brother so stressed out. She had brought him a beer, which he gratefully accepted, then silently returned to his work on the shelf. But, before he left he asked that she not mention his comment about the overspending to Katherine.

"He's constantly in a bad mood these days. We hardly ever talk anymore." Katherine shook her head as she watched Madison pick a dandelion from the grass.

"He was real quiet when he came over last week," Lauren said, then called out to her son, "Stop throwing sand, James!"

"You too, Keenan. If you can't keep the sand in the sandbox, you boys will have to come inside," Katherine said sternly.

Madison came over and presented her aunt with the dandelion.

"Thank you, sweetheart." Lauren took the sad, wilted flower in her hand and acted as if it were the most exquisite gift.

"Coffee?" Katherine smiled and stood up.

"Sounds great." Lauren followed her inside. "I noticed you haven't asked me to sit for you in a while. No date nights for you two?"

"Not lately. But you know I've started taking my own date night." Katherine took two mugs down from the cupboard and poured coffee into them.

"What do you mean?"

"Every Thursday night I go out to dinner by myself. It gives me time to just enjoy some quiet time and a meal where I can actually eat my dinner before it gets cold." Katherine grinned as she poured cream and sugar into both mugs.

"So, you don't feel weird eating alone?" Lauren asked as they took their coffees into the den.

Katherine smiled. "Not at all. I love the quiet. Sometimes I bring a book or just people watch. Plus I discovered this great little Italian place in the Wild Oak neighborhood. It's just this cozy little place with awesome Chicken Picatta and real cheesecake."

"That sounds so good. If I ever decide to accept one of Jake's invitations to dinner I'll make him take me there."

"He's still asking? I'd have thought he'd given up by now. Poor guy." Katherine frowned.

"Oh, don't feel sorry for him. He's getting plenty of dates from the other single teachers at my school. He's definitely not lonely. And I'm just not sure I could handle dating such a jock. I don't know anything about sports."

"I know. I know," Katherine said, holding up her hand. "You've said it all before. I just think it'd be nice for you to get out of the house and get back into the swing of dating. Just consider it practice. Plus it would be a great excuse to have a delicious meal at Tiramisu."

"Well, when you put it that way.... I might. We'll see." Lauren laughed, trying to picture herself on a date with Jake, the handsome P.E. coach at her school, who was well known to be quite the ladies' man.

After another cup of coffee and thirty more minutes of chatting, Lauren and James said their goodbyes, got back into the car and headed for the park. She had decided to go to the park near Nathan and Katherine's neighborhood that ran along a small creek. It had jogging trails that ran parallel to the creek, with a nice grassy area in front of the playground and plenty of shady trees.

Lauren laid out a blanket and read a novel while James played on the playscape, chasing around with the other kids. As the sun began to settle lower in the sky, the other kids began to trickle out and James asked his mom if she would kick the ball with him. They kicked his worn soccer ball back and forth easily for a while, enjoying the coolness of the air as dusk settled around them. Then just after Lauren had given him the 'five more minutes' signal, James put a little too much into it and the ball went rolling over to the jogger's path.

James ran after the ball, but it had met the path of a male jogger and he had already scooped it up. As James made his way up to him, the man held it out for him kindly. Lauren was about to shout out a Thank You! when she looked up and realized she recognized the man all too well. Her hand flew to her mouth in surprise and she averted her gaze back to James as he walked back towards his mother. She kept her eyes on James and silently prayed that the man wouldn't look at her and just get back to his jog.

"Lauren?" The familiar voice questioned as he made his way towards her. She looked up and sure enough she found herself face to face with the one man she had hoped to never see again. Daniel.

James' father.

Lauren had not seen him in almost seven years. She had privately kept tabs on him, occasionally googling him and finding out that he still lived in Austin. Five years ago she saw the article covering the ribbon cutting ceremony for his real estate brokerage firm. Since the firm location was downtown and she figured he still lived in that area, she had never run into him. It seemed today her luck had run out. He was standing right in front of her with that same old mischievous grin, the one that had initially drawn her in, but eventually she came to loathe. He had his hands on his hips and he was still breathing heavily from his run.

"Lauren." He stated her name this time and just stood there shaking his head in amused disbelief.

"Hi Daniel." Lauren managed a small smile, which probably looked more like a grimace.

"Wow. It's good to see you. You look great." He crossed his arms over his chest as he looked her up and down.

"Thanks," Lauren barely managed to say as her mind churned with various quick escape plans.

"Mo-om. Who is that?" James' little boy voice broke into her thoughts of turning and running for the car, and she faltered for words.

"This is, um, an old friend of mine. Daniel."

"I'm James. Nice to meet you." James was already stretching his little hand toward Daniel. Lauren cringed. Of all the times for him to decide to practice his manners.

"Hi, James. It's nice to meet you too." Daniel shook his hand in mock seriousness and smiled warmly. But Lauren noticed his slight frown as his smile faded, and Daniel stared at the boy. His eyes stayed on James as he asked Lauren, "So... are you married?"

"No. I'm... uh... a single mom." She tried her best to say it casually and then before he could say anything she quickly shot back, "Are you married?"

"Ahhh... no." Daniel shook his head, his face an expression Lauren couldn't really read. But he didn't waste any time turning the table back to her. "So, you're divorced?"

He sure is nosy! Lauren tried to come up with something to say.

"Hey, Mom. I'm starving. What's for dinner?" James interjected, pulling at her arm, and Lauren had never been so grateful for his quick return to his usual lack of etiquette.

"That's a good question, James. It is getting pretty late. We better get going." She turned away as she gave Daniel a wave of her hand. "But it was really good to run into you, Daniel."

"Yeah, yeah. It was...." Daniel said distractedly and then took a few steps toward her. "Hey! Maybe we could meet for coffee sometime. Catch up some more."

"Oh, I don't know. I'm pretty busy right now. With work... and you know...stuff," she stammered as she picked up her blanket. She busied herself with flipping it out and folding it, hoping that Daniel was getting back to his jog. But when she looked up, her eyes and face scrunched with dread, he was still standing in the same spot. She saw him studying James again as if he were trying to solve a puzzle. She quickly said again, "It was good to see you."

"Yeah, you said that," Daniel said, smirking a little.

"Right." Lauren laughed nervously as she shoved the blanket under one arm and grabbed her book from the ground, then began leading James toward the parking lot. She turned back with another feeble wave as Daniel remained grounded, arms still crossed, his face twisted into a confused frown, watching them leave.

Chapter 3

Once settled at her table, her wool coat and caramel handbag neatly piled on the seat next to her, she began to feel nervous. *This is ridiculous*, Katherine thought, chiding herself for acting like a schoolgirl with a crush. *I'm here to relax and enjoy an evening to myself, not to be all flirty with some boy who's probably a decade younger than me.*

Katherine was just placing her napkin in her lap when a woman with dark hair pulled into a tight bun appeared at her side and asked for her drink order. Katherine recognized her as one of the other waitresses she'd seen at Tiramisu before and asked for her usual glass of wine. As soon as the waitress turned to leave, Katherine felt an unnerving feeling of disappointment. She began to wonder if Jonathan didn't work out and was already let go.

She immediately felt silly for the extra fuss she had given to her appearance and the butterflies she had experienced throughout the day as she looked forward to seeing him tonight. *Well, it's definitely for the best*, she told herself, finally admitting that the last thing she needed was to have the hots for some waiter.

Katherine pulled out her phone and looked at her email inbox. Becca Thompson reminded her that the March PTA meeting was coming up next week, and "Did anyone have extra time in the mornings to work on the sets for the spring play??" Margaret Keller from Keenan's playgroup wanted to know if Katherine could host the next playgroup at her home and "we would be so grateful if you could whip up a batch of your famous lemon bars!!" A friendly reminder from Greystone Auto & Detail that her van was due for an oil change. Madison's school principal announcing yet another fundraiser, where Katherine would be coerced into asking every family member and close friend to donate so that Madison's class would win a pizza party. Katherine sighed and put her phone back in her bag. Always so much to do, and she was beginning to feel increasingly alone in managing the details of running their household.

"Good evening. It's good to see you again, Katherine." A deep voice cut into her thoughts, and she found herself looking into those impossibly gorgeous green eyes.

"Good evening, uh... " Katherine said, her voice cracking a bit. She cleared her throat and fussed with her napkin, as he sat her glass of wine in front of her.

"Jonathan." He unnecessarily reminded her of his name. "Are you keeping warm enough tonight?"

"Yes, thank you Jonathan." Katherine felt her cheeks grow warm under his gaze.

"Will you be having the salmon again tonight?" he asked her with a wink.

"Yes," Katherine said, continuing to let herself be dazzled by those emerald eyes. But she then quickly changed her mind. "Wait... no. Actually I think I'll have the, uh, spinach cannelloni."

"Excellent choice." Jonathan smiled and walked away.

She had no idea why, but she didn't like the idea of him presuming that she was so predictable. She recalled the early days of her marriage and how Nathan had always insisted on ordering for her, as if he would know better than her what she preferred to eat. She realized that he seemed determined to dominate all of the decision making when it came to their relationship. For years she had appreciated the easy way he took charge of matters, whether big or small. She could sit back and relax and let him steer the ship. However, slowly over the course of the past few months she had begun to resent his constant need to control everything. He even occasionally called her in the middle of the day to suggest what she made for dinner that night.

Her thoughts were interrupted by Jonathan leaning over to set down her bruschetta and olive oil. When she looked up at him, he was grinning as he studied her. She realized she had been frowning when he walked up to her table. "That looked like some heavy duty thinking."

Katherine felt her cheeks flush and she just smiled and looked down at the table. She expected him to walk away so that she could tuck into her bread, but instead he bent down onto one knee so that he was at eye level with her.

"You know, I used to be a bartender," Jonathan said with another wink.

Katherine just stared at him blankly, not sure how to respond.

"I mean, if you need to unload, I'm good at listening," he clarified with a warm smile.

Understanding his connotation Katherine laughed and shook her head. "Well, thank you very much for the offer. But it's really not that interesting." She paused for a moment, then for no apparent reason, she found herself saying, "I was just thinking about work."

"Oh, yeah? And what is it that you do? Brain surgery?"

Katherine laughed again and took a sip of her wine to give her a moment to figure out what her answer would be. And in a few seconds, she decided she would invent a completely different life for herself. After all, this was her night to escape from reality. So, why bore this boy with details of laundry piling up and cleaning up spilled juice?

"I'm a marketing executive for a company in Dallas." The lie rolled off her tongue easily. "I'm just here during the week to work for a client in Austin."

"Ah... That explains why such an attractive lady is dining alone. I've been losing sleep at night trying to figure that one out," Jonathan said, obviously quite comfortable flirting with her. Katherine blushed at the thought of him thinking about her late at night, lying in bed.

Over the course of the next hour, as Jonathan brought her salad and entrée, refilled her water and her wine glass, he asked her questions about her job and what it was like to commute between the two cities. Katherine was a little surprised that it was so easy to just make it up as she went. She had thoroughly enjoyed playing the role of a young single professional. She often wondered what her life would have been like if she hadn't met Nathan and gotten married right out of college and started a family so soon.

The restaurant was slow that night and as his other customers left, Jonathan spent more time lingering at her table, bending down on one knee, getting a little closer each time. She could smell his cologne, and see the specks of gold in his green eyes. With a pang of guilt, Katherine found herself making sure to keep her left hand under the table so that he wouldn't see her wedding ring. Even though he had revealed that he was a student at the University of Austin, probably making him at least eight or nine years younger than she was, Katherine couldn't help just letting herself bask in his obvious interest.

As she drove home that evening, she found herself taking a longer route than necessary. She turned up the radio, rolled down the windows and let herself replay the evening in her mind. She hadn't felt so charged in a long time. Not only from the thrill of pretending to be someone entirely different; but also because of how Jonathan made her feel. Young, interesting, attractive. When she got home, she didn't even get angry that there were still dishes in the sink from dinner and toys scattered across the living room floor. And it didn't sting as bad when she walked past Nathan's office and announced, "I'm home," only to have him give her a curt wave without even turning to glance her way.

Chapter 4

*N*ot even a week went by before the call came. Lauren was cooking dinner while James played in the backyard, throwing a ball for their Great Dane, Burley. She was distracted as the chicken started popping in the pan and the pasta water began boiling over, so that she didn't even check the caller ID. But when she heard his voice on the other end she wasn't surprised at all.

"Lauren. It's Daniel." He sounded weary as if he'd been struggling with whether or not to make the call.

"Hey Daniel. So weird running into you the other day." Lauren tried to keep her voice casual, as her heart rate picked up. She waited a second, heard him sigh and then the words she knew were coming, but still startled her that he got down to business so quickly.

"So, how old is James? I'm just going to take a wild guess - seven?" Daniel asked.

"Um, yes, almost." Lauren tried to keep the irritation from her tone.

"So, who's his father?" he asked boldly, startling her again with his bluntness.

"Daniel, that is none of your business," Lauren announced with barely any conviction.

"He's mine, isn't he?" His voice was much lower now, but there was no mistaking what he'd asked.

"What?" Lauren said to buy time, wincing as she tried her best to breathe steadily.

"Is it just a coincidence that you gave him my middle name?"

"Look, Daniel, this isn't the best time for me. I'm in the middle of cooking dinner and it's about to burn." Lauren was tempted to just hang up the phone, but knew that wouldn't help matters.

"I'm not a fool, Lauren. He looks just like me."

"I can't really talk about it right now," she told him as James came noisily through the back door yelling for Burley to follow him.

"Ok, well, when is a good time? Because we're going to talk about this," Daniel insisted.

"Mo-om. Who are you talking to? I'm starving!" James interjected loudly.

"Can I call you back after I get James to bed?" Lauren asked. "It'll be sometime after 8:30."

Another loud sigh from Daniel and then, "Yeah, sure."

The phone clicked off and Lauren continued to hold it to her ear, staring at James realizing their simple, tidy life she had grown so comfortable with was about to change.

Lauren barely made it through dinner, James' bath and story time. She tried to keep up the usual cheery banter with James while the wheels of her mind churned with anxious thoughts of the conversation that lay ahead with Daniel. Even more unsettling was the realization that she was soon going to have an even more difficult conversation with James.

When James was old enough to ask, she told him that his father lived far away and though he loved James very much, he was busy with his work and couldn't come for a visit. As James got older he began pressing her with further questions, such as where this faraway place and what did he do that kept him so busy. So she

finally told him that he was in Africa taking care of an endangered tribe of elephants. This story fascinated him and placated him at the same time. Although Lauren felt guilty for lying, she believed she was ultimately protecting James from a man that wouldn't want to be a part of their life anyway.

After two extra stories, James was finally asleep at 8:45. Lauren picked up the phone several times, pulling up the last incoming number, her finger trembling over the send button, but she hung it up each time. Giving up, she slammed the phone down, poured herself a glass of iced tea and took it out onto the patio. She sipped the sweet tea, listening to the crickets and the cool breeze rustling the leaves in the trees that surrounded their fence line. She had almost completely convinced herself that this day would never come. That she and James were safe in their own little world. Of course she was constantly bombarded with the guilt of James not knowing his father, but she had finally absolved herself by her strong belief that Daniel could care less and that even if she had told him he would have wanted nothing to do with James.

Daniel had always complained about noisy, whiny children in restaurants or the movie theatre when they had been dating. The one time she dared to ask him if he ever wanted children, his reaction was so concrete. He didn't want the complications; he wanted to have the freedom to travel and be able to go out spontaneously. So, she never even considered telling Daniel when she found out she was almost nine weeks pregnant. Even when her family insisted it was the right thing to do, especially after James was born, she held steadfast that she was doing the right thing. Daniel had made it obvious that he had already moved on with that little bimbo. It still angered her when she relived the humiliation she felt when Kelly answered the door to his apartment, so smug that she had taken Lauren's place so quickly. They weren't even officially broken up! Daniel had said he just needed some space. Space to get closer to Kelly.

Lauren finished her tea, went back inside and was just rinsing out her glass when the doorbell rang. She glanced at the clock, wondering who would come by the house so late.

She opened the door and found herself eye-to-eye with a very annoyed, but annoyingly handsome Daniel. He was in business attire, but his shirt was untucked and slightly wrinkled. His dark hair was disheveled as if he'd been running his hand through it over and over, something Lauren remembered him doing whenever frustrated.

"What are you doing here?" Lauren blurted out, equally frustrated at his surprise visit.

"You said you would call me back. I got tired of waiting."

"How did you know where I live?" She asked.

"They call it the Internet," he replied dryly and peered over her shoulder. "I take it he's asleep."

"Yes, but I really don't appreciate you just coming over like this. It's late."

"Look, Lauren. We can either do this the easy way or the hard way. Just answer my question. Is he my son?"

Lauren stared at him for a few seconds, then warily waved him in. She closed the door and led him to the living room. She sat down on the sofa and he sat opposite her in one of the armchairs.

"I'm just going to go ahead and assume your silence is confirmation. So, let me move on to my next question. Why the hell didn't you tell me?" Daniel had raised his voice on the last sentence and Lauren immediately shushed him, looking nervously over her shoulder towards James' bedroom.

"Daniel." Lauren took a deep breath before continuing in a matter-of-fact tone. "You made it pretty clear the type of guy you were when things ended between us. Not to mention the way you made it clear that you never wanted anything to do with children."

"The 'type of guy' I was? I don't even know what that means, but I sure as hell don't see how that gives you the right to hide the fact that I have a son? You could have at least had the decency to let me know."

"Why in the world would I even think for a second that you would have cared? You had already moved on with your blond bimbo."

"Who are you talking about?" Daniel asked in irritation.

"Kelly? Remember? Or didn't she even tell you I stopped by that night? She said you were 'busy' and that she would let you know I came by. But let me guess...I'm sure you two were too 'busy' to have that conversation," Lauren said, putting disgusted emphasis on the word busy both times.

Daniel looked at Lauren with confusion and frustration. He stood up and began pacing in front of the fireplace. "I don't know what you're talking about, but there was never anything going on between me and Kelly. We were business associates, that's all."

"Well, she seemed pretty cozy in your apartment that night," Lauren pointed out. "Which, by the way, isn't exactly the most appropriate place to be conducting business."

"This is ridiculous. You're completely avoiding the real issue here." Daniel stopped pacing and flopped back down into the chair. "Whatever you thought was going on with Kelly... you were wrong."

"Well, what did you expect me to believe after the fight we had? You told me that you needed space and that I was getting in the way of your career goals. Or did you forget that part?"

"No, of course not. I was young and trying to focus on growing my business. I just felt like I needed room to breathe." Daniel slapped his hand to his forehead and looked intently at Lauren. "Why do we have to rehash all this? You're totally sidestepping the big issue here. We have a son together and you never once thought that it might be the right thing to tell me?"

"That is so unfair. I have struggled with that decision over and over. But I decided not to tell you because I didn't think you would care. And I could not have handled that kind of rejection. Not just of me, but of my child. Our child." She barely whispered the last two words.

"We're back to the same thing - that wasn't your decision to make. It was mine and you didn't even give me a chance." Daniel sat back down and eyed the pictures of James on the coffee table. He picked one up and just stared at it for a few minutes. Setting the picture back on the table, he glanced at his watch and sighed. "I have a meeting with my lawyer tomorrow. After I talk things over with him I'll get back in touch with you."

"Wait. Why do you need to talk to your lawyer?" Lauren asked him with concern.

"Why do you think? I want to be involved in my son's life. And you've made it obvious that I can't trust you."

"Trust *me*? I'm not the one with reliability issues. What is it you think I'm going to do? Run off and take James so you can't see him?"

"Well, you've pretty much already done that for the past seven years." Daniel stood to his feet and glared at her. "Like I said, I want to be in his life, but I need to know what my rights are, so I'm going to let you know what we figure out."

Lauren just stared at him for a few minutes, trying to process everything. She took a deep breath and let it out slowly. "Look, I don't intend to keep you from getting to know James. But you need to understand that you can't just barge in on him and say 'Hey, I'm your father.' We need to take this slowly."

"You've already had the past seven years on your terms. Now, we're going to do things my way." Daniel strode toward the front door, put his hand on the door handle and turned to face her. "I don't have to tell him who I am right away, but I don't want to waste any more time. After I talk to my lawyer I intend to start spending time with him."

"Daniel, I've already said I'm not trying to stop you. I understand you're angry with me. But please try to see it from my side. I was only trying to protect James."

"You didn't protect him. You denied him. And me." Daniel pulled open the door and let himself out. "I'll be in touch."

Lauren watched him walk down the pathway to his silver BMW parked in her driveway and once he had slammed his car door and backed out onto the street, she closed the door, locked it and slid down to the floor, letting the tears fall.

Chapter 5

Katherine was only five months away from graduating with a degree in education when she met Nathan at Southwestern University. The sun was shining through the scarce clouds in early December, warming the cool air to a temperature worthy of shorts and sweatshirts, as Katherine stood at the top of the expansive stairs leading up to the library. She was passing out flyers for a fundraiser to help the animal shelter raise funds and adopt out the ever-growing population of homeless dogs. As Nathan ran up the steps, late for a group study session, he practically knocked Katherine over. He had his cell phone pressed to his ear, his father at the other end lecturing him on the importance of planning ahead. Katherine stumbled a bit, but kept her balance by grabbing onto Nathan's arm.

Laughing she had good-naturedly scolded him "Slow down, Flash!" She then plucked his phone from his hand and waved it around, "You really should just concentrate on one task at a time."

Nathan, distracted by Katherine's blue eyes, twinkling with mischief under a sheath of strawberry blond bangs, forgot that his father was on the line. She handed him the flier with the information to play with a dog for an hour, then drink "free" beer for a donation of $50 to the shelter. "It's a very worthy cause," she told him.

"Will you be there?" he asked and she nodded her head.

"Ok then. I'm in." He grinned as she handed his phone back.

Nathan showed up to the Paws & Beer fundraiser at the last minute as Katherine was corralling the dogs back into their crates. When Katherine saw him walking across the grass toward the tented area, she gave him a raised eyebrow as she looked pointedly at her watch. He told her he had been working on an architecture class project for building a homeless shelter, figuring he could appeal to her obvious philanthropic side. Even though she had a feeling he made it up, she let it go because he was looking incredibly gorgeous in a light green polo that accented his light brown hair and hazel eyes.

Nathan was eager to play with the one year old German Shepherd/Collie mix that had quickly become Katherine's favorite. Then after writing a check and enjoying his bottle of Shiner Bock, he asked her if she would like to spend the evening with him. Katherine had been tempted to accept his offer as she watched him running around, his muscular arms taut as he tried to keep Queenie from running after a squirrel darting up into a tree. He was a tall drink of water, but she knew she could not afford to get distracted.

Katherine sighed as she scooped up the dirty clothes from the floor of their closet. As she carried them downstairs to the laundry room, she once again wondered how different her life would be if she and Nathan hadn't gotten married so young.

For as long as she could recall she wanted to teach elementary school. She loved the idea of having the structured days, writing up lesson plans on the weekends and having her summers off. She had planned to use that time to travel and see a different part of the world each year. In her mental timeline she saw herself finding the perfect teaching job after graduation. She would take her time to find the right guy to marry. Then wait a few more years before having children, so that she could travel with her husband as well.

She hadn't dated anyone seriously since she parted ways with her high school sweetheart the summer before she left for university. Even though her young heart was tender with the pain of her first break-up, she had enjoyed the freedom of being single. She pledged a sorority, volunteered at the local animal shelter, and went on casual dates here and there. All the while, dedicating plenty of time to her studies and maintaining her 3.5 GPA. She was focused and determined to stay on track for the future that she had envisioned for herself, until the day she met Nathan Montgomery.

Chapter 6

*L*auren usually loved Fridays. The students seemed to be more energetic and easier to please. The teachers were in a good mood knowing only a few more hours separated them from the weekend. Even the principal tended to smile more and sometimes hum happy tunes as she made her way through the hallways. But this Friday Lauren felt a grey cloud over her head, and that cloud had a label on it with the name Daniel.

After Lauren's students had filed out of her classroom for lunch, she closed the door and called Katherine. She answered on the fourth ring, out of breath.

"Hey. I'm just bringing some groceries in. Hold on a sec." She could hear the rustling of the paper bags, then Katherine telling Keenan, "Grab this for Mommy and put it on the counter, ok sweetie?"

"Do you want me to call you back?" Lauren asked as she heard several objects falling, then Katherine telling Keenan to stop rolling the apples across the floor.

"No, it's ok. You sound upset. What's going on?" Katherine knew Lauren didn't usually call during work days unless it was something important.

"He came over last night. He knows."

"Whoa." Katherine took a deep breath and exhaled slowly. Lauren had already called her sister in-law and filled her in on the run-in with Daniel at the park. Lauren had told her how she could see it in his face that he was processing James' age, the dark hair and eyes.

"How did he know where you live? I thought you were unlisted."

"Yeah, so did I."

"Did he say how he found out?"

"He said the Internet. I don't know. That's not even the least of my worries right now."

"So, was he pissed?"

"What do you think?"

"Well, I told you a long time ago that you needed to let him know. It would have been a whole lot easier."

"Katherine, I really don't need a lecture right now, ok? I mean, he said he's getting his lawyer involved and everything."

"His lawyer? Are you kidding?" Katherine clucked her tongue. "Oh, Lauren, I am so sorry. So, what are you going to do?"

"What can I do? I guess his fancy lawyer is probably going to want to take me to court to try to work out some formal custody agreement. I don't understand why he couldn't just leave it to us to work out by ourselves."

"Well, I guess partly because he's mad at you and then there's the whole domineering thing too." Katherine sighed loudly. "I hate to say it but I have a feeling he's going to be a big pain in the rear about it."

"Yeah, me too. Well, I better get going. I'll let you know when he calls me again." Lauren put her phone down and tried to concentrate on grading her students' spelling tests, putting all thoughts of Daniel out of her mind for the moment.

On the way home from school, Lauren decided to stop at one of her and James' favorite spots, The Coffee Bean. She ordered a Mocha with extra whipped cream for herself and a vanilla bean scone for James. They sat at a table near the windows and Lauren sipped the remaining whipped cream as it melted into the hot coffee. The beverage didn't seem to have its usual soothing effect on her. Her stomach had been in a constant state of churning since Daniel's visit two nights ago.

Lauren couldn't stop the nagging thought that Daniel really didn't care that he had a son, but he was just doing this to retaliate in his own selfish way. She hated the thought that he would involve himself in James' life just to spite her. He didn't seem to have changed much at all over the past seven years. He was still a big jerk, but unfortunately the only thing that had improved with time was his looks. He had filled out more, but in a toned muscular way. He wore his dark brown hair a little longer, curling a little near his collar and falling over his forehead, almost reaching his dark brown eyes. Sure, he had some lines on his face that hadn't been there, but they almost made him look even more determined and confident, if that was possible.

Lauren recalled how Daniel had become so resolute in advancing his career as a Realtor, that he just completely pushed their relationship to the back burner. He had been so attentive in the beginning. He called her every night and they talked for hours. They enjoyed getting outdoors together- hiking, jogging, and kayaking on the lake. They met for long, leisurely lunches during the week, and on the weekends Daniel took her out to the finest restaurants for dinner. He surprised her with flowers and sweet cards for no reason. They had only been dating a year when things began to change.

Lauren remembered how hurt she was when he backed out of going with her for the spa weekend he had gifted her for her 25th birthday. It was more important for him to spend that weekend working on his plans to become a broker.

"Daniel, I don't want to go by myself," Lauren had pleaded. "You said we would do this together. I'll feel weird being there alone."

"You can ask one of your girlfriends to go with you," Daniel said simply as he speared his next bite of steak. "You're always saying how you never spend time with your friends anymore."

"Yes, but we made plans to do this together. I was looking forward to it." Lauren had attempted her best pout.

"Lauren, I have to meet with this broker. She's flying in all the way from California."

"*She*? You didn't mention it was a woman before." Lauren's pout had become a scowl.

"Lauren, please don't do this," Daniel had said impatiently. "Whether she's male or female is not important. She happens to be one of the most successful brokers in L.A. and she's willing to help me get started with my firm. Can't you see how important this is for my career?"

It was utterly frustrating to Lauren that she still felt an overwhelming attraction to this man after all the pain he had caused her. His emotional coolness and appearance of always being in control just pulled her in that much more. Months after their break up she realized how much better off she was without him. He definitely wasn't the type of man she would want to be in a long term relationship with. She remembered all the times she had caught him looking at other women when they were out, but she had done her best to hold her tongue, not wanting to appear overly jealous and insecure.

Putting her past feelings aside, the thing she really dreaded was telling James that this emotionally unavailable man was his father. Not to mention the panic that coursed through her when she imagined Daniel taking James on outings without her. What kind of things would they do? Would Daniel think it appropriate to take a seven year old to a gentleman's bar? Or take him to a sporting event with his guy friends where they would all be drinking beer and using foul language. Daniel didn't know anything about taking care of a child, and he certainly made it clear years ago that he never intended to find out.

Chapter 7

Katherine was feeling a little guilty. She couldn't stop thinking about Jonathan. It was incredibly ridiculous that this guy was having such an effect on her, but she just kept replaying their conversation in her head. She kept picturing him crouched down next to her, intimately asking her questions. She recalled the way his eyes crinkled and the little dimple that appeared when he laughed. And oh, the way he looked at her when she was talking. It was as if he was fascinated by every word that came out of her mouth.

It was Saturday night and she was just getting home from the monthly PTA board meeting. The meeting had gone on longer than usual due to the planning of the upcoming spring festival. Several times during the meeting her mind had wandered to thoughts of Jonathan and she all but had to slap herself to keep her head in the discussion. She had even nodded her head to the fundraising chairman's suggestion that Katherine take on the duty of baking all of the goodies for the cake walk. She hadn't even realized what she had committed herself to. But then Carisa hugged her goodbye as they were leaving and trilled, "You are just so generous to do all the baking for the cake walk. I sure hope you make some of those lemon bars you did last year. They were incredible!"

Katherine's stomach sank. She had vowed last year that she

would never volunteer to bake for the festival again. Staying up all night three nights in a row baking 12 dozen cookies, 5 pies, 3 pans of brownies and lemon bars had definitely not been the best of times. Even though Nathan had helped her quite a bit, she still did most of the work on her own. And she knew there was no way Nathan would be up for lending a hand this year.

On the drive home, she once again found her mind drifting to thoughts of the young handsome waiter. She ran through imaginary possible conversations they might have next Thursday. He would ask her about her work again and then question if she felt lonely being away from her hometown. She pictured herself flirting back with him, gazing into his eyes and telling him how she didn't feel lonely when she was at his table. She thought about what she might wear on her next visit. Maybe her cute little cocktail dress, the green one that she'd bought a few months ago and still hadn't had a chance to wear.

Katherine shook her head as if trying to wake herself from a dream. *I'm being ridiculous. I have to stop this. I'm married. I'm a mother, for crying out loud.* She was pulling into their neighborhood and the closer she got to home, the guiltier she felt. But, why should she feel guilty? What was this anyway? Just harmless flirting. *It's not as if Nathan cares about anything I do these days.*

She let herself into the house quietly and went into the kitchen to get a glass of water. She was surprised to see that Nathan had put away the dinner dishes and washed the pots and pans. Katherine couldn't remember the last time Nathan had cleaned the kitchen for her. Another little pang of guilt. She went upstairs and found Nathan on their bed, his laptop in front of him, his eyes glassy and red.

"How'd it go?" Nathan asked as he rubbed his eyes.

"Waaay too long." Katherine yawned. "And somehow I managed to volunteer to bake again."

"Oh no. That just about did you in last year," Nathan said as he continued to type.

"Yeah, well, maybe I'll just buy store bought goods this year," Katherine said, kicking off her shoes.

"Somehow I do *not* see that happening."

"I know." Katherine sighed. She always ranted about the moms who brought store bought baked goods to school functions. Didn't the job of being a mom come with the requisite duty of learning how to bake?

Katherine went into the bathroom and began to wash her face. She took her time, noticing the dark circles under her eyes. She needed to get more sleep. The last thing she needed was another all night bake-a-thon. As she expected, Nathan didn't even make mention of helping her. She brushed her teeth vigorously, trying not to let her anger go past a simmer. She tidied up Nathan's ever messy side of the vanity and walked back into their bedroom. She just stood at the foot of the bed for a few moments, watching Nathan type away at his laptop.

He finally looked up at her. "Are you coming to bed?"

"Yes, in a minute. I might call Lauren and see if she'll help out by baking some cookies."

"Can't you wait until tomorrow? It's late."

"You're one to talk." Katherine pointed at his laptop and rolled her eyes. "And I can see that your eyes are totally bloodshot."

"I just have to finish this email and I'm done for the night."

"Really?" Katherine didn't disguise her surprise.

"Yeah, I'm tired. Aren't you?" Nathan looked up at her again and this time their eyes stayed locked on one another. For a moment Katherine could see that college boy she fell in love with so many years ago.

"A little," Katherine said, then began to undress slowly, letting her dress fall to the floor.

This time Nathan looked up and kept his eyes on her. She was glad she happened to be wearing one of her nice matching bra sets.

"But not too tired for this," she said, walking over to his side of the bed. She carefully picked up his laptop and set it on the floor. Nathan made no objections whatsoever and Katherine completely forgot about Jonathan as her husband made love to her for the first time in months.

Chapter 8

An entire week had passed before Lauren heard from Daniel again. With each passing day she found herself toggling back and forth between being angry that he was taking so long to contact her and utter relief to not hear from him. She had almost hoped that maybe he decided to just give up altogether on the whole being a dad thing. This thought had her emotions in an even bigger turmoil. She felt horrible for James, thinking that his own father finally knew about him, had even seen him and talked to him, but decided that he did not want to be a part of his life. Then the anger at Daniel would rise to the boiling point all over again.

Lauren thought back to the last time she saw Daniel. He had been so cold- he made it seem like she was the problem in their relationship, as if she had no right to be upset about his lack of interest in her. After a year of making her feel like she was the luckiest woman in the world, suddenly all he cared about was advancing in his career and of course, along with it, came Kelly. Lauren still couldn't believe how quickly he replaced her with the woman that was supposedly just a business associate. Thinking about it again was bringing up so many emotions that she thought she had successfully buried all those years ago.

So, when the phone finally rang Tuesday evening and she recognized his number she was completely on the verge of emotional upheaval. She was tempted to just let his call go to voicemail, but she figured Daniel might just show up on her doorstep again. Which, honestly, wouldn't be the worst thing in the world. She hated herself for being that pathetic, but seeing him again had actually been nice. Aside from him being completely angry with her for keeping his son a secret. She knew he had every right to be upset, but she also wanted him to fully comprehend the reason why she'd done it. He'd hurt her and she needed him to validate those feelings. Somehow she didn't think that was going to happen, and she knew she needed to just keep her focus on what was best for James.

"Hey, it's me," Daniel said coolly. But at least the animosity from their last conversation was missing.

"Hi." Lauren waited a few seconds then added, "I was starting to think you weren't going to call."

"My lawyer had a big case last week, so we weren't able to talk about it until just yesterday," Daniel said and paused for a moment. "So, would it be okay if I came over sometime this week and I can go over the details with you? I'd also like to see James as well."

"As long as you mean seeing him at our house while I'm there, it's fine. I'd like to see how he reacts to you first. And you need to give him some time before you let him know who you are."

"How much time are we talking? He's already gone seven years without a father." Daniel's voice was beginning to have an edge again.

"Daniel, can we please just take it slow? We aren't going anywhere. There's no point in springing this on him all at once." Lauren tried to remain pleasant as she dug her fingers into her palms.

"Ok. Ok. But I don't want to drag this out. We need to set a limit. I'm thinking no longer than two weeks." Daniel was in his usual take charge mode.

"Two weeks? That's way too fast. I want him to have time to get to know you a little."

"Ok, fine. A month tops."

"Fine. One month," Lauren said through gritted teeth.

"Good. So, the only night I have free is Thursday. Can you make that work?"

Lauren rolled her eyes. As usual, things always had to be Daniel's way or the highway.

"Sure. You can come over after dinner. We're usually done by 7:30, then he goes to bed at 8:30, so that'll give you an hour with him. Then we can talk."

"Ok. I'll see you then." Daniel ended the call.

After she hung up the phone Lauren paced the house trying to detangle her nerves. *How dare he try to demand that everything be on his terms.* She was James' mother. She knew what was best for him. What did Daniel know about children? Nothing.

She peeked into James bedroom and watched him for a few minutes. He was sitting on his bed with some of his Hot Wheel cars, pushing them around his bedspread, making little "vrrooom vroom" noises. She smiled as she pondered how quickly time had gone by; he would be seven in three months. He had already asked several times about plans for his birthday party. Lauren had mixed feelings as she realized he may actually have his father attending this year's party.

She walked in and sat down next to him on the bed and gave him a big hug. "How's my big boy?" she asked him, picking up one of the little cars and driving it around in circles.

"Good," he answered, letting go of his tiny blue Camaro. He then grabbed a book from his nightstand. "Can you read SmellyFish to me?"

"Sure, baby. But before we read, I need to talk to you about something, ok?" Lauren said and moved the cars to his bedside table. James nodded and looked up at her with curiosity.

"So, do you remember the man in the park the other day? The one who caught your ball?"

"Oh, yeah. I remember," James said, nodding his head enthusiastically. "He was tall."

"Yes. He is tall." Lauren laughed a little at James' gesture of putting his hand way up in the air. "Well, he's coming over to our house tomorrow night after dinner."

"How come?" James wanted to know.

"Well, remember I said he was an old friend of mine? I used to know him a long time ago."

"Was he your boyfriend?" James asked with a little boy grin.

"What?" Lauren said in surprise, and despite the tension of the situation, she laughed again. "Who told you about 'boyfriends'?"

"Sean from school says his mom has a boyfriend, but that he hardly talks to him, just to his mom. Sean says he doesn't like him."

"Oh, I see." Lauren took a moment to figure out how to proceed from there. "Well, yes, I guess he kind of used to be my boyfriend. But we lost touch with each other."

"Kind of like we lost touch with my dad?" James asked and Lauren felt her heart sink to her toes.

"Um... yes, kind of like that." Lauren could feel tears pricking the backs of her eyes. She cleared her throat and blinked a few times.

"Anyway, he's going to hang out with us for a little while before bedtime. Then I'll talk to him about some grown up things for a bit," she told him, trying her best to make it sound like a casual situation. "So, let's be on our best behavior and use our manners, okay?"

"Okay, Mommy," James said, followed by a big yawn. "But can we read SmellyFish now?"

Lauren kissed the top of his head and said, "Of course, sweetie."

Chapter 9

On Wednesday morning Katherine still felt as if her marriage had taken a turn for the better. Nathan hadn't gone into work on Sunday for the first time in weeks. He had made chocolate chip pancakes while Katherine whipped up her famous fruit salad casserole. They had sipped their coffee together, reading the newspaper on the patio while the children played in the backyard. They even went shopping as a family, buying spring flowers at Home Depot and doing the weekly grocery trip at Whole Foods. Although he went into his office when they returned home and spent several hours on his computer, it was a huge improvement to the weekends in the past couple of months. And Nathan had made it home in time for dinner both Monday and Tuesday night. That was huge progress in Katherine's mind.

Several times she had caught her mind wandering to Jonathan, but just as quickly she managed to dismiss those thoughts. She had seriously contemplated finding a new restaurant to visit on her Thursday night outing. She figured she'd had her fun – having the attention of a cute young man, the opportunity to flirt a little. It may have even given her a little spark that Saturday night when she had initiated things with Nathan in the bedroom. She felt that maybe, just maybe, things were getting back on track with her marriage.

She managed to make it through her morning errands without a single thought of Jonathan. She picked up the dry cleaning, dropped off the overdue books at the library and bought the ingredients for one of Nathan's favorites – chicken and dumpling casserole. Once home, she made herself a salad with crisp romaine lettuce, slices of deli turkey, avocado, tomatoes and cucumbers. She ate her lunch while she checked her email and looked up some new recipes that she thought Nathan might enjoy.

However, the day started taking a downward turn in the late afternoon. She had just arrived home with the children from an after school playdate at the park. Her cell phone rang with the familiar tune of Nathan's ringtone – U2's 'One', the song they had danced to at their wedding.

"Hey, I'm not going to make it home for dinner." His voice was muffled and she could tell he was outside, probably at the Johnson site.

"Oh, no. I'm making your favorite tonight. Chicken and dumpling casserole," Katherine said, not hiding her disappointment.

"Just keep some warmed in the oven for me, okay? I gotta go," he said and ended the call.

Katherine stared at the phone for a moment as his name and photo disappeared from the screen. His cold attitude had her heart sinking to her toes. It felt as if the past few days hadn't even happened.

"Mo-om!" Madison's yell from the living room interrupted her pity party. "Keenan spilled his cheddar bunnies all over the floor!"

Katherine took a deep breath and tried to shake off her hurt feelings. No big deal, she told herself. She was determined to not let this minor set-back ruin the rest of her day.

"So, it's my Mom's birthday next weekend," Katherine said to Nathan as she came down from putting the kids to bed. Nathan was sitting in the living room, slouched in the leather recliner Katherine had bought him for their second anniversary. The TV was on some sports channel. He didn't bother to look up, just continued to stare at the screen.

"We're going to have to leave here by one so that I can help my sister with the cake." Katherine stepped in front of him and waved a hand in front of his eyes.

"Next Saturday? I can't go anywhere at one. I'm meeting the plumbing contractor at the Johnson's site," Nathan said with a frown and picked up the remote to change the channel.

"Nathan, I told you about this weeks ago. You told me your schedule was clear." Katherine tried not to raise her voice as anger stirred within her.

"You said the party was in the evening. You never said anything about leaving early to make a cake." Nathan continued to avoid eye contact.

"Yes, but you know it's a two hour drive and that I'd want to get there early. Why couldn't you have scheduled the meeting in the morning?"

"That's the only time the guy could meet. And we're already way behind schedule."

"And so what am I supposed to do? Go without you?" Katherine stood in front of him, her hands on her hips. When he said nothing, she grabbed the remote from his hand.

"Hey!" Nathan yelled and tried to grab it back from her.

"I am trying to talk to you, Nathan," Katherine said between clenched teeth. "If you can't change the meeting then you'll have to drive up without us. Or just stay home."

"You know, it actually would be a good idea if I stayed here and caught up on work," Nathan said calmly. Katherine felt her blood begin to boil.

"You're kidding, right?" Katherine glared at him, still holding the remote.

"No, why would I be kidding? Gas prices are so high right now, it doesn't make sense for us to both drive out there."

"That's just great, Nathan! You hardly spend any time with us anymore and now you're going to miss my Mom's birthday?" Katherine yelled.

"Your mom won't even notice I'm not there. You girls just natter the whole time anyway." Nathan stood up and reached for the remote. "Can I have the remote back now?"

"No! I am so tired of you blowing us off because of work!" Katherine's voice rose even higher.

"Keep your voice down! You'll wake up the kids," Nathan snapped.

"Like you care! You don't care about anything that goes on around here anymore!" Katherine continued to yell. "All you ever do is work!"

"I *have* to work! How else are we going to pay the bills?" Nathan's voice began to rise as well.

"Yes, I know you *have* to work. Just not *all the time!*" Katherine yelled, "You're the one that wanted me to quit my job, remember?

That was *your* idea, not mine." She thrust the remote at him and turned to stomp up the stairs. She was barely surprised that Nathan didn't follow her as he used to do when they argued. Now he was probably just glad that she was gone so that he could get back to watching ESPN.

When she reached their bedroom, Katherine flopped herself down on the bed and picked up the phone to dial her mother's number, but it went straight to voicemail. Katherine hung up with a dramatic sigh, remembering that it was Wednesday night and her mother was at church. As she walked into the bathroom to get ready for bed she also remembered that tomorrow night was her night out. She no longer felt the resolve to put a stop to her routine at Tiramisu. And the thought of seeing Jonathan again slowly began to ease the anger and
disappointment she had felt moments earlier.

Chapter 10

*B*y the time Thursday evening rolled around, Lauren was so nervous she could barely eat dinner. She picked at her salad while James chatted happily about school, his upcoming soccer game, and the new Lego movie coming out.

Lauren managed to get the kitchen cleaned up before the doorbell rang promptly at 7:30. She took a deep breath and walked toward the front entrance, James and Burley tagging along behind her. She paused at the hall mirror and took a peek at her reflection, checking for any parsley in her teeth.

Daniel stood there looking as handsome as ever, wearing jeans and a light blue button-down with the sleeves rolled up. His hands were in his pockets and Lauren thought he looked a little nervous.

"Hi," Lauren said and managed a small smile.

"Hey," Daniel replied and looked down at James who was hanging onto his mother's leg. "Hello James."

"Hi," James said quietly, then his voice became more animated. "Do you want to play with my Spiderman Lego set? It's really fun."

"Uh...sure." Daniel smiled at James then looked back at Lauren.

"Come on in." Lauren moved aside for him to walk inside the entrance hall.

"You can come see my room. That's where all the cool stuff is,"

James said, practically bouncing down the hallway.

"OK. Show me the way," Daniel said cheerfully and turned to catch up with James. Burley followed them both, his tail wagging happily.

Lauren followed as James led Daniel down the hallway to his room. She hovered for a moment at the doorway as James gave Daniel a little tour of his bookshelf, toy area and a rundown of his Lego creations. Feeling satisfied that the two of them would be okay on their own for a bit, she walked to the kitchen and poured herself a large glass of wine.

She stood looking out the kitchen window, sipping her wine until Burley came over and nudged her thigh with his head, letting her know he needed out. She opened the back door and walked out onto the patio, while Burley wandered out to water the grass and then returned to her side. She stood on the patio and scratched his ears absently, letting the cool night breeze roll over her. She smiled as she heard the sound of James' laughter coming from inside.

She went back in and sat down in the living room, feeling restless. She picked up a book and tried to read to distract herself, but found herself reading the same sentence over and over. Frustrated, she put the book down and began pacing the living room. Glancing at the clock she realized only twenty minutes had passed. She sat back down on the sofa, turned the TV on and flipped through the channels. She watched about fifteen minutes of a home improvement show, then got up again. Quietly, she made her way down the hallway toward James' room.

"You really made this yourself?" Lauren heard Daniel asking. "This is really amazing."

"Yeah, my Mom helped a little. She's really good at stuff," James was replying as Lauren walked in to see Daniel holding up the robot they had made together for the science competition at the library last year. He had won first place, which Lauren had been convinced was due to the little green dog on a leash they had added at the last minute made from a piece of packing foam.

"Hey," Daniel said to Lauren when he noticed her in the doorway. He set the robot back on James' bookshelf.

"Hey," Lauren said. "You boys having fun?"

"Of course, Mom. Daniel is really cool," James said in a serious voice and Daniel laughed, catching Lauren's eye. Lauren held his gaze for a moment and smiled, then turned her attention to James.

"Hey, sweetie. Go brush your teeth, ok?" Lauren instructed.

"Do I have to go to bed now? Can't I hang out with Daniel a little longer?" James whined.

"James, it's time for bed. Now please go brush your teeth." Lauren gave him a stern look and he slinked off toward the bathroom.

"Do you want to wait out in the living room for a few minutes while I get him tucked in?" she asked Daniel and he nodded and left the room.

Once Lauren had James tucked into bed, she found Daniel sitting on the sofa looking through the photo album she kept on the coffee table. He was looking at a page where James was barely two years old, sitting in a swing at the park with a huge smile. Lauren sat down next to him and waited while he thumbed through a few more pages. Finally Daniel looked over at her, his face tight with emotion.

"I missed out on so much," he said softly.

"I know. I'm sorry." It was all she could think to say. As she continued to look at Daniel she slowly began to see things from his perspective. How would she feel if she had just met James for the first time, realizing she'd missed out on seven years of his life? The most precious years, his baby years, learning to talk, walk and discover everything about the world around him. She felt something for Daniel that she hadn't expected to tug at her heart. Compassion.

"Look, Daniel, if you really want to be part of his life, I'm not going to come between you. I want him to know his father, but only if it's something that you really want," Lauren said.

"Of course I want to be a part of his life. And yes we could make it all legal and tidy. That was the point of my meeting with my lawyer. But he did say that the easiest thing would be for us to work something out between ourselves. And honestly, that's what I'd like too."

"Good, because I don't want this to be difficult, especially not for James. It's going to be hard enough for him to adjust to the changes as it is." Lauren sighed, worrying about that impending moment when she would have to divulge the truth.

"Well, I'm glad we can agree on that," Daniel said matter of fact. "But I don't want to wait much longer to tell him who I am. I think that will make things even harder for everyone."

"I understand, but I'd really like to give him some time to get to know you."

"Great. I'd love to spend time with him again. What did you have in mind?"

"Are you free Saturday afternoon?" Lauren asked.

"I have a meeting first thing in the morning, but I can come over as soon as we're finished," he replied, then, looking thoughtful for a moment, he asked, "So, what exactly have you told James about his father?"

Lauren hesitated, but decided she better just tell him the truth, especially since James might say something. She began slowly, dreading his reaction. "Well, I, uh... I told him that his father lived too far to be able to visit."

"Too far? As in where 'too far'?" Daniel asked with a note of annoyance.

"I told him that you lived in Africa," she said and Daniel just stared at her.

"Africa?" Daniel finally repeated. "Why would I live in Africa?"

"Because you had to look after an endangered tribe of elephants?" Lauren posed the statement as a question, speaking quickly, as if he might not understand what she'd just said. But she knew better- he heard her perfectly. She cringed while she waited for the outburst.

But the reaction she received was completely opposite of what she had expected. To her surprise, Daniel burst out laughing. Lauren found herself giggling a little as well.

"Is that seriously the best you could come up with?" Daniel asked, shaking his head. "So, what now? We tell him I'm back from Africa because the elephants aren't endangered anymore?"

Lauren laughed again and was relieved to see Daniel was able to find some humor in the situation.

"I don't know. I hadn't really thought that far ahead," she admitted. She hadn't even considered having to backtrack and tell James that she'd lied to him. That was one thing she'd really rather avoid altogether. "Would it be so bad if we just stuck with that for now?"

Daniel kept his eyes on hers for a few seconds, his expression unreadable, and Lauren felt sure he was going to make this hard on her, but he once again surprised her.

"That's fine. We can stick with it for now." He smiled a little, and Lauren let out the breath she had been holding in. However, he quickly amended, "But we'll need to tell him the truth someday soon."

"Yes, you're right." Lauren nodded solemnly.

"Well, then I guess I'll see you on Saturday," Daniel said, getting to his feet. Lauren stood up as well and they started for the front door.

Daniel opened the door, then paused a moment and turned around to face her. He asked softly, "Do you think he'll be glad? I mean, to find out I'm his dad?"

Lauren had never seen Daniel look unsure of himself. It melted her heart a little. She smiled and nodded earnestly. "Yes, I think that he will."

Chapter 11

"*H*ey, I'm getting off early tonight and I'm going to meet some friends over at The Pavilion," Jonathan said as he kneeled down next to Katherine's table. "Would you...uh... want to go with me?"

Katherine hesitated for a moment, taking in Jonathan's eager expression. She knew she should say no, but the argument with Nathan had caused something to stir in her. She didn't want to sit around waiting for Nathan to pay attention to her or spend time with her. She didn't want to have that crushing feeling of only being half listened to or that she was practically invisible. So even though she knew deep down that she was getting in over her head, she said yes.

The Pavilion was a fairly new club that had opened in North Austin. It had quickly become popular due to the live music, huge dance floor and covered patio. That evening a band called The News was playing, delighting the crowd with cover songs from the late 80's. As Katherine and Jonathan walked in they were greeted with an upbeat version of The Cure's "Just Like Heaven". Strolling through the club with Jonathan next to her, feeling the bass of the music thump throughout her body, made her feel ten years younger and she felt her spirits lift a little bit more.

Jonathan led them through the maze of high top tables and out onto the patio where his friends were already seated at a table near the outside bar. Jonathan fist bumped the two guys at the table, then introduced Katherine to the group. She took a seat next to Sylvia, an attractive girl with olive skin and dark hair. Jonathan asked her what she would like to drink and headed towards the bar.

Katherine felt a little self-conscious as the conversation flowed easily between the friends at the table. She figured, like Jonathan, they were all much younger than her, engrossed in a world that seemed a lifetime ago to her. Late nights, caffeine infused study sessions, partying all night and sleeping in until noon, sitting around watching movies all day on a Sunday. Nothing like the constant whirlwind of activity it took to keep a family household running. She took her phone out of her bag to check for any calls from Nathan, knowing there wouldn't be any. He hardly ever called her when she was out, except for a rare occasion when he couldn't locate something for the children such as Madison's favorite stuffed kitty that tended to get tucked into the couch cushion or flung behind a dresser by Keenan.

"So, how do you know Jonathan?" Sylvia asked, breaking into her thoughts.

"I, um, met him at Tiramisu."

"Do you work there?" Sylvia asked, flipping her sleek black hair over her shoulder.

"No, I eat there," Katherine said and found herself laughing.

"What's so funny?" Jonathan asked as he set down a gin and tonic in front of Katherine. He grabbed a chair from the nearby table and sat down in between the two girls.

"I was just telling Sylvia about how I'm your favorite customer," Katherine said and took a sip of her drink. Jonathan raised an eyebrow and smiled. She then asked, "So, where do you all know each other from?"

"We met in Family Law last year," Jonathan explained. "We were assigned to sit in on a court case together. We started going out for a drink afterwards and just kind of kept the tradition going after the class ended."

"What was the case?" Katherine asked.

"It was a custody battle between a couple who were getting a divorce," Sylvia said. "Basically, the husband was trying to get sole custody of the kids just to upset the wife. He worked all the time and didn't spend time with the kids before the divorce. She caught him cheating with his secretary. It was really sad."

"How awful," Katherine said, shaking her head. "What was the outcome?"

"The husband won custody because the wife had gotten drunk one night and gotten in a car accident," Susan, the girl with radiant red hair said. "She testified that she had never gotten drunk like that before, but it was the night she found out her husband was cheating on her and she was so upset she just went a little crazy."

"Wow. That's terrible." Katherine sipped her drink, taking in the story.

"Anyway, it was sad to see how hard she cried when the judge announced the decision," Sylvia said and looked at Jonathan. "I even saw Jonny's eyes mist up a little."

"I told you, my allergies were acting up that day," Jonathan said, taking a swig from his beer.

Sylvia and Susan looked at each other and giggled.

Katherine turned to Jonathan and patted his leg. "I think it's good for a man to show his emotions."

Jonathan laughed and took another swig from his beer. "Like I said, it was allergy season."

"Yeah, yeah. We all believe you," Susan said, shaking her head, then turned to Katherine. "So, are you going to U.T. as well?"

"No," Katherine said. "I, uh, graduated a while ago."

"Katherine works in marketing," Jonathan said with a hint of pride. "She's actually from Dallas."

"Oh, that sounds very interesting," Sylvia said. "My brother is a marketing manager at Geneva downtown. He heads up a team that's currently utilizing 'shock advertising.' Have you heard about that?"

"Um, yeah, sure..." Katherine racked her brain for something to say, but all she came up with was, "I hear it's very controversial."

"Well, personally I don't agree with the tactic at all. It's very alarming, not to mention the damage being done to young people's impressionability."

"True..." Katherine wasn't completely sure what the term meant, but she concluded that it was ads that shocked people. What she did know was that she needed a way out of having a discussion on the topic. Hearing the strains of a song by The Fixx, she exclaimed, "Oh, I love this song! Jonathan, do you want to go dance?"

"Sure," Jonathan agreed easily. He finished his beer in a long gulp and grabbed Katherine's hand. Pulling her to her feet, he said, "Come on. Let's go boogy."

Katherine couldn't remember the last time she had danced. Nathan had never really been into dancing. He had been good natured about dancing at their wedding, but after that, he put his foot down. If Katherine felt the urge to dance, she'd have to go with her girlfriends.

The News broke into a rendition of New Order's 'Bizarre Love Triangle', and even though it was early, there were several other people already dancing. Katherine felt a little awkward at first, but Jonathan started being goofy and she joined in as he mimicked different styles of dancing, like the robot and the swing. Jonathan grabbed Katherine's hand and spun her around and she found herself having so much fun she had completely forgotten about Nathan and their troubled marriage for the moment.

After another drink and an hour of dancing, Katherine walked out of the club laughing and holding onto Jonathan's arm. The cool evening breeze was welcoming as they had worked up a sweat on the dance floor. Jonathan walked Katherine to her car and stood by her as she pulled her keys from her bag. She looked up at him. "That was so much fun."

"Yeah, it was awesome. I haven't danced that much in years." Jonathan smiled down at her.

"I know. That band was so good!" Katherine didn't want to leave, but she knew it was very late. "I guess I'd better get going."

"So, you've never told me where you stay," Jonathan said as he leaned against her car.

"Stay?" Katherine questioned, thinking kids of his age must use that term in place of 'where do you live'.

"Yeah, do you stay at a hotel or corporate housing?"

"Oh! I stay at the, um, Marriott near my branch office," Katherine said feeling weird about lying. Again.

"I could follow you there if you want. Just to make sure you're okay?" Jonathan offered.

"No," Katherine said a bit too abruptly, then more softly, "It's okay. I'm fine. Really."

"Ok. Well, then, I guess I'll see you next week?" Jonathan asked, his voice a little lower as he came closer to her. "Or maybe sooner?"

Katherine just smiled nervously. As he closed the distance between them, she knew she was in trouble. Before she could think, his lips were pressed against hers and she felt his hands slide around her waist. She melted into him and found her hands going up to his strong shoulders, then to his neck and through his soft hair. He kissed her gently at first, but the kiss quickly grew more intense and Katherine let herself get lost in the passion.

It seemed like they stood there in the darkened parking lot, making out like teenagers, for an hour. Finally Katherine pulled away, but stayed in his arms and murmured in his ear, "That was even more fun than the dancing."

Jonathan laughed softly and looked down at her, his green eyes filled with desire. "So, is that a yes?"

Katherine tilted her head to the side. "A yes to what?"

"To seeing me again? Sooner than next Thursday?"

Chapter 12

*L*auren was attempting to grade her class's book reports, but she couldn't seem to focus. She had barely slept the night before, her mind racing with thoughts of Daniel. She had mixed feelings about seeing him again, especially about James spending more time with him. She was so nervous that James would get attached to Daniel; only to have his little heart broken if Daniel decided he couldn't handle being a parent after all.

She was still very uncertain about the right time to let James know that Daniel was his father. But she knew Daniel, and he was definitely going to push for sooner than later. This was something she knew was going to be hard to get used to: the concept of raising James with Daniel, now having to consider his opinions or more likely, demands. She had gotten so used to the routine of being a single mom. She had listened to Katherine and Nathan argue about so many issues related to her niece and nephew and had always been secretly glad she didn't have to deal with that.

She impatiently pushed the reports aside. She should probably just take them home to work on over the weekend. It was already quickly approaching bell time, as the school had early dismissal that day.

She wandered over to the window that overlooked the school

playground. As she watched the children scrambling around the play equipment, she realized that there was another aspect of the situation bothering her. She had tried to ignore it all week, but she had felt her old feelings for Daniel trying their best to rise to the surface. No matter what she did to push them down, there they were: raw and painfully potent. She still wanted to talk to Daniel about how he hurt her, but she realized it was silly and petty compared to the situation they were now dealing with.

"Does somebody have a little Spring fever?" A deep male voice cut into her thoughts.

Lauren turned from the window to see Jake Martin, the P.E. coach, taking up much of her classroom doorway with his 6'4, 250 pound athletic frame. He was extremely good looking, with dark hair and brown eyes, and he definitely wasn't lacking in confidence.

"I was just taking a little break from grading book reports," Lauren said and walked back over to her desk.

"Well, you definitely look like you could use a break," Jake said, looking her up and down. "How about you join me for happy hour later?"

"That sounds nice, but I couldn't possibly. I have a lot of work to catch up on, plus I couldn't find a sitter on such short notice." Lauren was always polite when she turned down Jake's offers, which came at least once a week. But Jake never seemed put out by her rejection; he always took it in stride.

"I could help you grade those book reports, you know," he offered, coming over to her desk and picking one up. "A little wine and we could make our way through these in no time."

Lauren laughed at him as he wiggled his eyebrows up and down.

"I'm serious, Lauren. I studied English as my minor. I'm not all looks and no brains." He teased her with a sexy grin.

"Oh, really? Well, in that case that's an awfully hard offer to resist, Mr. Martin." Lauren flirted back. "I had no idea you were such an intellectual."

"I am indeed. I'd love to prove it to you some time with a game of scrabble. I'll go easy on you." Jake winked.

"How did you know I love to play scrabble?" Lauren asked, putting her hands on her hips.

"Oh I have my ways," Jake said with a sly grin.

Just then the school bell rang and Jake gave Lauren a little salute. "Just let me know when you're ready."

Jake turned and strolled back down the hall, and after a few moments of children noisily making their way down the hall, James appeared at her door, escorted by Mrs. Cohen, his first grade teacher.

"Good afternoon, Ms. Montgomery." Mrs. Cohen was in her sixties, very sweet and adored by all of her students.

"Good afternoon. Glad it's the weekend?" Lauren asked.

"Yes. Very much. I have big gardening plans ahead of me." Mrs. Cohen smiled.

"That sounds like a productive way to spend your weekend. I hear the weather is going to be great."

"Yes, I love our early springs," Mrs. Cohen said. "I'll see you tomorrow, James."

"Bye Mrs. Cohen," James said and went over to hug his mom.

"Hi, baby. Did you have a good day today?" Lauren asked him as she hugged him back.

"Yeah, it was good. We got to paint today and I painted you a really pretty picture," James told her.

"Oh, I can't wait to see it!" Lauren exclaimed. "You want to get a snack? I need a few minutes to tidy up."

James nodded eagerly and went over to his mom's drawer where she always kept a supply of after school snacks. He opened it and pulled out a package of crackers and began fussing with the plastic wrapping.

"I saw Mr. Martin heading down the hall. I'm guessing he was stopping by with another irresistible offer?" Karen, one of the other third grade teachers, said as she came into Lauren's room.

"Yes. How ever did you ever figure it out? You're a regular detective," Lauren said sarcastically.

"Why don't you just say yes? He's totally hot and there's no way you don't think so too."

"You're just jealous because he hasn't asked you out lately," Lauren joked.

"Well, you know I would have to turn him down anyway because I just might be getting serious with someone else," Karen stated proudly.

"Really? You'll have to fill me in on the details soon," Lauren said.

"I will, once it's more solid," Karen said. "So are you going to go out with Jake or not?"

"My mom already has a boyfriend." James' voice peeped up and surprised Lauren.

"Oh, she does, does she?" Karen said, her eyes widening in surprise. "She's never told me about this boyfriend of hers."

"He's just a friend, James. Remember?" Lauren felt her cheeks burning.

"I know. But he's really nice," James said thoughtfully as he munched on a cracker. "I think he should be your boyfriend. Then he could be my dad, right?"

Lauren felt her cheeks blush even more. "He's just an old friend I ran into last weekend," she explained to Karen, waving her hand dismissively.

"Oh, yeah? Is he as hot as Jake?" Karen asked.

"Yeah, he was pretty sweaty when we met him." James said and the two women laughed.

"Hot and sweaty. Sounds like my kind of man." Karen winked.

"Don't you have some papers to grade or something?" Lauren asked.

"I'm going to expect to hear the story on this 'friend' over lunch next week," Karen said with a wave and sauntered out of the room.

"So, when can Daniel come over again?" James asked as Lauren began packing her school bag.

"Actually, we're meeting him at the park tomorrow," Lauren told him and was pleased to see his face light up.

"Really? Cool! And he's going to play with me, right?" James asked with a hint of worry in his voice.

"Yes, of course," Lauren laughed and hugged him again.

Katherine was walking into Whole Foods to pick up something to make for dinner when her cell phone rang. She didn't recognize the number and was tempted to let it go to her voicemail, but at the last moment she answered the call.

"So, dancing queen, how are you feeling today?" Jonathan's sexy voice came over the line.

Katherine was surprised, but thrilled he called so soon. "I have a little bit of a headache and my ears are still ringing, but other than that I'm doing great."

"Are you at work?" he asked as a Whole Foods employee began announcing the granola special over the loudspeaker.

"Um, actually I just popped into Whole Foods for some coffee and then I'm heading back to the office," Katherine said as she turned around and walked back out the door to escape the noise.

"Mmmmm.... coffee sounds good," Jonathan said sleepily.

"Are you still in bed?" Katherine asked with envy.

"Yep. I know, it's almost noon, but I couldn't sleep last night. I couldn't get my mind off you," he said provocatively.

Now that the alcohol and nostalgia from the night before had faded, Katherine felt self-conscious. She wasn't quite sure what to say.

"Did I make you uncomfortable?" Jonathan asked as the silence lingered.

"No, you just caught me a little off guard. I'm just in work mode I guess," she said as she sat down at one of the picnic tables in front of the store.

"Well, how about I get you out of work mode? What would you say to playing hooky today?" Jonathan asked.

"Well, I really have a lot of work to do," Katherine said, twisting a lock of hair in her fingers.

"Ok, how about just lunch then? I know a great park. We could have a picnic."

Katherine hesitated as she watched a couple walk across the parking lot, their arms wrapped intimately around each other's waist.

She closed her eyes and remembered their kiss the night before. When was the last time Nathan had kissed her like that?

"Katherine? Did I lose you?" Jonathan was asking.

"Nope. I'm here. I was just checking my schedule. Looks like I'm free for a couple hours. Where should I meet you?"

When Jonathan had suggested a picnic, she had imagined him showing up with a couple of sandwiches in paper sacks from a local deli. But when Katherine had parked her car and walked through the path down to the shore of Lake Austin she found Jonathan waiting for her with a genuine picnic basket and a bottle of wine.

He was sitting on a navy blue blanket reading a book, but when he saw her approaching he put the book down and jumped to his feet. He walked toward her and met her halfway, grabbing her into a hug that lifted her from the earth. She giggled as he set her back down and looking up at him she felt herself melting. He surprised her again by pressing his lips to hers for a tender, but lingering kiss.

"I thought I'd just get that out of the way," he said with a wink. "I didn't want you wondering for the next two hours when I was going to kiss you."

"I like that strategy." Katherine relinquished the anxiety she had felt on the drive over and took his hand as they strolled toward the picnic blanket.

They spent the next hour and a half talking and eating the delicious lunch he had prepared for them - fresh mozzarella, prosciutto and roasted red pepper sandwiches on crusty artisan bread, arugula with basil vinaigrette, sweet potato chips and a bottle of pinot grigio.

Jonathan shared that he hadn't been interested in entering the corporate world after he graduated with a degree in business. He said he needed a little more time before he settled into the serious role of official adult. So, he had taken a few courses at a culinary school, then landed a job as a sous chef at one of Austin's finer restaurants. He worked his way up to head chef and this satisfied him for a few years, but he eventually grew tired of the hustle and bustle of working long, late hours in a hot kitchen. He still loved to cook, but on a smaller scale: for himself, family or friends. His family had finally convinced him to go to law school, since his father, uncle and brother were all lawyers. So, although he looked very young, he was really only two years younger than Katherine, which she was very glad to discover.

He had grown up and gone to high school in suburban Houston, then moved to Austin to go to the University of Texas. Katherine did her best to keep the spotlight on him, but he eventually managed to put the ball in her court.

"So... enough about me. I want to hear about you. Where are you from? Where does your family live?"

She immediately thought about her husband and children. She mentally scrambled for an answer that would satisfy the parameters of her invented self.

"Well, my parents and sisters live in San Antonio," she began truthfully. "I grew up there, and then I went to school in Georgetown."

"How'd you end up in Dallas?" he asked, stretching out on his side and resting his head on his hand.

"I followed my college boyfriend there after we graduated. He had a job offer at a big architecture firm," she said, trying to keep things as close to the truth as possible, so she wouldn't have to back track later and try to remember a big pile of lies.

"And so how did you end up as a hot shot marketing guru and land a cool job that allows you to travel to Austin?"

Katherine laughed and waved her hand, "I'm not a hot shot. It's really not that glamorous. I guess I just got lucky."

"I'm the one who's lucky. Lucky you ended up at my table." Jonathan reached out and touched her hand. "I'm really glad I met you."

"I am too," Katherine said whole-heartedly. A flock of mockingbirds flew overhead just then and landed noisily in the tree above them. They both looked up at the gaggle of birds, momentarily caught up in their own thoughts.

"So, I'm guessing it didn't work out with him?" He looked up at her with raised eyebrows.

"Who?" Katherine asked in confusion.

"The college boyfriend," Jonathan reminded her.

"No, I guess not," she answered and before she could ponder the magnitude of the statement, he reached out and pulled her down next to him.

"Well, I'm glad," he said huskily as he wrapped his arms around her and kissed her.

They enjoyed another make out session, not quite as lustful as the night before, but still full of the passion that Katherine craved. Then, reluctantly, they packed up the basket, folded the blanket and made their way towards the parking lot.

"So, I guess you're heading out tonight, huh?" he asked her as she leaned against the door of her car.

"What?" she questioned, but then quickly remembered that he

was referring to her returning to Dallas, her supposed hometown, for the weekend. "Oh, yes."

"Will you call me tonight and let me know you got back okay?" He looked at her with such genuine sadness it almost made her heart ache.

"Ok," she barely whispered as she realized that she would miss him just as much.

Later that evening, Katherine was just starting dinner when she heard Nathan's truck pull up in the driveway. She sighed as she stirred the pasta sauce and recalled how that sound used to lift her spirits. Now she just felt a sense of pending disappointment. She knew that he wouldn't come through the door whistling happily and wrap his arms around her as if they hadn't seen each other in days. Instead it was almost always the same these days: Nathan would come in, and after the kids clambered over him for a few minutes he would either go straight to the living room to watch TV or to his office until dinner was ready.

But tonight he surprised her by coming straight over to her at the stove; he hovered for a few seconds breathing in the scent of garlic and tomatoes. She turned to him with expectancy, but he just looked at her with tired eyes and said, "I need to talk to you."

Like clockwork, Keenan and Madison came rushing into the kitchen to greet their father. He lifted Madison up into his arms while Keenan hugged him around his legs.

"Daddy, daddy.... Can you play sharks with me tonight?" Keenan was asking.

"No, Daddy is going to play kitty cats with me!" Madison yelled at her brother.

"Hey, hey, no arguing. I'm not sure if Daddy can play tonight. Maybe just for a few minutes," Nathan said as he set Madison down.

"Well, first we are going to eat dinner. So, go wash up," Katherine said and started to pull some plates from the cupboard. Then she turned to Nathan, "What do you want to talk about?"

"We'll talk after dinner," he said with little emotion.

Finally, after she got Keenan and Madison into their pajamas, their teeth were brushed and stories were read, Katherine descended the stairs to find Nathan in his office. During dinner and the kid's bedtime routine she had felt her stomach twist in knots as she anticipated what Nathan wanted to talk about. Considering his somber mood at dinner, she knew it couldn't be anything positive.

She stood silently in the doorway for a few moments and just watched Nathan as he intently typed away at his computer. She was hit with a sudden wave of sadness as she thought about how in love they were not too long ago. She didn't even really know when the feeling had started to dissolve. It seemed as if it almost happened over night, but it had definitely been that way for a long time now. It wasn't just him, she realized. She felt flat as she gazed at her husband. Even if by some miracle he waltzed over and swept her into his arms, would she even want him to? She didn't think so. She let out a big sigh.

"What time did you get in last night?" Nathan asked after he finally turned to see her in the doorway.

"I don't know... it was kind of late, maybe 11:30." Katherine had been certain Nathan was asleep already when she came in. The house was dark and quiet and when she tiptoed into their room it had looked as if he were sleeping.

"I heard you, Katherine. It was one o'clock in the morning,"

Nathan stated and waited for her reaction.

"I guess I lost track of time. After dinner I went over to the Internet Cafe and had a cup of coffee and read for a bit." Katherine tried to keep her voice even and hold his eye contact.

"Why did you lie the first time I asked?"

"I don't know. I guess I didn't want you to be worried."

"Worried about what?" he asked

"That I was out so late," Katherine stated simply, realizing how childish it sounded. But she wanted him to say something that made her feel like he still cared. A part of her wanted him to figure out that she'd been out with another guy. She wondered if he would even be jealous.

"Well, I think maybe you should cut back to once a month on the girl's nights. At least until the Johnson project is sorted out."

"What? Why?" Katherine was surprised. This was not where she saw the conversation going at all. He honestly didn't even care about how late she'd been out. For some reason that hurt her more than it should.

"We can't afford it right now. Your little dinners are expensive."

"I need that time, Nathan. That's my only time away from the kids, the only thing I do for myself." Katherine couldn't believe what she was hearing. She felt like her freedom was being taken away.

"I don't even know if I'm going to make a profit on this deal anymore." Nathan's voice began to rise.

"Fine, I won't go out to dinner. I'll just meet the girls at the Internet Cafe and have a latte. But I need this time. It's the only thing that keeps me sane sometimes." Katherine felt like a teenager trying to get her daddy to let her go out on a weeknight. She felt a surge of resentment toward Nathan for making her feel like she had to ask for permission to leave the house.

"Ok, fine. But no more dinners." Nathan turned back around to face his computer screen. So that was it? No mention of *'maybe you should try to come home at a decent hour.'* No *'It's dangerous for an attractive woman to be out that late at night.'* How about *'What are you doing during all those hours you're out?'* Did he really not even think it was a possibility that she might get hit on by other men? Apparently not.

Katherine remained in the doorway, staring at the back of Nathan's head, feeling her anger surge. "Are you still not going to my Mom's party tomorrow?"

"No, I'm going to catch up on some work," he said without turning around to look at her.

"Great," Katherine said sarcastically and left the room.

Chapter 13

It was a beautiful day on Saturday; the bright blue sky dotted with fluffy cotton ball clouds, pleasantly cool for early April. Lauren had asked Daniel if he would meet them at a park not far from their neighborhood. When Lauren and James arrived just before noon, the park was already crowded. Kids of all ages ran to and from the playscape, sandbox and swing sets. Parents and grandparents stood hovering around the perimeter, drinking coffee, talking, and tapping at their phones. Lauren spotted Daniel sitting on one of the benches reading the newspaper. She greeted him and sat down next to him, while James took off to explore the playscape.

Lauren gently rustled his paper and smiled at him. "I didn't know anyone read the actual newspaper anymore."

Daniel smiled back at her. "I'm just an old fashioned kind of guy."

"Really?" Lauren questioned with a raised brow.

"Yeah, really," Daniel affirmed, smiling back. "I even still pay my bills with checks."

"You have a checkbook? Now we're talking prehistoric," Lauren teased him.

"Hey, if I recall correctly, weren't you the one that didn't want to switch from a dinosaur computer to a laptop?" Daniel countered.

"You said you didn't trust that it would keep all your information if it wasn't plugged into something?"

"You're right. I wasn't ready for that technological advance. But I'm on board now. Bring on all the modern conveniences." Lauren recalled the conversation back when he'd tried to talk her into going wireless. She was pleased that Daniel remembered as well.

After about five minutes, James came running back to the bench, out of breath and happy. He stood in front of Daniel. "Can you come play castle with me?" he asked excitedly.

"Castle?" Daniel questioned and looked at Lauren with apprehension. Lauren just giggled.

"Yeah, I'll be the King and you can be the mean dragon trying to get me," James explained. "Usually Mommy is the Princess and I'm the dragon. But I bet you're even scarier than me!"

Daniel laughed at that and let James lead him to the tall playscape. Lauren watched as Daniel put on an excellent show of being a menacing dragon, trying to grab James by climbing one of the many ladders or just reaching up through the bars of the bridge. James was loving it, running back and forth laughing happily.

Daniel finally came back to sit down next to Lauren, beads of sweat on his forehead.

"I may be able to cancel my gym membership. That's the best workout I've had in years," he said grinning.

"Yeah, he keeps me on my toes, that's for sure," Lauren agreed.

"You've done really well with him," Daniel said sincerely, taking Lauren by surprise.

"Thank you," she replied and glancing at him she saw respect in his eyes. "It hasn't always been easy, but I've done the best I could."

"I guess you had help from your family?" Daniel asked gently.

"Yes, my mom lived with me when James was a baby. Then my sister-in-law babysat for me when I went back to teaching. I wouldn't have been able to do it without them."

"And did they think it was a good idea not to tell me?" he asked with a hint of frustration.

"No, they thought I should have contacted you." Lauren sighed recalling the fights with Nathan and their mother. At one point Nathan had threatened to call Daniel himself. Lauren had cried and begged him not to. Katherine was the one who finally told Nathan it was Lauren's decision to make and to back off.

"Things could have been a lot different if you had," Daniel said somberly.

But before Lauren could respond, James flung himself in between them, requesting another round of King and dragon.

They spent another hour at the park, taking turns chasing James, kicking a ball together in the big grassy field. Then Lauren pushed James on the swings while Daniel took a business call from a real estate agent. It was close to one o'clock when Daniel suggested they go get some lunch.

They agreed on a deli that was not far from the park. Lauren ordered tarragon chicken salad on a croissant and the boys both ordered turkey and cheese on sourdough rolls. They grabbed their sandwiches and some bottles of sparkling water and took them out onto the shaded patio.

"Mmmm...," Lauren said as she bit into her sandwich. "All that running around. I was starving."

Daniel watched her as she took three enormous bites one right after another. He laughed, "Wow. I've never seen you eat like that."

"Well, back when we were dating I guess I had to eat like a bird so you wouldn't think I was a big fat pig!" she exclaimed.

"You were never and probably never will be a fat pig," Daniel said laughing again.

James laughed too at the silly statement and chimed in, "The only time Mommy was fat was when I was in her tummy. I know because I saw the pictures. Her tummy was huge!"

"Really?" Daniel looked at James with big eyes. "Can I see those pictures?"

"No!" Lauren gave Daniel a little punch on the arm. "Absolutely not."

"Come on. I'm being serious. I'd like to see what you looked like pregnant." Daniel looked at her intently as he tore off a huge hunk of his own sandwich.

Lauren felt a little tug in her stomach. She couldn't tell if he was just teasing her, but it felt good to have his attention in that way. She felt her cheeks growing warm and she changed the subject. "How's your sandwich, James?"

"Yummy!" he yelled, holding it up in the air. "But, can I have some chips?"

"Sure." Lauren dug in her purse for a couple dollars and handed them to James.

"I'll be right back!" James announced and took off inside to buy his chips.

"So," Daniel said and cleared his voice, waiting for Lauren to look up at him. "When can I tell him?"

Lauren glanced nervously through the glass doors of the deli and watched as James handed the cashier the money. "I thought we already agreed on a month."

"Come on, Lauren. It's obvious he likes me. And I want to be in his life. I want to be a father to him. What's the point in waiting?" Daniel's eyes were so intense. Lauren held his gaze; she saw sadness there and felt her guard slowly being dissolved.

"I don't know. I just think it's going to be a lot for him to take in."

"Lauren. I'm his father. I want him to know," he said firmly, then softened his tone. "Please."

"You're right," Lauren said. "But you can't just change your mind later. You have to promise not to just disappear on him."

"I'm not going anywhere. I promise."

"Ok," she gave in. "But not here. How about we go back to my house after we finish lunch and tell him there?"

"Perfect," Daniel said just as James came running back to their table.

Lauren and Daniel sat in opposite arm chairs in the living room, while James sprawled on the rug with his Transformers figures. Lauren was twisting her hands and watching James, who was making loud fighting noises, while Daniel looked anxiously at Lauren waiting for her to say something. Finally, when Bumblebee was about to toss Arcee across the floor, Daniel cleared his throat, slapped his hands on his knees and said, "So."

Lauren glanced nervously over at Daniel, then back to James who was lost in his world of Autobots. "James, honey, can you come here for a minute?"

James scampered over and sat down in his mom's lap, still

fidgeting with the toys in his hands.

"There's something very exciting that I want to tell you," Lauren began. "It's about your dad."

When Lauren saw that she had James' full attention as his arms relaxed, his eyes on hers, she continued, "Remember how I told you that he lives far away because of his job?"

"Oh, yeah, of course. The elephants. They keep him really busy, right?" James said in a serious voice and Daniel had to conceal a little snicker.

"Yes, that's right. The elephants kept him very busy, but he did such a good job with them. So much so, that the elephants are doing great now. They are absolutely the most healthy elephants in the world," Lauren said, her eyes darting back and forth between James and Daniel. Daniel was nodding his head encouragingly.

"So, he, uh... now that the elephants are doing better, he doesn't have to be in Africa anymore." Lauren continued and took a deep breath. "So, the thing is... well, he's... umm...."

"James, what your mother is trying to tell you," Daniel interrupted, "is that I am your father." James' head spun to look at him, his eyes wide.

"*You're* my Dad?" James said, his mouth gaping. "Really?"

"Yes, I really am," Daniel said, his eyes misting. Looking over at Lauren, he saw a tear trickle down her cheek.

"That's awesome!" James exclaimed, hopped off Lauren's lap and ran to Daniel. Daniel took him into his arms and held him as James squeezed his little arms tightly around his father's neck. Then he pulled back and studied Daniel very seriously for a minute, slowly nodding his head. "You know I thought you kinda looked like me."

Daniel and Lauren both burst out laughing, bringing tears to their eyes all over again.

James had pleaded with Lauren that Daniel - his dad, stay and have dinner with them. Saturday night was their game night and they often made homemade pizza. James chose Battlefield and they took turns playing against him while the other one worked on the pizzas.

Daniel impressed Lauren with his idea to use a garlic pesto sauce in place of the traditional tomato sauce and they all agreed that Daniel's pizza was the best. After they polished off three pizzas, iced tea for Lauren and Daniel and sparkling cranberry juice for James, they moved into the living room for a game of charades. James had them all laughing with his incredible impersonations. By the time they finally persuaded James to go to bed, both Lauren and Daniel were yawning.

"Well, I better get going," Daniel whispered as they walked out of James' room.

"Yeah, it's been a long day," Lauren said and headed down the hallway, Daniel following her.

When they reached the front entrance, Lauren turned around and found herself inches from Daniel. She looked up at him and smiled, "Tonight was nice."

"Yeah, it really was," Daniel said, his blue eyes serious but tender. "James is a pretty amazing little guy."

Lauren just nodded and then not sure what to say or do next, she found herself leaning forward to give him a hug. Daniel wrapped his strong arms around her and it felt good to be nestled up against his warm chest. They stayed like that for several minutes, Lauren enjoying taking in his scent, listening to the faint beat of his heart.

When she reluctantly drew back she went to give him a kiss on the check, but Daniel turned his head and placed his lips firmly on hers.

She was surprised at first, and was about to protest and pull away, but her resolve quickly melted and she found herself unable to deny her feelings any longer. They kissed for several minutes, slow and tender at first, as if they were searching for what once was between them. As the kiss intensified, Daniel backed her up against the door, pressing his body firmly against hers. Lauren gave in completely and let the desire that had been building up take over.

"Mommy?" James' little voice sounded out from his bedroom.

They both parted quickly and looked at each other with surprise.

Catching her breath, Lauren called out, "I'll be right there, sweetie."

Daniel gave her a naughty little grin and one more firm kiss on the lips. "I'll call you tomorrow."

Then he opened the door and let himself out. Lauren smoothed down her hair and headed for James' room, a huge smile on her face.

Chapter 14

*I*t was Sunday afternoon and Katherine was in a sour mood. She had reluctantly woken up at dawn to get an early start back to Austin from her mother's house in San Antonio. She had a headache from the champagne the night before and the children had argued in the back seat during the entire hour and a half drive home.

When she arrived home, the huge pile of laundry Nathan had promised to fold remained in a heap on the living room couch, and there was a bunch of dirty dishes in the sink. She barely greeted her husband as they came into the house and he seemed he couldn't care less. The children gave their father a quick hug, and then made a beeline for the playroom to turn on the television. Katherine sighed and dumped their overnight bags on the floor and went upstairs. Walking into the master bedroom, she took in the sight of the unmade bed and half empty glass of watery iced tea on the nightstand, let out another big sigh and lay down amidst the disheveled covers.

She awoke to the sound of the lawn mower and glanced at the alarm clock. It was already 2:00 in the afternoon. She lay on the bed staring up at the ceiling for a few more minutes relishing the quiet of the house. Then she got up, tidied the bed, and walked over to the window. Nathan had just finished mowing the lawn and Madison was scooping weeds into a garbage bag. Keenan was trotting around the lawn with a garden shovel in one hand and a long branch in the other.

She went down to the kitchen and put together a plate of white cheddar cheese and whole wheat crackers. She took the platter out to the patio, then went back to retrieve a pitcher of lemonade and plastic cups. She yelled out to Nathan that she was going to the grocery store.

When she pulled her car into the crammed parking lot, she circled around until she found a shaded spot in the back, plugged her phone into the car charger and dialed Jonathan's number.

"Hey, Kat. I was just thinking about you." Jonathan's voice was a soothing balm for her tender heart, which had ached all day at her Mom's birthday as various relatives asked where her husband was.

They talked for an hour, mostly about what they had done over the weekend. Jonathan told her about the party he had gone to Friday night with his friends. She tried not to be jealous when he told her that he had driven Sylvia home because she'd had too much to drink. He said he had slept in late, and then studied all day on Saturday until he went into work for the dinner shift. It made her smile when he told her that the restaurant had been incredibly boring and lonely without her there.

Katherine gave him a doctored version of her weekend. She told him she had gone to her mother's 50th birthday party and that she had enjoyed the time spent finishing the cake with her sisters and catching up on each other's lives. What she couldn't tell him was how her son had grabbed a fistful of icing from the cake while everyone was outside and that they didn't notice the gaping bald spot until it was time to sing Happy Birthday. Or how Madison had dumped the contents of her unmarried aunt's purse on the living room floor in front of everyone, revealing a pregnancy test kit. But what she wanted to confide in him the most was how her heart had felt crushed all day, even as she kept her smile in place and kept up her cheery banter. How she felt the bitter seed of resentment as she realized the cold truth: that her husband couldn't be there because he didn't care. He was too busy to notice that his wife had fallen into an affair.

"Kat? Did I lose you?" Jonathan's voice broke her thoughts.

"No, you didn't lose me," Katherine said quietly. "I'm still here."

"You sound sad."

"I guess I'm just really tired."

"Yeah? I wish you were here. I'd make you dinner and give you a nice relaxing shoulder rub," he told her.

"You don't even know how good that sounds," Katherine said wistfully, trying to imagine his hands on her shoulders. "So, you're a chef, a lawyer and a masseuse?"

"Hey, I'm a man of many talents." Jonathan laughed. "But seriously, I need to see you. Like yesterday."

Katherine laughed then. "A very demanding man of many talents."

"Yes, demanding. And determined. Meet me for lunch tomorrow?"

"I can't tomorrow," Katherine told him, as she already had a conference scheduled with Keenan's teacher during lunch. "What about Tuesday?"

"I shall be a patient, demanding man of many talents and wait until Tuesday."

"Okay," Katherine laughed again.

Chapter 15

"*I* met my dad yesterday. My real, live dad! He came back all the way from Africa to meet me," James was telling his cousins loudly as Lauren and Katherine shared a smile. They were in Lauren's backyard, seated at the patio table sipping iced coffee, while the kids ran around the swing set.

"So, I see James is ecstatic. What about Daniel?" Katherine asked.

"He was so emotional. I noticed he even teared up for a moment," Lauren said, recalling how good it felt to know that Daniel truly cared for James.

"You mean real tears? Mr. Cool? Wow." Katherine shook her head in disbelief.

"I know. I was a little surprised too." Lauren took a sip of her coffee. "But, you know, after spending some time with him I think he's really changed."

"Impossible. Maybe he's just putting on an act in front of James."

"No, I don't think so. He seems very sincere. He's completely at ease around James. It's like being a father just comes naturally to him." Lauren was silent for a moment. "It's weird though. All that talk about not wanting kids back when we were together."

"It's always different when they're your own."

"That's true. Plus, he's older now."

"Hmmm...true. So, you really think he's a changed man?"

"Yeah, I do. He's kind and attentive. And he's not just like that when James is around."

"What do you mean?" Katherine asked.

"Well...." Lauren broke off, grinning at the memory of their kiss.

"Uh-oh. That look. Don't even tell me." Katherine held up her hand, but Lauren's smile grew even wider as scarlet crept across her cheeks. "You kissed him, didn't you?"

Lauren just nodded and continued to grin.

"Lauren! What were you thinking?" Katherine said as if she were scolding one of her children.

"Oh, Katherine. It was just a kiss. No big deal," Lauren said, but she knew it was pointless kidding herself that it didn't mean anything to her. She had lain awake for hours imagining what might have happened if James hadn't interrupted them. She knew she had the good sense not to go to bed with Daniel, but she had wished their kiss could have lingered much longer. Maybe they could have made their way back to the living room, to the couch...

"I can tell by your face that it wasn't 'no big deal'."

"Okay, okay. It was pretty fabulous." Lauren could not stop smiling.

"Was it a kiss or a make-out session?"

"Well, it could have been a longer make-out session, but James interrupted."

"Oh, yikes! Did he see y'all?"

"No, thank goodness. That's something that I'm definitely not ready for."

They were quiet for a few minutes as they just sat and watched the happy cousins run around the yard together.

"Ok, so what happens next? You two get married and live happily ever after?" Katherine said sarcastically.

"Katherine, please don't be like that. Just be happy for me. Two weeks ago I thought he was going to be a tyrant and try to make me pay for keeping James a secret from him. He had every right to be angry and I don't blame him. I couldn't imagine what it must feel like for him to have missed out on so much of James' life."

"I'm sorry. I'm really not trying to make you feel bad. I just don't want to see you get hurt."

"Yes, I know. That's why I'm going to take things as slowly as possible."

"Good. So, we can wait until next week to start shopping for wedding dresses?" Katherine joked.

"Funny." Lauren punched her in the arm lightly. Then she gave her sister-in-law a little sly smile. "But it wouldn't hurt to look online a little."

Katherine laughed. "It never hurts to look."

The women sat in silence again, sipping their coffees. The ice had now melted and their glasses were frosty with condensation.

"You know, I totally misjudged him. I thought he was going to be difficult and cold-hearted. But I saw a side of him I've never seen before. I can tell he really cares about James. And of course James adores him already," Lauren said with a smile.

"Well, that's natural, I guess. I mean I spend almost every waking minute with Madison and Keenan, while Nathan sees them for about an hour a day tops. And sometimes he completely ignores them. But they still act as if he were the coolest person on earth." Katherine frowned, looking over at the kids as they chased each other around one of the big oak trees.

"Things are still bad, huh?" Lauren put her hand on Katherine's arm. "Do you want me to talk to him?"

"No, I don't think it would do any good. I mean, not to degrade your sisterly influence on him or anything. He's worried about money, but I'm sure it will smooth over soon," Katherine said, not convincingly.

"Well, what about you? Are you still having your solo date nights?" Lauren asked.

"Mm hmm." Katherine nodded as she took a long sip of her coffee.

"And how's that going?" Lauren prodded.

"It's fine," Katherine said, wiping the dripping water from the icy cup, not meeting Lauren's eyes. She had to work really hard to keep the smitten grin from appearing. The same type of smile that she'd just chastised her sister-in-law for. When she looked up and saw Lauren studying her face she asked, "What?"

"I don't know. You just had a funny look on your face."

"No, I didn't," Katherine protested childishly.

Lauren was about to say something else when her phone rang. After glancing at the screen she quickly answered with a bright "Hello." She stood up and went into the house, leaving Katherine sighing with relief that she didn't have to answer any more questions about her night out.

She longed to confide in someone about her situation with

Jonathan, but that person definitely could not be her husband's sister. She hadn't had time to meet up with any of her other friends lately. And there was no way she would tell her mother. She was a devout Catholic, attending mass twice a week. She was sure she would tell Katherine that she would burn in hell. She had heard it all when Katherine's older sister's husband cheated - about how a marriage was a sacred institution and no one took their wedding vows seriously anymore.

Lauren came back through the sliding glass door, unable to hide her bliss.

"Let me guess? Daniel?" Katherine asked, raising an eyebrow.

"Yes, as a matter of fact. He wants to take me and James out for dinner tonight," Lauren said.

"Well, all I can say is: guard your heart. And make sure he takes you somewhere expensive."

That night Lauren couldn't fall asleep. Her mind was toggling back and forth between the conversation with Katherine earlier and the past few days spent with Daniel. She knew she wasn't imagining it. Daniel was different. He was patient and kind. He was present when spending time with them, making sure to give both her and James equal amounts of attention. It was so hard for her to reconcile this new Daniel with the man she had known seven years ago.

Lauren remembered how Daniel never seemed to be fully with her; he was often preoccupied and she felt as if he wasn't really listening to her. In the first few months of their relationship, she let it go because he made up for it with fancy dinners, flowers and sweet sentiments. *You're so beautiful. I'm so lucky to have you. I miss you when we're not together.*

After dating for about five or six months, Lauren was clearly no longer a priority for Daniel. His business became his all-consuming focus. And apparently, so did Kelly.

Chapter 16

Tuesday morning Katherine dropped Madison off at the elementary school and then Keenan at preschool. She had agreed to meet Jonathan for lunch at 11:30 and still had a couple of hours to fill. She longed to go to her favorite day spa and let herself be pampered with a facial and pedicure, but that would definitely not go over well with Nathan's newly imposed strict budget.

Aside from discussions involving the menial topics of running the household, she still had not spoken to Nathan. She was so angry she could barely stand to be in the same room with him. Sunday night he had gone into her purse and taken out all of her credit cards. He didn't even tell her. When she was in the checkout lane at Target Monday afternoon, she was shocked to see that her Target card was missing from her wallet, along with all of her other department store cards. She thought that they had been stolen! But after texting Nathan, his cold reply came back: *Too much spending. Cards are locked up.*

Katherine had been so furious she could hardly see straight walking out of the store. Nathan had been the one who insisted that Katherine stay home with the children. He had said that he was making enough money so that she didn't have to work anymore. And when she had offered to go back to teaching a year ago, he once again contended that he felt it was best if she focused on the children and taking care of things at home. Which was fine with her, as long as they didn't have to struggle to make ends meet.

She was still trying to come up with an excuse to tell Jonathan why she wouldn't be able to dine at Tiramisu this coming Thursday. She figured she could use the standard "I have to work late" excuse, but that was what Nathan told her all the time and she just couldn't stomach it. She knew Jonathan was going to be disappointed no matter what reason she gave. She had wracked her brain all morning and still had not come up with something reasonable.

She was wearing her heather grey suit that she had worn when she had first interviewed for her teaching job. She didn't think she really needed to convince Jonathan that she was working. But she did want to look professional. Not so much for him, but for herself. Today she didn't want to be the stay at home mom who usually ran errands in work-out clothes.

Keenan had noticed that she was dressed up and commented that she looked fancy. He had asked if she was going to an important meeting, like Daddy. It had made Katherine laugh, but she immediately felt a little tug of guilt. Of course it was just as easy to brush that guilt right off her conscience as she recalled how Nathan had barely interacted with her the past few days. He didn't even bother to say sorry for missing her mother's birthday party.

She went into the little boutique shop that was in the same shopping strip as the café where she was meeting Jonathan later. She had made sure to pick a place that was far enough from where she might run into anyone she knew. As she walked through the aisles of the store, glancing at the jewelry and knick-knacks, she felt good to be dressed up, her face made-up and her hair twisted up into a loose knot. She even wore her best black heels that she had only worn twice; once last year to Nathan's office Christmas party and at the wedding of one of her college friends.

She noticed the two young sales clerks eyeing her and was sure they were envious of her, wondering what important job she must have. She held her head a little higher, enjoying the attention. After browsing the scarves and handbags, she went next door to the book shop. She picked up the latest novel by one of her favorite authors, found a comfy chair and read until it was time to meet Jonathan.

Jonathan was waiting for her at a table near the window, looking incredibly handsome in a black t-shirt and jeans. Katherine was pleased, but nervous when he stood up to greet her with a kiss. She had quickly searched the tables as she walked in for anyone she knew, but she still felt a little uneasy.

"How's your day been so far? Busy?" Jonathan asked as she settled in across from him.

"Yes. Very busy," Katherine said and took another glance around the café. She made sure to keep her hands in her lap in case Jonathan tried to reach for her across the table.

"I already ordered you a sparkling water," Jonathan said, surmising that Katherine had been looking for their server.

The waitress appeared just then, delivering her water and his coke, and took their lunch order: a Cobb salad for Katherine and a burger and fries for Jonathan.

"So," Katherine said a little anxiously. "What have you been up to today?"

"I went to the gym, studied a little bit," Jonathan answered and then gave Katherine a long glance. "You seem preoccupied. Everything ok?"

"Yes," Katherine said and took a long sip of her water. "I just have a lot going on this week with work."

"Tell me about the project you're working on," Jonathan said, his blue eyes intense on her.

"Well, I'm, uh, working with a small start-up company called M & K Enterprises", she began. Katherine was extremely glad that she had drilled her sister about her marketing job at their mother's party last weekend. Rachel loved to talk about her work and had told her in great detail about the current project she was working on. Katherine reiterated as much as she could from their conversation. Jonathan listened with interest and asked her questions that she answered either ad lib or from the information her sister had relayed.

Their entrees arrived and they made small talk in between bites. Jonathan happily shared his French fries with Katherine, something that Nathan always complained about. *If you wanted fries, why didn't you just order your own?* Nathan would say when she tried to sneak some from his plate. He never understood that she only wanted a few and if she ordered her own she would eat way more than she needed. Of course he hadn't complained about it when they were first dating. But there were a lot of things that he seemed to be much more relaxed about back then.

As they waited for the check she told Jonathan that she wouldn't be able to dine at Tiramisu this Thursday night because she needed to get back home for a family event. Jonathan looked disappointed, but told her he understood, then asked if she'd meet him during the day for another picnic at "their park" and she eagerly agreed.

They were just walking out of the café when Katherine turned to see Lauren and James at the counter. The clerk was handing Lauren a brown to-go bag and a couple of drinks. Her heart began to race. She quickly turned her back to them and rushed Jonathan out the door and down the sidewalk out of view of the cafe's windows.

"In a hurry?" Jonathan asked as he took a couple big steps to catch up to her.

"No, I'm just glad to have some fresh air. You know, I'm cooped up in the office all day." Katherine glanced back to make sure Lauren wasn't coming out the door already. The coast was clear, but as she turned back around, she noticed Lauren's car parked along the street right in front of them. She grabbed Jonathan's hand and picked up the pace even more. "Come on, slow poke."

"What is this? An after lunch jog?" Jonathan laughed as they turned a corner. There was a little alcove in between the shops on the next block and Katherine tugged him into it. She grabbed him around the neck and pulled his lips down onto hers. Jonathan murmured in between kisses, "Mmmm... You couldn't wait to get your hands on me, huh?"

Katherine laughed nervously as she pulled away from him. "Something like that."

"Well, I'm certainly not complaining," he said and pulled her back for another kiss.

Katherine allowed the kiss to continue for a few minutes, hoping that she had given Lauren enough time to get into her car and drive away. Her heart was still racing, both because of the intensity of the kiss and the prospect of being caught. She pulled away again and ran her hand along Jonathan's smooth jawline. "I'd better get back to work."

"So soon? I thought we could take a nice walk. Or jog, if you feel the need," he joked.

"I would love to, but I have a meeting I need to get back in time for." Katherine looked at her watch for emphasis.

"Ok. I'll call you tonight during my break," Jonathan said as they emerged from the alcove. He noticed Katherine looking nervously down the street and he laughed, "What are you looking for?"

"Nothing. I just thought I saw someone I knew. From work," Katherine added quickly. She smiled, gave him a little wave and turned to go, almost running smack into a store sign. She giggled nervously and called out, "See you later."

"Ok." Jonathan was laughing at her and shaking his head as he headed toward his own car.

That evening, after the kids had gone to bed and Katherine was cleaning the kitchen, the house phone rang, but it stopped before she could rinse and dry her hands. After a few minutes, Nathan called out from his office, "It's Lauren. She wants to talk to you."

Katherine grabbed the phone and as she picked up she heard Nathan saying, "I'll try not to. Good night, sis."

"Hey Lauren," Katherine said and then heard Nathan click off. "What were you and Nathan talking about?"

"Oh, I was just telling him not to work so hard," Lauren said.

Katherine snorted, "Well, thanks for trying, but I won't hold my breath."

"I'm sorry. I know it must be hard. But I'm sure it won't always be like this," Lauren said, then paused and added, "Hey! Were you at Antonio's Cafe today?"

97

Katherine cringed. So she had seen her! She had thought about it the rest of the afternoon and couldn't come up with any good reason for being on that side of town, especially dressed up in business attire, not to mention with a gorgeous young man on her arm. So she had finally decided she would just flat out deny it.

"Nooooo...." Katherine said in a sarcastic tone. "What in the world would I be doing on that side of town?"

"I didn't think it could be you. But, then you definitely have a twin. And she was with a really good looking guy."

"Really?" Katherine said as if barely interested. Then asked, "But what were you doing at Antonio's? That's nowhere near your school."

"Oh, James had a dentist appointment down the street and we popped in to pick up lunch afterward. When I was paying I saw this girl leaving that looked exactly like you. It was weird. But come to think of it, she was dressed in a business suit. That should have clued me off right away," Lauren said with a laugh.

"Yeah, you know me. Always in jeans or yoga pants," Katherine said and tried to laugh, but it came out more like she was choking. "Hey, I need to go get the kids ready for bed. I'll talk to you later, ok?"

"Sure. Next time I see your twin I'll be sure to get a picture for you," Lauren teased her.

"Funny. Bye." Katherine hung up the phone, sat down and let out a big sigh. Was it really necessary for Lauren to point out how unusual it would be for her to be dressed up? She quickly realized how silly it was to let that menial comment bother her when she had come so close to being caught. She really needed to be more careful the next time she saw Jonathan. However, should there even be a next time? Just how long was she going to carry on for? She hadn't really given much thought to how her little fling would end.

Oh, how she craved the attention Jonathan gave her. The way he made her feel young and interesting and alive. What was her alternative? Sit at home and watch overpaid actresses being lavished with love and affection? She was slowly starting to understand how some housewives got so addicted to soap operas. If their husbands weren't giving them the romance they craved, they could get a good dose of it on TV. And here she was with the opportunity to experience it live.

The problem was that she was beginning to have real feelings for Jonathan. She loved spending time with him. He made her laugh. She loved hearing him talk about his classes, his friends and his co-workers. When she talked, he really listened to her, making comments and asking questions. Unlike her and her husband, they had actual conversations. Nathan was always only half listening. It seemed as if his mind never stopped thinking about his work. He was even distracted with the children and sometimes impatient with them. The more Katherine thought about it, the angrier she became toward Nathan. And the angrier she became, the easier it was to justify continuing to see Jonathan.

Chapter 17

By the following week Daniel had appeared at Lauren's door each and every night to spend time with James. The two of them would throw or kick a ball back and forth in the yard, play with Burley or construct Lego creations in the living room while Lauren busied herself with grading papers or housework.

"Can't Dad stay for dinner?" James begged almost every night. Daniel helped Lauren in the kitchen, while James colored at the table or played with his toys in the living room.

Daniel and Lauren tucked James into bed together, taking turns reading stories. Then when it was time for Daniel to go home, he would corner Lauren at the door and they would make out until James called out, asking Lauren for water or declaring that he was too hot or too cold.

Daniel would laugh and shake his head. "Does he have a surveillance camera on us or what?"

As they said goodbye Thursday night, Daniel told her he had an agent's dinner to attend Friday night, but that he wanted to take Lauren out for a real date Saturday afternoon.

"You mean just us?" Lauren asked as she leaned against the front door.

"Yes, just you and me." Daniel gave her a sexy grin as he drew her into his arms and kissed her good night. He paused and looked toward James' room, expecting him to call for his mom. When he only heard silence, Daniel wiggled his eyebrows. "He must be asleep."

Daniel leaned down to kiss Lauren again, but this time James' voice called out, "Mom, I hear a weird noise coming from my closet." They both burst out laughing.

"I'll pick you up at eleven," Daniel said with a wink and let himself out.

Katherine volunteered to take James with her and the kids to lunch and a movie on Saturday. Even so, she continued to chide Lauren about going out with Daniel. "Didn't he already cause you enough pain seven years ago?"

"And this time if he breaks your heart, you won't be able to just cut him out of your life and get over him. You'll have to see him every time he comes to spend time with James."

She gave her sister-in-law a pass, figuring that Katherine's attitude was due to the strain on her marriage with Nathan's late hours and grumpiness. Sure, Katherine has some valid points, but Lauren couldn't discount the changes she'd seen in Daniel. Her fear of him being an inadequate father had been long forgotten, watching the two of them rough house and joke around as if they'd known each other all their lives. Lauren saw that glint of pride in Daniel's eyes when he looked at his son.

Lauren couldn't recall the last time she took so long deciding what to wear. She finally settled on her white jeans, a soft grey sweater and short black suede boots. She wanted to look appealing, but casual and relaxed. *It's not that big of a deal, it's just a date*, she kept telling herself, but by the time the doorbell rang her stomach was a ball of nerves and she felt like she did when she and Daniel just met: completely smitten.

"Hey," Daniel said softly as he casually leaned against her doorframe. "You ready to go have some grown-up fun?"

Lauren smiled and gave James a big hug as he came running up to the door. James gave Daniel a quick hug too, before running back to the living room where he was playing a board game with his cousins.

Katherine popped her head around the corner of the hallway to get a peek at Daniel and to give Lauren a look that once again warned her to be cautious with her heart. "You kids behave yourselves."

"We'll do our best," Daniel winked at Lauren as they walked out the door.

Settling into the leather seat of Daniel's pristine Saab, she realized how long it had been since she'd been in a car that didn't have toys and crumbs strewn all over or handprints on the windows. Daniel started the engine and popped in a CD. The upbeat music of Coldplay filled the car and he looked over and raised an eyebrow at her. Lauren smiled back, memories of their early dates filling her mind.

"I thought we would head out to the lake," Daniel said, lightly drumming his hand on the steering wheel.

"Wait, let me guess - you own a boat?" Lauren asked with a smirk.

"Well, actually I do. But I thought we'd wait and do that with James. I think he would love it. Plus it's still a little cool out for boating."

"You talked constantly about the day you would buy a boat." Lauren reminisced as she watched Daniel out of the corner of her eye, and saw that he was smiling proudly. "I remember that time you took me to the boat show. We were there for hours. And we had to get on every single one of them. I was so wiped out."

"Yeah, but do you remember how I took you to your favorite restaurant that night? Then let you pick the movie? I mercifully sat through the sappiest movie of all times as compensation."

"If I recall correctly, you fell asleep during the first half hour and I had to wake you up when it was over," Lauren said, giving his arm a playful punch.

"I didn't fall asleep!" Daniel said indignantly, but started laughing when he saw the expression on Lauren's face. "Okay, okay. You caught me. But, still. I endured thirty minutes."

Lauren smiled and crossed her arms, looking out the window. She felt a little pang of tenderness creep over her.

"Do you remember the one I liked the best?" Daniel broke into her thoughts.

"Yes, I remember what it looked like and the color, but I have no idea what kind it was."

"A bow rider. The Cobalt R7. 430 HP."

"Ahhh.... Of course. 430 HP. Great choice."

"430 horsepower," Daniel said with a sideways grin.

"Right. I knew that." Lauren smiled. "So, you bought it?"

"Yep. Two years ago. I take it out from April to October at least once a week," Daniel said with pride. "I have her docked over at Wilson's Cove."

"I can't wait to see it," Lauren said with sincerity. "And you're right. I think James will love it."

They spent the rest of the fifteen minute drive through the hill country in comfortable silence. Daniel let Lauren pick out the next CD and she chose the upbeat music of INXS. Lauren occasionally glanced over at Daniel, admiring his profile, and each time he would return her gaze with a little smile and a wink. By the time Daniel pulled into a small alcove overlooking the lake and turned off the engine, Lauren felt as if they had just picked up where they left off seven years ago.

Daniel quickly got out of the car and came around to open Lauren's door for her. She gratefully took his hand as he helped her out. He held onto her hand as he led her over to a large rock that was near the edge of the look-out point. They sat down and took in the view of the quiet lake for a few minutes, savoring the cool breeze and the sun barely peeking through the tall cedar trees.

"Before I bought the boat, I used to come out here a lot. Sometimes I'd hike down to the bottom of the hill. Or just hang out here. Great way to clear my thoughts."

"About what? The boat you had your sights on?" Lauren joked. But Daniel remained serious.

"Yeah, sometimes. But that's not all." Daniel continued to stare out at the lake and frowned a little. "Sometimes I thought about you. I wondered what you were doing. If you were dating someone or had gotten married. I tried finding you a few times, but you were unlisted."

Lauren sat in stunned silence. After she found out she was pregnant, she had changed her number and purposely remained unlisted. It wasn't because she didn't want Daniel to find her, but because she worried that if she was listed and he didn't contact her it would hurt too much. She also didn't want to be tempted to take him back just to have him betray her all over again. Especially not with a baby involved.

"Did you ever even consider telling me?" Daniel asked.

She breathed in and let out a big sigh. "Of course I did, but every time I thought about it I pictured *her* in your apartment, drinking wine and practically telling me you two had just gotten out of bed."

Daniel glanced over at Lauren and nudged her with his shoulder. "I promise you I never even kissed Kelly. Boy, did she try, but I wasn't interested in her. I was so focused on building my business. I just got caught up in achieving my goals. I was selfish and self-centered. But, I never meant to hurt you."

"Well, you did," Lauren said with emphasis. "I knew your business was important. But I wanted to be there for you. And you shut me out."

"I know. I was an idiot. I'm sorry," Daniel said softly. "But you made mistakes too."

The two of them sat for a few minutes in silence, listening to the cackling of crows and the wind rustling through the trees.

"I know I was wrong to keep James from you. I was just so hurt that all I could think about was how I could keep from dealing with any more pain. And I guess if I'm really honest with myself, maybe I wanted to punish you a little bit." Lauren finally spoke. "But then I just got too busy taking care of James to really think about anything else. Of course there were many nights that I would lay awake wondering if I did the right thing. Wondering if I had told you about the pregnancy, maybe you would have seen it as a positive thing. But I was just so scared that you would think I was trying to trap you. And

I didn't want you to decide to stay with me only for the sake of a baby."

"Lauren, you don't have to explain anymore."

"No, let me finish. I need to get this off my chest," Lauren insisted. She had already had this conversation with Daniel in her head so many times over the years. "You always told me you never wanted kids and how much of a bother they were. I never in a million years had any reason to think you would be interested in a baby. I just did what I thought was right to protect me and James."

"I know. I was kind of a meathead about kids back then. But the moment I realized James was my son, I felt something I'd never experienced before. It's just different when you know they're your own flesh and blood."

"Yes, it is," Lauren said quietly. "The second they placed him in my arms I was in love. A complete selfless, overwhelming love."

"I totally get that now." Daniel took her hand in his. "And I'm just really glad that I can be a part of his life."

"I am too," Lauren said, squeezing his hand.

He then took her chin in his hand and turned her face toward his. "Can we start over?"

Lauren nodded, trying to hold back the tears that had been threatening to flow during their conversation. Daniel leaned in and kissed her tenderly. Then he wrapped his arms around her, embracing her in a way that left Lauren with no doubt as to his sincerity.

"Are you hungry?" Daniel asked as he let go and pulled her to her feet.

"Starved," Lauren answered.

"Well, let's go get some lunch."

They spent the rest of the afternoon enjoying a leisurely meal at the Iguana Grill, a Mexican restaurant that overlooked the lake. The view of the lake was spectacular from their table on the patio. Gentle ripples lined the crystal blue water with just a few boats speckled here and there. The sky mirrored the lake, a perfect blue dotted by perfect white cotton ball clouds. They ate two baskets of chips with spicy salsa then split an order of sizzling beef fajitas. Lauren had a margarita and Daniel drank a Mexican beer.

They talked about everything from James to Lauren's class at school to Daniel's business, and even the old days when they were dating. They kept the conversation light and laughed often. By the time they were back in Daniel's car heading toward home, Lauren felt assured that not only could she trust Daniel, but that he had indeed changed for the better. He was more attentive, spoke with compassion and even though he still displayed an air of confidence, it wasn't peppered with the egotistical manner that had once defined his character.

When they arrived at Lauren's house and came through the front door, James practically knocked Daniel over with a big hug.

"Hey, buddy. Did you have fun with your aunt and cousins today?" Daniel asked as he scooped him up into his arms.

"Yep. We ate fried chicken and mashed potatoes! Then we went to see Journey to the Center of the Earth. It was so cool!" James announced.

"That sounds awesome," Daniel said as he set James back down.

"What did you guys do?" James asked as they walked into the living room.

"We took a drive out to the lake and had some lunch," Daniel said, taking notice of Katherine, who was just getting up from the couch, eyeing him with interest. "Hi Katherine. Good to see you again."

"Hi Daniel," Katherine looked over at Lauren and asked, "So, you two had fun?"

"Yes, it was very nice," Lauren answered with sincerity. "Thanks again for taking James out."

"Sure. Anytime," Katherine said, gathering her purse and keys. "Well, we'd better get going. I need to start sewing Madison's costume for the Spring play."

"Oh, you're going to be in a play?" Lauren asked her niece, smoothing Madison's curly crimson hair.

"Yes! I'm going to be a butterfly!" Madison said proudly, waving her arms and spinning in a circle. "Daddy said I'll be the prettiest one on stage."

"Yeah, but Daddy probably won't even be there. I heard Mommy say that to Grandma on the phone," Keenan interjected.

"Keenan!" Katherine scolded her son. "That isn't what I said at all. I just said that he might get stuck at work and he would do his best to be there. Now stop teasing your sister."

"Come on, I'll walk you out," Lauren stepped in. She glanced over at Daniel who was busy asking James about the movie he'd gone to. "We'll be right back."

As Katherine corralled Madison and Keenan into the car, she said to Lauren, "Call me when you can talk. In Private."

Lauren nodded, smiling from ear to ear, and waltzed back into the house as if she were walking on air.

An hour later when Daniel announced it was time for him to go,

James whined, "Aww Dad, can't you just stay the night here? We could have a sleepover."

Daniel looked over at Lauren with a sly grin and held his hands up in question.

Lauren just laughed and shook her head. "I don't think so, James. Daniel needs to sleep at his house."

Just as James was beginning to protest with another onslaught of *Aww, Mom*, Daniel told James he needed to talk to his mom alone and could he give them a minute. James nodded and slowly slinked toward his bedroom.

"Hey, I have an idea," Daniel said as he pulled Lauren toward him.

"I bet you do, but, Daniel, I'm not sure I'm ready for..." Lauren began, but Daniel put a finger over her lips.

"No, I didn't mean that. Not that it isn't extremely appealing," he said, running his hand over her arm. "But I meant that James could spend the night at my house."

"Ohhhh...," Lauren said, feeling disappointed but relieved at the same time. The thought of having a 'sleepover' with Daniel made her stomach do funny things, but she knew that would be moving a little too fast. "Well, I don't see why not. Just make sure he brushes his teeth and uses the bathroom before bed. Do you have a room for him?"

"Yeah, I have a guest room," Daniel said. "I'll even cook him breakfast in the morning. I bet he'll love my famous omelet."

"Well, then. I guess I'll go pack up his things."

Chapter 18

Katherine was just hanging up the phone with Lauren as Nathan strolled into their bedroom. Lauren had given her the play-by-play on her date with Daniel and Katherine had to admit that she was impressed. She still had her doubts, but she was beginning to see that maybe Lauren was right about Daniel being a changed man.

"Who ya talking to?" Nathan asked casually as he walked past her and into their bathroom.

"Your sister. She went out with Daniel today, remember?" Katherine said as she followed him.

"Oh, yeah," Nathan said absently, which Katherine knew was his way of disguising that he did not remember at all. She figured he only listened to about half of anything she ever told him.

"So, they had a very nice time. He took her for a drive into the hill country and they ate at that new Mexican place on the lake."

"Mm-hmm," he murmured as he uncapped the toothpaste.

"It would be nice to go out there and check it out one weekend."

Nathan started to brush his teeth and gave her a little shoulder shrug.

Katherine rolled her eyes, but Nathan didn't notice.

"So, Lauren thinks that Daniel's really changed. Plus, he's been totally bonding with James." Katherine went on, "And James adores him already. It's really cute to see them together."

Nathan frowned and spit toothpaste. "I don't know if she should trust that guy. The only reason I'm even somewhat okay with him coming around again is because he's James' dad."

"Well, at least he's trying. He brought her flowers and took her out somewhere unique." Katherine tried to keep the annoyance from her tone. She waited for Nathan to say something, but he just started to floss his teeth. She leaned against the counter, crossed her arms and waited for him to finish, then said, "Remember when you used to do that?"

"Do what?" Nathan asked as he wiped his mouth with a towel.

"Bring me flowers. Take me out on dates," Katherine said, catching her husband's gaze in the mirror.

Nathan turned around, shrugged his shoulders and said, "Yeah, of course I remember. That's what you do when you first start dating."

"It doesn't have to be like that, you know? Married people can do that too." Katherine followed Nathan back out into the bedroom.

Nathan sighed heavily as he sat down on their bed. "What are you getting at, Katherine?"

"When's the last time we had a date night? It's been ages." Katherine sat down on her side of the bed.

"Well, you know I've been bogged down with work. And we can't really afford it right now."

"It doesn't have to be expensive. We could just go on a picnic or something." Katherine tried to get him to make eye contact, but Nathan was more interested in picking at the stray threads on their comforter. "Nathan?"

"Look, Katherine, it's been a long day. I'm really tired. What do you want me to say?" Nathan said in a weary voice.

"Nothing. Absolutely nothing," Katherine said and walked out of the room.

Katherine went downstairs to the kitchen and put the tea kettle on to boil. She pulled out an Earl Grey tea bag and plunked it into a mug. While she waited for the water to boil she stood at the kitchen counter, drumming her fingers on the marble. As the steam began to pour out of the kettle, she let out a huff of air herself. *When did Nathan become so insensitive?* She poured the hot water into her mug and dunked her tea bag up and down, watching the hazel color begin to infuse the water. She stirred in a spoonful of honey and was just walking to the refrigerator for the cream when Nathan came into the room holding her phone.

"Who's J?" he asked, holding her phone up.

Katherine's heart quickened. She hadn't realized that she left her cell phone in the bedroom and she had completely forgotten that Jonathan had said he was going to call her later that night.

"J called you three times in the past five minutes. It must be important." Nathan handed her phone to her.

"Oh, thanks." She took the phone from him, trying to sound casual, her heart still pounding. However, scanning his face she quickly realized that he wasn't even interested in her answer. He didn't look the least bit concerned about the mysterious caller. But just in case, she quickly added, "It's just a mom from Madison's school. She's probably checking to see if I'm still bringing cookies for their class party on Monday."

Katherine set her phone down and went about getting out the cream. When she closed the refrigerator door and turned around she had expected Nathan to be gone, but he stood there leaning against the counter top.

"If it's that important to you, we'll go on a picnic tomorrow. We can either bring the kids along or we can see if Lauren will watch them. Okay?"

Katherine just looked at her husband for a few moments. Then she nodded her head as she walked over to pour the cream into her mug. She stood with her back to him and stirred her tea slowly, her hand shaking ever so slightly. She waited to see if he was going to say anything else. He finally walked over and kissed her on the cheek, then said softly, "I'm going up to bed. Good night."

"Good night," Katherine replied serenely.

She picked up the phone and looked at the display that read "3 missed calls from J". She carried her tea to the living room where she sat down on the sofa. She clicked on Jonathan's contact and selected the text icon.

She hesitated for several minutes, going over the conversation she had just had with Nathan upstairs. Then she thought about her husband's simple form of apology by offering to take her on a picnic after all. She didn't even want to contemplate how near she came to being caught with Jonathan calling her cell phone. She still felt a little shaky.

Finally, she typed out a quick text that said, *Sorry I missed you. Will call you tomorrow.* She then turned off her phone.

After finishing her tea and placing the mug in the sink, Katherine went upstairs, got into bed and curled up next to Nathan who was already snoring. She inched closer to him and put her arm around his waist, guilty tears streaming down her face.

The next morning, Katherine was making pancakes while Nathan sat in the living room with Madison and Keenan working on a puzzle. Just as Katherine was about to call them into the kitchen to eat, Nathan's phone rang. It was his boss calling to tell him that the Johnsons wanted to schedule an emergency meeting to go over some of the additions to their plans and could Nathan possibly come in today? Of course he could.

Katherine didn't even say anything. She just poured some coffee into Nathan's ceramic thermos and set it on the counter while he went upstairs to get dressed. Then she went about pouring syrup and cutting the children's pancakes into little squares, taking deep even breaths.

"We'll do the picnic next weekend, ok?" Nathan said as he came back down in jeans and a button down shirt. She just handed him his coffee and nodded silently.

Chapter 19

"So, what do you think?" Daniel asked as he showed Lauren around his condo. Lauren was pleased that he suggested she come to pick up James after their sleep over, so that she could have an official tour of his place. It was small, but cozy. Perfect for a bachelor, with a small living room, kitchen, dining area, master bedroom and guest bedroom.

"Very nice," Lauren said as she admired the contemporary furniture and the bold colors. She picked up a bright orange ceramic vase and asked, "You decorated it yourself?"

"Nah, a friend actually helped me out in that department. You know I'm hopeless when it comes to that stuff. The only thing I can take credit for is finding this gem and getting an awesome deal on it." Daniel smiled and put his arms around her.

"Yes, I'll agree to both those statements." Lauren melted into his arms and then she asked, "Who helped you?"

"Hmmmm?" Daniel murmured as he nuzzled the top of her head with his cheek. "You feel so nice."

"Who is the friend that helped you decorate?" Lauren asked, pulling back from him.

Before he could answer, James came out from the guest room with his backpack. He wore a frown on his face as he pleaded, "Can't

I stay another night, Mom? It's so cool here!"

"No sweetie. You have school tomorrow," Lauren reminded him.

"But I didn't even get to go in the pool!" he declared. "Look!"

Lauren walked over to the window and looked down below. There was a sparkling pool surrounded by chaise lounge chairs covered in bright striped pillows. Lauren became wistful herself to hang out by the pool as well. She couldn't help wondering if Daniel had other women here and had taken them for a swim. She knew it wasn't a matter of 'if'. It was more a question of 'how many'.

"Don't worry, buddy." Daniel ruffled his hair gently. "We can have another sleep over next weekend. And we will definitely go in the pool. Sound good?"

"But next weekend's like a million days away," James whined.

Daniel laughed and lifted him up into his arms. "It will be here before you know it, I promise. Now, can you go into the kitchen and grab the cookies I said you could take home with you?"

"You made cookies?" Lauren asked.

"Don't look so shocked. I know how to bake," Daniel said, mocking insult. "They were from a roll, but we cut them, put them in the oven and even managed not to burn them. Didn't we, champ?"

James nodded his head. "Yep. They were yummy! You can have some too, Mom."

Daniel set him down and James scampered into the kitchen. Then Daniel grabbed Lauren's hand and whispered intimately, "So, when are we going to get some alone time again?"

"That's a good question," Lauren replied as she looked up at him with a seductive smile. "What did you have in mind?"

"Oh, I don't know if you really want me to answer that," Daniel said quietly and pulled her in for a kiss.

"Ew. Gross!" James exclaimed as he came back into the room with the foil wrapped cookies.

Daniel and Lauren pulled away from one another, laughing.

"We'd better get going," Lauren said and picked up James' backpack. She glanced at Daniel with a mischievous grin, "But, I'll call you later so that we can finish our conversation."

"You'd better," Daniel said as he walked them to the door. As James walked out onto the front porch, he grabbed Lauren around her waist and snuck another quick kiss.

On the way home James chattered happily about Daniel; how much he liked his condo and about all the fun they had. He told her that Daniel made really yummy grilled turkey and cheese sandwiches. Then he asked a question Lauren wasn't expecting. "How come we can't live together in the same house?"

Lauren cleared her throat and tried to piece something together in her mind, but before she could speak James said, "Moms and dads are supposed to live together."

"Well, yes, that's true. But not all moms and dads live together. Remember your friend Sean? His parents have separate houses," Lauren said and peered at him in the rear view mirror.

"Yeah, but Sean says that's because they were fighting too much. You and Dad don't ever fight," James pointed out.

"Yes, that's true, sweetheart. But I haven't seen your dad in a very long time. We're just getting to know each other again. Maybe one day..." Lauren trailed off and realized that her words were something that her heart hadn't even allowed her to comprehend yet. She knew that it would be ideal for Daniel and her to get married and be a happy family. But was that realistic? What if Daniel didn't want that at all? What if he wanted to remain single and be able to date other women?

That brought her thoughts back to the "friend" that had decorated his apartment. She saw way too many feminine touches to know better than to think it was a male friend. But Daniel had conveniently dodged her question. Whoever this 'friend' is, she was probably better off not hearing about it.

For the rest of the afternoon Lauren's heart was heavy with pestering thoughts about her relationship with James' father. She was falling for Daniel again and even though he was showering her with affection, there was still a very good chance that it didn't mean as much to him as it did to her. Deep down she knew her sister-in-law was right when she had advised her to guard her heart. It wasn't realistic to just become a happy family overnight.

Can I trust him again? He did indeed seem sincere, but hadn't that been the way he acted when they'd first started dating the last time?

After James was fast asleep, and Lauren had showered and settled into bed with a book, she first picked up her phone to text Daniel.

James told me to tell you Good Night.
Thanks! I miss him already. Are you in bed??
Yes, I am.
Wish I were there.
Stop. You're making me blush.
Me too. :) I want to say good night in person.
How about we compromise? Over the phone?

Her phone immediately rang and she answered quickly. "Hey."

"Hey you." Daniel's low voice made her shiver. "Are you getting ready to doze off?"

"Not quite. I was planning to read for a bit first. What about you?"

"I have some work I need to do before bed, but I probably won't be too far behind you. James kinda wore me out." Daniel laughed.

"He has a way of doing that," Lauren said. "But it's worth it."

"Oh, absolutely," Daniel said. "Hey I have an idea. How about you two have dinner here at my place for a change this week?"

"Sure, that sounds good," Lauren said. Then against her better judgment, she added, "By the way, you never answered me about who decorated your place."

"Yeah I did," Daniel said. Lauren waited but he didn't seem to be going to give any further details.

"You said it was a friend. A girl friend?"

"Aw, Lauren. You don't have anything to worry about. It was actually one of my agents. And yes, she is female. But we are *just friends*," Daniel said with a hint of annoyance.

"Okay. Okay. I was just curious." Lauren immediately regretted bringing it up.

"I better let you get some sleep," Daniel said with a little less edge, but not quite as cheery as before.

"Okay. I'm sorry. I didn't mean to accuse you of anything."

"No worries. We're good. I'll give you a call tomorrow during lunch," he said.

They said their good nights and Lauren switched off her phone. She felt heavy as she chided herself for once again letting her jealousy cause tension between them. Even though Daniel said it was fine, she could tell he was annoyed with her. *Was she good enough for him?* She was a great mom, she loved her job, she knew she was attractive and interesting. But there was just something missing she couldn't quite place.

Chapter 20

Katherine knew she was hovering on the edge of total disaster. Jonathan had asked her if she would come for dinner at his house on his night off. She had eagerly agreed over the phone last Sunday after Nathan had spoiled their picnic plans to go into work. After cleaning up, she had packed up some snacks and taken the kids to the park. Then while Madison and Keenan ran around the playground, she talked on the phone with Jonathan for over an hour.

They were now talking on the phone every night, flirting unashamedly. Katherine didn't even bother worrying about talking to "J" at home now. She just closed the bedroom door and figured Nathan wouldn't be upstairs until after midnight as usual. He continued with his routine of holing up in his office right after dinner, ignoring everything else going on in the household. Madison and Keenan had long given up begging him to read them a story. Katherine didn't bother to say anything to him; Nathan always answered with a dry 'I get lots of time with them when you're out.' Katherine didn't dare say anything else, fearful that Nathan might make another fuss about her night out.

Katherine and Nathan were saying very little to each other as it was. They only talked when absolutely necessary, about matters concerning the kids and their schedules, household issues, and the new budget. When they were in the same room alone together, which was rare, they just went about their business in awkward silence. This only further fueled the fire in Katherine to seal her heart off to her husband. And it strengthened the desire to become closer to Jonathan.

But now, on the day of the planned dinner date at Jonathan's, as she sat on a park bench watching Keenan and Madison scamper around the playscape, she had a knot in her stomach. She shouldn't go to his house; she could be swept away by passion and do something that would damage her marriage beyond repair. But how could she not go? The thought of another night sitting home alone after the kids went to bed wasn't exactly appealing.

She stopped by the self-serve yogurt shop on the way home from the park and let Keenan and Madison fill their cups to the brim, pouring on as many toppings as they wished. She skipped her usual vanilla bean topped with mini chocolate chips as her stomach was still churning with nerves.

At home, she put on a video for the children while she took a hot bath and washed her hair. She took her time shaving her legs, still unsure if she was going to go through with this. It was both electrifying and terrifying at the same time. By the time she had blown out her hair to perfection and carefully applied her make-up, she was practically shaking with nerves. She had already selected her favorite lavender wrap dress and hung it on the closet door that morning.

Coming downstairs into the living room, she saw Keenan with his head resting on the end of the sofa, napping peacefully and Madison still staring at the TV, clutching her favorite bear. She paused for a moment, just taking in the sight of her children.

What in the world am I doing? This is crazy. She felt a horrible pang of guilt. *What kind of person does this anyway? I'm a good person. And a good mother. I can't do this.*

She rushed to the kitchen and grabbed her cell phone off the charger, then scrolled through her contacts until she pulled up his number. Jonathan's phone went straight to voicemail. *Dang it.* She waited a minute and tried again with no luck. She didn't feel it was right to cancel via a message, so she hung up the phone and started to work on dinner for Nathan and the kids. She would try Jonathan again in a little bit and cancel. Then maybe she'd just go have coffee with one of her friends once Nathan got home.

When the tacos were ready and she had rounded the kids to the table, she picked up her phone to try Jonathan again, but at that moment an incoming call from Nathan popped up on her screen. Katherine jumped, then breathed a sigh of relief. "Hey," she answered in a brighter tone than usual. "Dinner's ready."

"Hey. I'm gonna be late," Nathan said flatly.

"How late?" She tried to keep her voice pleasant.

"Just don't wait up. Something's come up here and I have to take care of it tonight," he said impatiently.

"But I'm supposed to be going out. I told you last night I was meeting the girls for coffee," Katherine reminded him, her tone becoming impatient as well.

"Look Katherine, this is a little more crucial than coffee with the girls. I'm trying to earn a living so that we can pay our bills."

"I realize that, Nathan, but it's also important for me to get some time off."

Nathan just sighed loudly into the phone. A few more seconds of silence and then, "Look, I gotta go. Please get off my case about this." Then he hung up the phone before she could say anything else.

Katherine stood for a few moments staring at the phone in disbelief. How had things gotten this bad? She was so hurt by his rude tone and the way he hung up on her. She then felt a surge of anger. There was no reason for him to treat her like an unruly child. And with that, her resolve immediately shifted and she dialed her neighbor's number to ask if she could watch the kids for her until Nathan got home.

Jonathan's house was in a mature neighborhood not far from downtown Austin. Katherine had looked up his address the night before and even though she had the route from her house to Jonathan's memorized, she pulled up the address again on her phone's GPS. Her mood was upbeat and confident during the twenty minute drive, the radio turned up high, the moonroof open, her hair blowing gently in the early evening breeze. She had drank a half glass of wine before leaving the house and it had soothed her nerves. But as she approached his street, her heart began to race and her palms felt clammy as she clenched the steering wheel.

What in the world am I doing? Do I really know this guy well enough to be going over to his house? She had asked herself these questions several times already over the past couple of days. And she had placated herself each time with breezy justifications. *Of course I know him well enough. I've seen him at work, met his friends, heard him talk about his family and have spent plenty of time with him.* Then of course there was the big question of What if he asks me to spend the night? Clearly she could not; that was out of the question. But the fact that she knew she really wanted to made her incredibly unsettled.

She drove slowly down his street until she came up to his address, pulling over to the opposite curb. She put her car in park and just sat there, studying his house. It was a modest white ranch style with green shutters and a neatly manicured lawn. It looked inviting with a nice potted plant and a little wrought iron bench on the porch. The windows were lit up with a warm yellow glow emanating through the encased windows which were framed with expensive looking drapes. It was nothing like what she imagined his home to look like. She had pictured something a little bit more becoming a bachelor lifestyle. Something in a darker color, with no window coverings, perhaps the lawn a little unruly.

After a few minutes, she put her car back in gear and continued driving. When she reached the stop sign at the end of his street she sat there for at least five minutes until a car came up behind her, pressuring her to move on. She drove straight, then pulled into the nearest driveway and turned back around. She drove slowly by his house a second time, and when she paused in front of it she noticed that Jonathan was standing on his front porch. He must have recognized her car, because he waved at her. Realizing her moment to escape without embarrassment had passed; she reluctantly waved back and pulled her car into his driveway.

"I was starting to think you got lost," he said as he opened her car door for her and held out his hand.

Katherine took his hand and let him help her out of the car. They were inches from each other and he smelled fantastic, a mix of masculine soap and his familiar cologne. He was dressed casually in jeans and a white polo shirt and his hair was still damp from a shower.

As she gazed up at him, a sexy grin played on his lips and his eyes sparkled. Katherine impulsively pushed aside her hesitation and let him lead her up his walkway and through the front door.

Chapter 21

"Hey Dad, I was thinking since I had a sleep over at your house, you could have one at mine tonight," James said as he dragged a French fry through the lake of ketchup on his plate.

"Um..." Daniel set down his burger in mid bite and looked over at Lauren. "Well, I didn't bring my pajamas or toothbrush."

Lauren returned Daniel's gaze and tried not to giggle. "James, we've talked about this before – your dad needs to sleep at his own house. Plus it's a school night."

"I know but I hate it when you have to leave," James said dramatically. "You could eat breakfast with us. Mom makes really good blueberry pancakes."

"You know what? I would love to try your Mom's blueberry pancakes. Maybe I could come over early in the morning and we'll all have breakfast together," Daniel suggested.

"But it's not the same as staying the night," James whined.

"James, can you clear your plate and take Burley outside for me?" Lauren asked.

"Ok." James slowly got up from the table with a long face.

Once James went out the back door with the dog in tow, Lauren stood up and began clearing the other dishes from the table. Daniel followed her into the kitchen, asking "Is he always so determined about things?"

"Yes, pretty much," Lauren said. " I wonder who he gets that from?"

Daniel laughed and Lauren gave him a playful punch.

"It's hard saying no to him." Daniel shook his head and began helping her put the plates into the dishwasher. They worked in silence for a few minutes then Lauren stopped, dishrag in hand, and looked over at Daniel. He met her intense gaze and waited a beat, then asked, "What is it?"

"Well, I was just thinking… you could stay in the guest room," Lauren said, surprising Daniel.

"Did you just say what I think you said?" Daniel asked.

"I mean, that is, if you wanted to. You don't have to. I know you weren't expecting to stay or anything," Lauren said quickly and turned her attention back to the dishes in the sink. She continued to ramble on, nervously. "You probably have work to do or something. Plus tomorrow's a school day."

"Lauren," Daniel said, gently turning her back around to face him. "Of course I want to spend the night with you."

"You do?" Lauren asked with uncertainty.

"Are you kidding me? How can I resist? Especially after James' offer of blueberry pancakes."

"Stop teasing," Lauren said, giving his shoulder another gentle punch.

"I'm serious. But it's not just about the pancakes." Daniel took her into his arms. "I want to spend as much time with you as possible. I love the idea of waking up and being able to see you and James first thing. I'm just surprised you extended the invitation."

"Well, like I said, you'll have to stay in the guest room, and you have to promise to behave yourself," Lauren said with a shy grin.

"Oh, I promise to behave." Daniel held his hand up with a serious expression, then he smiled and added, "It's you I'm worried about."

"I'll do my best," Lauren teased back.

James was thrilled to have his father spend the night. He insisted that Daniel read him several books, then stayed up an hour past his usual bedtime laughing and talking to Daniel about every topic under the sun. Finally, Lauren broke up the slumber party and scooted Daniel down the hallway to the guest room. She said good night to him at the door and gave him a soft, lingering kiss before making her way back to her own room.

Lauren lay in her bed for a half hour trying to fall asleep. All she could think about was Daniel right down the hallway lying in her guest room bed. She wondered if he was thinking about her or if he was already asleep. She remembered when they were dating that he had always fallen asleep so quickly. She knew how easy it was for men to just turn off their brains and tune out the cares of the day. Even so, she had put on one of her nice silk nightgowns, just in case Daniel decided to disregard her warning to behave and sneak into her room. She was partially disappointed that he hadn't, but she was also glad to know that he was upholding the gallant qualities of the new and improved Daniel.

She tossed and turned for another ten minutes, then threw the bed covers off and quietly left her room. She tip-toed down the hallway, peeking into James' room to make sure he was asleep and then continued stealthily toward the guest room. She stopped in front of the door, her heart beating fast. She thought about knocking, but then changed her mind and just quietly turned the unlocked doorknob. She carefully closed the door behind her and walked slowly toward the bed, a streak of silver moonlight guiding her. Daniel didn't stir; but she could see his bare chest rising with the deep breathing of slumber. She slipped underneath the covers and snuggled up against him.

"I knew you wouldn't be able to control yourself," Daniel whispered into the dark.

"I thought you were asleep," Lauren whispered back, propping her head up with her hand.

Daniel rolled over onto his side and faced her, "I was... until about five seconds ago, when you jumped on top of me."

Lauren laughed and protested, "I did not jump on top of you!"

"Shh..." Daniel placed a finger over her lips. He ran his fingertip down her chin and neck, then gently reached his hand behind her head and pulled her in for a delectable kiss.

"I take it you don't mind me invading your privacy," Lauren whispered when they parted.

"Oh, trust me. I'm not complaining," Daniel murmured as he kissed her again. "But I don't want to risk James waking up and coming to look for you."

"I know. You're right. I just wanted to make sure you were able to get to sleep. See you in the morning," Lauren whispered and slipped out of the bed. She made it out of the room quietly before Daniel could say anything else.

Getting back into her own bed, Lauren tried to shake off the feeling of rejection. She knew Daniel was right about James. She didn't want to confuse him. She felt a pang of regret for letting Daniel stay over. It was too soon.

Chapter 22

*J*onathan's house was cozy, and very nicely decorated in tones of pale yellows and muted browns. It was definitely not the bachelor pad she had envisioned. Katherine followed him down the hallway past the living room, admiring the plush tan sofas and chairs, accented by a thick wool rug, dark cherry end tables and colorful oil paintings. "So, did you do the decorating yourself?"

Jonathan laughed easily, "No, all the credit goes to my Mom. My parents contributed a hefty down payment for the house, but they also laid down three rules: First, I make the mortgage payments, second: my Mom got to do the decorating."

"And the third?"

"No wild parties."

"What? However do you manage?" Katherine asked incredulously.

"Honestly, I don't mind. I don't like having to clean up after a bunch of people who don't respect a nice house. So, when I want to get wild I have to do it at someone else's house."

"Interesting. So, how often is it that you 'get wild'?" She teased him, raising her eyebrows.

"Well, it depends if I have someone interesting to 'get wild' with," he teased back, winking and giving her his irresistible grin. He grabbed an open bottle of Pinot Grigio from a silver cooler and began pouring a generous amount into a pair of crystal wine goblets. He handed one to Katherine and they clinked their glasses gingerly.

"Here's to having someone to get wild with," Jonathan said and they both laughed easily.

They both took a sip, keeping their gaze on one another. Katherine was the first to break eye contact, walking over towards the oven.

"What is that wonderful smell?" Katherine asked, taking in the scent of garlic and rosemary.

"I'm making rosemary chicken and garlic bruschetta," Jonathan said and ushered her to a seat at the dining table which was set with brightly colored china, candles and a single red rose in a bud vase.

"This is really lovely," Katherine said as she sat down. She watched Jonathan as he put on a pair of oven mitts, took the chicken and warm bread from the oven and placed them on the table. He looked so handsome and she began to feel that nervous tingle in her stomach again. She took two big gulps of wine while he went to the refrigerator to pull out a small bowl of mixed greens. He smiled at her as he sat down and began to fill her plate with salad. She nervously smiled back and cleared her throat.

"Are you okay?" he asked. "You're very quiet tonight."

"I'm fine. It's just been a long week," Katherine said.

"Well, in that case..." He filled her wine glass again and topped his own off. "Do you want to talk about it?"

"I don't want to bore you with the details. Why don't you tell me about your week?"

"Okay. Well... it's been long and lonely without you," he began and winked at her. "But, the restaurant has been busy. I had a ten top last night that practically drank every bottle of wine in the house. One of the girls got so drunk that she went into the men's bathroom and then screamed when she saw a man in there with his pants down."

Katherine giggled. "Did she try to get your phone number?"

"Yes. But I told her that I already had a girlfriend who liked to sit at my table and get drunk."

"I have never gotten drunk at your table!" Katherine protested with a pout.

"I know. I wish you would, though." Jonathan gave her another slow sexy smile. "How about tonight? At this table?"

"Excuse me, but if I'm not mistaken, I'd think you were trying to seduce me," Katherine said, feigning innocence.

"I do believe that is the general idea," Jonathan said so seductively that it came out comical and Katherine laughed, feeling her guard come down a little more.

They spent the next hour enjoying the meal and finishing off the bottle of wine. Jonathan continued to talk easily about what he had been studying in his law classes that week. He also told her about going out with his friends a few nights before. He entertained her with another hilarious story involving Susan and Sylvia playing a trick on the bartender. And once again she experienced a twinge of jealousy. She was curious if he was interested in either of the two girls, as they were both very attractive. But what right did she have to be jealous?

Jonathan opened another bottle of wine and suggested that they take it out onto the patio in the backyard. They settled into two comfortable chaise lounges that were covered with comfy navy cushions. Jonathan had brought his Ipod out and placed it into the docking station on the table between the two chairs. He turned it on, choosing a playlist with mellow pop songs and poured them each another glass of wine. They sipped their wine in silence for a few minutes as they listened to the melodious sounds of an Ed Sheeran track.

"I meant what I said earlier," Jonathan said, glancing over at Katherine, his long legs stretched out, ankles crossed casually. "Well, except for the drunk part."

"What?" Katherine asked in confusion.

"About you being my girlfriend," he said hesitantly.

Katherine almost choked on her wine and sat up a little straighter.

Jonathan seemed to notice her discomfort and said, "That is, if it's okay with you."

Katherine fidgeted with her wine glass and tried to come up with a response. But before she could even answer him, Jonathan stood and held out his hand to grab hers. He pulled her to her feet, took her wine glass out of her hand and set it down on the table. Then he guided her away from the lounge chairs and took both of her hands in his. 'Thinking Out Loud' had just begun playing and as Jonathan pulled her into his arms, Katherine let herself melt into him.

She rested her head on his warm chest and could hear the faint sound of his heartbeat. They swayed slowly to the music, enjoying the warmth of each other. Katherine felt dizzy breathing in his tantalizing scent, with the cool evening breeze grazing her bare arms. Even with her eyes closed she could sense the moon and stars beaming down around them. Everything else seemed to fall away. *Baby, we found love right where we are.* Jonathan quietly sang along with the last line of the song.

As the song ended, Katherine looked up at him and he gently pressed his mouth to hers. The kiss was tender, but searching, then began to intensify as Jonathan ran his hands up to her neck then into her hair. Katherine tightened her grip on his shoulders and pressed her body closer to his. Still kissing, Jonathan slowly led her over to one of the lounge chairs and gently pushed her down. She laid back and he lowered himself lightly on top of her, engaging her once again in a passionate kiss. They kissed each other hungrily and Katherine ran her hands up into his shirt and over the smooth muscles in his back.

They continued to kiss each other hungrily for several minutes, until Jonathan pulled back gently and murmured, "Let's go inside."

As he led her back into the house through the kitchen and down the hall, Katherine's heart began to race. She was still feeling a little dizzy from both the wine and the passion. She knew she needed to clear her head, but she wanted to remain in the moment and relish the feelings of lust and desire. She expected he was going to take her into his bedroom, and she quickly realized that if she allowed this to carry on, there would be no turning back. She was about to protest, but he turned into the living room and sat down on the sofa pulling her down next to him.

"There's something I need to tell you," he said and the seriousness in his tone surprised her. "It's something I've been meaning to tell you, but I just haven't found the right moment."

Katherine knew that it was highly unlikely that sentence could be leading up to anything positive. The possibility of what he might be about to say to her became clear and she felt sick to her stomach.

"Katherine, you know how much I like you and obviously I am extremely attracted to you," he began, his eyes searching hers. "And I don't want you to feel like I've been leading you on, because that has never been my intention."

Katherine's mind was fuzzy from the alcohol, but she slowly grasped where this conversation was going and she couldn't have been more shocked. Looking around at the beautifully decorated room, the vases with flowers and the delicate statues on the coffee table, she knew exactly what he had to tell her.

Jonathan took a breath, seemingly unaware of Katherine's state of turmoil, and continued, "I am trying so hard not to let temptation take over... but as much as I want to... And trust me, I do. But, I can't go to bed with you."

Katherine stared at him, her eyes practically glazing over. She shook her head as if to clear the fog and asked incredulously, "You're married?!"

"What?" Jonathan looked just as shocked. "That's not what I was trying to..."

"You're married." Katherine stated it, this time as an accusation. "It all makes sense. Your mom didn't decorate the house. It was your wife!"

"What are you talking about? Why would you even think that?" Jonathan frowned and followed her gaze around the room. He then turned back to her and tried to put his hand on her arm, but she jerked away and stood up.

"I can't believe you," she shouted. "All that talk about me being your girlfriend! What in the world is wrong with you?"

"Katherine. You've got it all wrong. I am not married," Jonathan said, remaining calm. "Please. Sit back down."

"Then what is it?" Katherine asked and flopped back down on the far end of the couch, leaving a good deal of distance between them. "What else could you possibly be trying to tell me? That you're engaged? Certainly you're not going to tell me that you're gay. Because there is no way that a gay guy kisses a girl like that."

Jonathan laughed a little and resolutely stated, "No, I am not engaged. And I am definitely not gay."

"Ok, then what? Just say it already!" Katherine exclaimed, getting to her feet again.

"Katherine, can you just sit down please? I promise you, it's not that bad," Jonathan said.

"Ok, fine." Katherine reluctantly sat again and waited for him to speak.

"I'm a born again Christian," Jonathan said tentatively. When Katherine just stared at him as if he were speaking another language, he continued, "A friend of mine invited me to his church about six months ago. I wasn't really sure what to expect, but when the pastor started talking about having a real relationship with God, it just all made sense to me. I felt as if he was speaking directly to me. He talked about how so many people are walking around with an empty feeling inside. That they're always yearning for more, but when they achieve everything they want in life, they just aren't satisfied. I realized that I've had that feeling for a long time now, but I just didn't know how to describe it. He said that the gaping hole in our hearts is a need to be one with our Creator."

Katherine remained silent on the other end of the couch, just listening, so Jonathan took a breath and went on, "Then the pastor explained that because of the choice Adam and Eve made to sin, we're all separated from God. But the good news is that we can all be reconciled with God through Jesus Christ."

Katherine? Aren't you going to say anything?" Jonathan tried to inch closer to her, but she backed up a little and crossed her arms over her chest.

"I don't know. I'm just not really sure what you expect me to say." Katherine was still trying to digest the peculiar turn the evening had taken. The earlier effect of the wine had completely worn off and she was beginning to feel very uncomfortable.

"I'm not expecting anything. I just wanted to let you know what's in my heart and where I'm coming from," Jonathan said, his eyes searching hers intensely. "This is a big part of my life and I want to share it with you."

"Ok. I get that part. But, I just... I'm just not sure how to respond," Katherine said honestly.

"I totally understand." Jonathan was finally able to get close enough to take her hand in his. "This is all still pretty new to me too, you know. That's why it took so long for me to tell you about it."

Katherine remained silent, but didn't pull away from him.

"I hope I didn't scare you away," Jonathan said lightly. "I'm not trying to push anything on you, I promise. I just needed you to know where I stand."

"You haven't scared me away, Jonathan. It's just late and I'm really tired. Can we talk about it tomorrow?"

"Of course. I'll walk you out."

Jonathan went to get her purse and keys from the kitchen, and met her at the front entrance. They walked in silence out the door and down the dimly lit path to the driveway. Katherine was about to open her car door, but Jonathan pulled her into his arms, hugged her, then gently kissed her on the forehead, "You promise I didn't scare you away?"

"I promise," Katherine whispered.

"Call me tomorrow?" he asked.

Katherine nodded, touched his cheek tenderly and then got into her car.

Chapter 23

*L*auren could not focus on the lesson she was attempting to teach her class. Her mind kept wandering back to last night and how wonderful it had been to wake up to the sound of James and Daniel laughing in the kitchen. She dressed, brushed her teeth and put on a little bit of makeup before joining them.

Daniel had already brewed a pot of coffee and then he helped Lauren make the blueberry pancakes and turkey bacon. Every time James wasn't looking he would sneak a kiss or whisper something clandestine into her ear, making her knees go weak. They had taken their breakfast out onto the back patio where they enjoyed the cool Friday morning. It was still early so they took their time eating, talking and laughing. Everyone was melancholy when it was time to leave for school and work.

Lauren was just pulling her car into the school parking lot when her phone chimed with a new text. Daniel had written, Can't wait for our next sleepover ;). Lauren still hadn't been able to stop smiling. It was so reminiscent of when they had first started dating, only better.

Daniel had definitely changed, and that made her want to make some changes herself. She decided she would try to be more confident and not worry about what he was doing every minute they were apart. This time around, even though she could barely wait to see him again, she had plenty to keep her busy in the meantime. She had her job and James to focus on. She wasn't going to make Daniel the center of her universe again.

She was older now and felt that she had wisdom that only being a parent could bring. There was no need for her to feel like a silly little girl around Daniel. They had a child together, for Pete's sake. She was determined to show Daniel that she could be just as self-assured as he was. Even so, she couldn't deny that she was falling for him head over heels all over again. But it felt oh so good.

She was still walking around with her head in the clouds as she went into the teacher's lounge to warm up her lunch. She ran smack into Jake as she rounded the corner into the kitchen.

"Whoa." Jake had to grab her by both arms to steady her. "Are you ok?"

"Sorry," Lauren said, feeling foolish as she looked up at Jake. "Yes, I'm fine."

"What's for lunch?" Jake asked in his easy manner as he watched her go over to the refrigerator.

"Chicken and pasta. Would you like some?"

"No, thanks. I just ate. But it's nice of you to offer to share." Jake grinned at her. "How's the boyfriend?"

"What?" Lauren asked in surprise.

"Karen told me," Jake said casually.

"Nice of her to mind her own business," Lauren muttered under her breath.

"What was that?" Jake queried.

"Nothing." Lauren put the plastic container into the microwave and pushed the start button.

"Does that mean happy hour tonight is out of the question?" Jake asked playfully.

"I'm afraid so," Lauren said, shrugging one shoulder.

"Ok, well... if you change your mind, you know where to find me," Jake said with another wink and then he sauntered off.

Lauren laughed and shook her head as she pulled the pasta out of the microwave. While her food was cooling, she pulled her phone from her pocket and sent Daniel a text. *Thinking about you...* After a few moments, he replied, *Nice thoughts, I hope. ;)*. Lauren felt her face flush and she glanced around as if someone might be peering over her shoulder. Quickly she typed out, *Always nice.* His reply came back immediately. *Same here... Can't wait to see you tonight.*

Katherine had barely slept the night before. She was feeling ashamed for more than one reason. She couldn't believe how she had reacted when she suspected Jonathan was married. What a hypocrite she had been, getting angry at him for something she herself was guilty of. Instead he had told her he was a Christian and wanted to keep himself pure, while here she was committing adultery! What would Jonathan think if he found out? She had never felt like such a complete and utter fraud in her entire life.

She had gotten herself way too deep into a situation that left her feeling like the criminal and the victim at the same time. Was Nathan's emotional detachment and lack of affection really a valid excuse for having an affair? After all, he was just working long hours to support his family. But did that justify the way Nathan treated her, talking rudely to her all the time and completely neglecting their relationship? If he was so stressed out, shouldn't he talk to her about it? Wasn't that what married couples did? Support each other in times of difficulty?

Now, to make matters worse, she was guilty of corrupting a newcomer to Christianity. Katherine's family had grown up Catholic, so she wasn't really that familiar with all the beliefs of born-again Christians, but she figured that they took the marriage vows very seriously. What would Jonathan think if he found out? She knew the right thing was to end things with Jonathan, but she couldn't imagine how. She genuinely cared for him and the attraction went beyond physical. She didn't want to give up spending time with him. She didn't want to go back to her lonely life, waiting around for Nathan to give her the slightest bit of attention.

She still hadn't called Jonathan even though she had desperately wanted to. She just wasn't sure what to say to him. She knew that her little charade could not continue indefinitely. It was not as if she was going to leave Nathan to run off with Jonathan and live some fantasy 'happily ever after'. She would never do that. She would never leave her kids. But what about Nathan? She wasn't quite sure about that right now. It was a horrible thought to have, but here she was having it. She never imagined that she'd feel that way about her husband. Had she really become that bad of a person?

She was relieved that she would have the distraction of having Lauren and James over after school. She needed all of these racing thoughts to stop for a while, before she went completely nuts. Lauren had texted her earlier saying that she wanted to talk about something. She knew it was about Daniel. Katherine lamented the fact that she couldn't talk to Lauren about her situation with Jonathan. *Definitely a downfall of cheating on your best friend's brother*, she said to herself with a groan.

Maybe she just needed to try harder with Nathan. She would ask him if he could set aside some time this weekend so that they could really talk. They wouldn't have to spend any money going out; they could just sit in the living room after the kids went to bed. Maybe even open a bottle of wine. *Yes, that's it. We'll just relax, have a heart to heart, share some wine. I'm sure he'll open up to me. Then we can put this little bump in the road behind us.*

By the time Katherine picked up Keenan and Madison she was feeling a little bit lighter. She decided she was going to do the right thing and try to repair her marriage. She stopped by the little bakery on the way home and picked up some cupcakes for the kids and a slice of chocolate cake for her and Lauren.

Lauren showed up beaming with joy. Katherine was happy for her friend, but a little part of her felt deflated with jealousy. After the kids had their cupcakes and a glass of milk, they tore out the back door, already wild on their sugar high. Katherine poured mugs of coffee for herself and Lauren and they settled on the patio chairs with the chocolate cake.

"So?" Katherine asked with a knowing look as she took a big bite of the luscious cake.

Lauren sipped her coffee, peering over the rim with a little grin, her cheeks turning crimson. "We had the most amazing night."

"You're going to have to give me a little more detail than that," Katherine probed.

"Well, James kept asking if Daniel could stay the night, so I said he could stay over in the guest room," Lauren began, unable to stop grinning. "Then after James was asleep, I snuck into Daniel's room."

"What? Are you serious?" Katherine asked in surprise. "I never knew you were so cheeky."

Lauren giggled. "I know. I kind of surprised myself actually. But I just couldn't help it."

"Well, go on..." Katherine pleaded.

"It was wonderful. It felt almost scandalous, like we were a couple of teenagers sneaking around in our parent's house," Lauren sighed.

"That sounds fun," Katherine admitted. "So, did you...?"

"No. We just kissed and then I went back to my room. It was perfect. I'm glad he didn't push for anything more. I definitely want to do things right this time around," Lauren said. "And apparently he does too. I'm telling you, Katherine. He's a changed man."

"Well, I'm proud of you. There's absolutely no need to rush things. How did he act in the morning?" Katherine asked.

"He was super sweet. He texted me today saying he couldn't wait to come over tonight."

"Wow. So this is getting really serious. Let's go look at those dresses this weekend," Katherine teased.

Lauren's face crumbled.

"What? I was just kidding."

"No, it's fine. I've just been trying to not even let myself go there. I mean, it's been wonderful and exciting, but I have no idea how serious Daniel is about me," Lauren said, pushing the remains of her cake around the plate.

"Don't worry. I'm sure he feels the same as you. He's probably just as nervous about the situation. Maybe even more so," Katherine reassured her.

"Why do you say that?"

"Well, because you kind of have the upper hand. You get to decide when and how much he sees James."

"I've never thought of it that way," Lauren said uneasily. "I would never deny James time with his father just to manipulate Daniel."

"No, I didn't mean it that way." Katherine backtracked. "But I'm sure he realizes that if he screws things up it's going to get real awkward."

"Why do you think he's going to screw things up?" Lauren asked defensively.

"I don't. I'm really hoping that he doesn't. I just think you should enjoy your time together and take things slow. See where it leads."

"You're right. I'm not going to over analyze it."

"I know I've said it before – just be careful."

"Yes I know. You don't have to keep reminding me."

The two women sat in silence for a few minutes while they watched the children play tag.

Lauren perked up a little. "Can you still watch James for us tomorrow?"

"Of course." Katherine nodded and after a moment, added, "I have an idea. How about if James stays the night here tonight? That way you and Daniel can have some quality alone time."

"Really? Do you think that's a good idea?" Lauren looked nervous.

"Sure. You and Daniel need more one on one time to really see if this thing is going to work or not."

"Ok. As long as you're sure having James tonight isn't a problem."

"Of course not. It's not like I have plans. Nathan will work late as usual and by the time he gets home, I'm too tired to even talk." Katherine smiled, trying to hide the anguish she felt over her failing marriage.

Katherine wished she could talk to Lauren about everything. Even if she did ask one of her friends that wasn't related to Nathan, she knew the answer already. She should end things with Jonathan and work toward mending her marriage. But after hearing Lauren's recount of her and Daniel's steamy evening, she couldn't help but get swept up in the romance of it all. She wanted that nostalgic feeling. The one she had every time she was with Jonathan. How in the world was she going to give that up?

Chapter 24

*L*auren had never been happier. She and Daniel had spent the night cooking together, sharing a bottle of wine as they prepared fettuccini Alfredo with chicken and asparagus. They ate their dinner on the patio, talking and laughing. They kept their conversation light, but they also talked a lot about James with Lauren telling him stories of when he was younger. And even though Daniel didn't say anything, Lauren could detect a sadness in his eyes that she knew came from missing out on his son's younger years. Lauren's respect for Daniel grew even more as she realized that he had never complained or mentioned the fact that she had kept his son from him since that first meeting.

After dinner they cleaned up the kitchen and then went into the living room. They curled up on the couch together and flipped through the TV channels, trying to find a movie that wasn't animated or rated G. They finally settled on 'Lover Come Back' with Doris Day, but they only made it halfway through the movie before Daniel initiated a kissing marathon. He scooped Lauren up into his arms and carried her into her bedroom. Once again, Daniel was a perfect gentleman; he kissed her good night, then went to the guest room.

Lauren slept in late and found Daniel in the living room sipping coffee. After spending a half hour cuddling and talking on the couch, they decided to go out to breakfast at a small café downtown. They were seated in a booth next to the window that offered views of the shops and the people walking by enjoying their Saturday. They ordered French toast, eggs and bacon. Lauren was extremely pleased when Daniel remembered to order her mocha latte with extra whipped cream. Afterward, they walked around, holding hands, peering in the shop windows and stopping every now and then for a kiss.

When they came across a small gift boutique, Lauren insisted they go inside despite Daniel's humorous protests about potpourri and scented candles making him nauseous. Lauren reminded him of the time she'd snuck lavender sachets in his sock and t-shirt drawers back when they were dating. When Daniel had come home from work he had told her that he couldn't stop sneezing during his client meeting. They were both laughing as they entered the shop, but immediately Daniel stopped and Lauren sensed him stiffen. She followed Daniel's serious gaze and found the object to be a woman standing near the cash register. The woman had turned as the door chime sounded and was looking directly into Daniel's eyes, her facial expression a mix of surprise and hesitation.

The woman approached them and eyed Lauren for a moment before turning to face Daniel. She said in a low, intimate voice, "Hello, Daniel."

"Hi, Sarah," he replied, and Lauren could tell he seemed a little nervous.

The woman stepped forward and put her arms around Daniel and hugged him. To Lauren's astonishment, Daniel wrapped his arms around her as well. She was tall, almost as tall as Daniel, her perfect porcelain skin accented with dark eyes and long, sleek dark brown hair. The hug seemed to go on forever and Lauren impatiently cleared her throat, but she seemed to have suddenly become invisible.

"How have you been?" Daniel asked in a tender voice when they finally parted.

"I'm doing really well," Sarah answered, smiling and showing off perfect white teeth. "I went back to school. I'll receive my Masters in a couple of months."

"Wow. Sarah. That is really great... I'm so happy for you," Daniel said with enthusiasm. Lauren started to become annoyed with the way they were acting as if she weren't even there.

"What about you? How's your business?" Sarah asked him, and Daniel went into a detailed explanation of how his firm was growing, the addition of five new agents to the team, and on and on.

Finally Lauren's patience ran out and she walked out of the boutique. She took a deep breath and glanced back through the windows seeing that Daniel was still completely engrossed with Sarah. So, she started down the sidewalk not even thinking about where she was heading.

She had only made it half a block when she heard Daniel calling her name behind her. She refused to turn around, just kept walking as fast as she could, but she heard his footsteps closing in on her.

"Lauren, slow down. Where are you going?" Daniel asked breathlessly as he caught up to her side.

"It's okay, Daniel. You don't have to chase me down. It was quite obvious Sarah was much more interesting to you," Lauren said sarcastically.

"Lauren, just stop for a second, okay?" Daniel tried to grab her arm, but she pulled away from him.

"Daniel, just leave me alone. I really don't want to talk to you right now." Lauren had slowed her pace and was a little breathless herself.

"Just stop walking for a minute. You're being ridiculous." Daniel was still following her closely and Lauren stopped abruptly and spun around so that they nearly collided with one another.

"The only thing that is ridiculous is that I was beginning to think that you've changed, but it is so clear that you haven't. The second a pretty girl comes on the scene, I'm invisible!" Lauren yelled at him, trying hard not to let the tears well up.

"Lauren, you're overreacting. Can't we just sit down somewhere so we can talk about this?" Daniel glanced around looking for a bench, but Lauren was already on the move again.

"I told you, I don't want to talk to you. Just please go," Lauren pleaded angrily, not looking at him.

"How are you going to get home?" he asked her impatiently.

"I don't know. I'll call a cab or something. You don't need to worry about it." She picked up her pace again, rounding a corner and ducked into a bookstore. She headed straight for the ladies room so that he wouldn't be able to follow her anymore. Then she scrambled for her phone in her bag and called Katherine.

"What happened?" Katherine exclaimed thirty minutes later as Lauren got into the front seat of her car.

Lauren glanced back at James, seated in between his cousins, and shook her head at Katherine, "I'll tell you when we get home."

"Where's Dad? I thought you were on a date with him?" James asked from the backseat.

"He, um, had to go to a meeting," Lauren lied.

"Well, can he come over to our house today? I didn't get to see him." James began to pout.

"Not today, James!" Lauren snapped. She was trying so hard not to burst into tears in front of him.

They rode the rest of the way back to Lauren's house in silence. When her phone rang and she saw that it was Daniel calling, she immediately switched her phone off.

Chapter 25

Katherine still had not returned Jonathan's calls. When he texted her, she just replied that she needed some more time. She knew she couldn't just break things off with him in a text, but she wasn't ready to have that conversation with him quite yet. She had managed to keep busy, with babysitting James Friday night and most of Saturday. Then she spent the rest of the afternoon at Lauren's. First listening to her vent about Daniel, and then watching the kids again while Lauren took a long bath and a nap. When she finally crawled into bed Saturday night, she was too tired to even care that Nathan was still clicking away on the computer in his office.

But Sunday afternoon she was determined to get Nathan to do something as a family. She informed him at breakfast that she would like for them to go to their favorite park for a hike. She expected for him to find some work related excuse to duck out, but surprisingly he agreed. He wasn't exactly enthusiastic, but she wasn't going to let that tiny infraction bother her.

Katherine packed drinks and snacks, dressed herself and the children in jeans, t-shirts and tennis shoes. They piled into Nathan's truck and headed out for the hill country. During the twenty minute drive, Nathan and Katherine were silent, listening to the radio while the children talked and giggled in the backseat. About halfway there,

Katherine's phone rang and Nathan grabbed it from the console and handed it to her. Holding the screen away from Nathan's view she saw that it was Jonathan calling and she quickly rejected the call.

"Who was it?" Nathan asked.

"Oh, it's just one of the moms from PTA," she answered, feeling her face go hot. "I don't really feel like talking right now."

Katherine set her phone on silent mode and slipped it into her pocket. Nathan just stared ahead at the road oblivious to his wife's guilty conscience.

They arrived at the wilderness preserve and Nathan pulled the truck into a parking spot near the trail entrance. The area was a vast forest of towering cedar and oak trees with multiple trails that coursed through the hillside. At the bottom of the hill the creek that led into Lake Travis snaked along the trails. Madison and Keenan quickly scrambled out of the car, racing toward the hiking path.

"Wait for us, you two!" Katherine called out as she got out and walked around to the bed of the truck to get the backpack that served as a cooler.

"I'll get it," Nathan said, shooing her toward the path. "You go catch up with the kids."

Katherine walked swiftly to the main entrance and past the sign with the trail map and caught up with the children who had already both found long sticks. Madison was using hers as a walking staff and Keenan was happily hitting the brush along the side of the dusty path. Katherine laughed and lifted her face up to the sun, breathing deeply and feeling the warmth soothe her. They walked along slowly, waiting for Nathan to catch up with them. After ten minutes when he hadn't appeared on the trail, Katherine told the children to stop to wait for their dad. They perched together on a big rock and after a few minutes, Nathan's voice broke into the silence of the woods.

"I'm sorry, Mr. Johnson, but I already have the electrical inspection scheduled. If we delay again the inspector won't be able to come out again for another two weeks." Nathan came into view with the oversized backpack slung over his shoulder and the phone pressed to his ear.

Katherine rolled her eyes and let out a huge sigh. She should have known better than to think he'd leave work behind for the afternoon. She motioned for the kids to start down the trail again. Nathan trailed behind them talking to Mr. Johnson in a voice Katherine knew to be his calm under pressure tone. But it was obvious he was angry and frustrated.

When he finally ended the call, Katherine turned around and said, "Couldn't you have just turned your phone off for the afternoon? This is supposed to be family time."

"Don't start on me, Katherine. I'm here, aren't I?"

"That's debatable," she mumbled, but he heard her.

"What is that supposed to mean?"

"Nothing."

"Can't you stop nagging me for just one afternoon?" Nathan said, his jaw set tight.

The comment caused anger to flash through her. "I am not nagging! I simply want my family to spend some time together. Is that too much to ask?"

"We *are* spending time together," Nathan pointed out. "I took one phone call and you fly off the handle."

"Oh, quit exaggerating Nathan. You just can't ever stop working, can you?"

"Well, maybe I could if you could ever stop spending money like it's flying out the window," Nathan accused.

"What? You think our money problems are *my* fault?" Katherine yelled. "I wanted to go back to work, Nathan!"

"Keep your voice down. You're embarrassing me," Nathan hissed.

Katherine felt her face grow hot once again. "Embarrassing you? In front of whom? The trees?" she asked incredulously.

"Mommy! Daddy!" Madison's little voice peeped up. "You can't fight during our family time!"

"You're right, baby." Katherine looked down to see Madison peering up at her. She lifted her up onto her hip and brushed past Nathan to catch up with Keenan.

"I'm going to go wait in the truck," Nathan muttered and turned around.

"What a surprise," Katherine muttered back.

Chapter 26

"Somebody had a bad day."

Lauren looked up from her desk to see Jake standing in her doorway. She had been slumped in her chair staring out the window for the past five minutes.

"Kids give you a hard time today?" he asked and Lauren just shook her head.

Jake slowly strolled into the room. "Boyfriend trouble?"

"I'd really rather not talk about it," Lauren said.

"No problem. How about I treat you to a drink?" Jake said as he perched on the corner of her desk.

She shook her head again and sighed. "I don't think I'd be very good company."

"Ok, if you say so," Jake said breezily and stood up. He walked back toward the door with one hand up in a goodbye gesture.

Lauren started gathering up her things, when suddenly she stood up and walked quickly to her door, looking down the hallway each way until she saw Jake about to turn the corner toward the gym.

"Jake! Wait!" she called out.

Katherine had finally called Jonathan back. After the fight with Nathan at the nature trail, she found talking to Jonathan comforting and reassuring. He wasn't angry with her for leaving him hanging for a week, dodging his five calls and most of his eleven text messages. He was sweet and understanding, but most of all, happy to talk to her. She told him that not only had she needed time to process their last conversation, but that her work schedule had been extremely hectic. He conceded that the week of silence had allowed him the much needed time to think about their relationship as well. He asked her if she could meet him for lunch and she easily said yes.

Once again, Katherine carefully selected a restaurant that was far from the areas of town she might run into anyone she knew. So that she would have an excuse to dress up, she told Jonathan that she was visiting with a client that morning near the Southwestern café she chose. She dressed in a pale blue silk blouse, grey pencil skirt and black heels. Her hair was pulled into a loose ponytail, her bangs lightly framing her face.

As soon as she spotted him, already seated on the patio, her stomach did a little somersault. He was wearing a long sleeved green shirt and khaki shorts, his eyes hidden behind dark aviator sunglasses.

"Hello, stranger," Katherine said breezily, trying to induce a light tone to stave off any awkwardness.

Jonathan stood up and kissed her on her cheek before pulling out a chair for her. She breathed in his now familiar scent and felt her stomach stir again.

"How did your client meeting go?" he asked politely as they sat down.

"Oh, it was fine. Routine stuff," she replied with a wave of her hand. "What have you been up to today?"

"Studying. Thinking about you," he answered and took off his glasses, revealing warmth in his gaze. She realized once again how difficult it was to resist him.

"I've been thinking a lot about you too." Katherine surprised herself as she said it. She reached out and placed her hand on his. He lifted her hand and slowly brought it to his lips.

"I've really missed seeing you," he murmured as he brushed his lips against her hand again, then wove their fingers together.

"Me too," she barely whispered as she felt her legs go weak. She ran her other hand lightly across his jaw line and said, "You know, I'm not really that hungry."

"Are you sure?" Jonathan asked. Then when Katherine lifted her eyebrows, he nodded and said, "Me neither. I actually had a really big breakfast."

"My car or yours?" she asked.

Katherine giggled as he stood up, took her hand and pulled her to her feet. Jonathan led the way back out into the parking lot, pointed to where his truck was parked and steered her toward it. As soon as they were seated inside, Jonathan pulled her to him and covered her mouth with his. They kissed each other hungrily until they were both breathless.

"I'm surprised we didn't steam up the windows." Jonathan laughed as they both came up for air.

Katherine laughed as well and peered out into the parking lot. "If someone saw us they might call the police for excessive PDA."

"Nope. Trucks are considered private property. So, we can make out all we want in here without worrying about getting arrested."

"Oh, really? Is that what they teach you in law school these days?"

Jonathan put both his hands on her face and kissed her more slowly this time, as if savoring every moment with her.

"I want more than anything to take you home and take you to my bed," he whispered.

"Oh, Jonathan," Katherine breathed in reply and kissed him again. When she pulled back, gazing at him lustfully, she said, "I understand. I don't want to rush things anyway. I'm perfectly happy just making out with you for now."

"It is kind of fun, huh? I feel like a teenager," Jonathan said.

Katherine sat back against the leather seat, sighing. They were quiet for a few moments. Then she turned to him trying to make out how to ask the question she had on her mind.

"What is it?" Jonathan asked, sensing her curiosity.

"So, have you ever... I mean, you've been with other women, right?" She stumbled over the awkward question.

"Are you asking me if I'm a virgin?" Jonathan said with barely disguised amusement.

"Um, well... yes. I guess I am." Katherine felt her cheeks grow warm.

"No. I'm not. I am guilty of having sex before marriage," he stated with mock shame. "But, as I said, I've only been born again for about six months. And I can proudly say that I have not had sexual relations since then."

"Hmmm... interesting," Katherine mused. "So, would you say there were a lot of women before you became abstinent? "

"Are you asking me for a number?" Jonathan continued to grin.

"Well, isn't it supposed to be good for you to confess your sins and all?" she quipped.

"I suppose so..." He rubbed his chin as if in deep thought. "But, I feel a little as if I'm on trial here."

"Well, don't you need to get used to it?"

"Uh, I'm kinda hoping I'll be on the other side of the witness chair."

Katherine laughed and nudged him playfully in the arm. "I'm sorry, I didn't mean to get all nosy on you."

"No, no. That's fine. You have plenty of justification to ask the questions. I'm just not so sure if you're going to like the answers." Jonathan's tone was still light hearted, but Katherine sensed that underneath it, he was serious.

"Look, I'll be the first to admit that I'm a sinner. Even now that I've cleaned up my life and admitted that I need God, I'm still human. It's taking all the inner strength that I have to resist seducing you."

"I'm sorry to say, but I think you've already done that."

"You got a point."

"Not that I'm complaining."

Jonathan gave her a smile and took her hand in his. He was silent for a few moments. He gazed out the front window and blew out a breath of air. "I was pretty wild BC."

"BC?"

"Before Christ."

"Ah." Katherine nodded in understanding.

"I think that's why it means so much to me to do this thing right. I don't want to be the man that I was before. I know I caused a lot of pain, especially to myself." Jonathan looked over at her. "I'm going to do my best to treat women with respect from now on."

"Women? As in plural?" she questioned.

"Well, I don't know how much I should say, because I already scared you off for a week there."

"I'm sorry. It's just that I…"

"No, it's fine," he cut her off. "I'm glad you took some time. Like I said, I needed it too. But, I just want you to know that the next woman I sleep with is going to be my wife. And I don't want to be hasty here – or to scare you off - but there is a real possibility that I'd like that woman to be you."

Lauren was already on her third glass of wine.

She had agreed to ride with Jake in his convertible Corvette to the sports bar he had insisted upon. She was actually quite enjoying the evening at first. Jake ordered a pitcher of beer, a carafe of white wine and a plate of various fried foods. They played a round of darts, in which she managed to throw all of hers several inches from the actual dartboard, including one that came very close to hitting a man walking to the restrooms. Jake had gone over to apologize to the scowling man while Lauren hid behind the barstool and giggled.

They attempted a game of shuffleboard, but Jake grew quickly weary of constantly reminding her to "ease up a bit", as all her disks went careening across the sanded board smacking into his hand.

Finally, they sat down and talked and laughed about various stories they each had about incidents in her classroom or at PE. As Jake was making his way through the fried zucchini and jalapenos, she realized he wasn't all that bad. She was actually enjoying talking to him, with his easy way of making her laugh and the common ground they had with work. She didn't feel inferior or too silly, the way she often felt with Daniel. Why did Daniel always seem to give her the feeling that she wasn't good enough?

"Another round?" the waitress stopped by their table, interrupting Lauren's thought of scooching a little closer to Jake so that he might possibly try to kiss her.

"We're good, Sugar," Jake answered, giving the waitress a wink.

"Do you flirt with everyone?" Lauren asked, realizing that was one area of commonality that Jake and Daniel shared. But at least the overpowering feeling of jealousy wasn't present with Jake.

"No, I don't flirt with *everyone*. Just women. And it's not flirting - I just like to make y'all ladies feel good about yourselves." Jake defended himself in his thick southern drawl. "My mom taught me right – always do your best to make a lady feel special."

"Well, don't you think she meant just *one* lady?"

Jake shrugged. "I'll get there. It takes time to find the one that you want to spend your life with. I'm still young. Plenty of time."

Jake refilled Lauren's wine glass and she started telling Jake all about Daniel and how he had thrown himself at another woman during their date. Jake tried to reassure her by saying that all men had a wandering eye and that it wasn't meant to be taken personally. But as Lauren took another huge gulp of wine and began ranting about how Daniel was toying with her son's emotions, Jake knew he was in over his head. He went to pay the tab, leaving Lauren to soothe herself with the remaining curly fries that Jake hadn't polished off. She was about to finish off the rest of her wine, when Jake deftly stepped in, removed the glass from her hand and steered Lauren out of the bar.

When they pulled up in front of her house, Lauren wasn't quite as drunk, but still tipsy enough to make the decision to enlist Jake as ammunition to rile Daniel.

"Would you like to come inside for a minute?" she asked as Jake opened the car door for her.

"Sure," Jake agreed easily with a shrug of his shoulder and followed her up the path.

The door swung open before they even reached the front porch and Daniel stood with arms crossed, taking in the scene of Lauren waltzing up the path, her arm tucked into Jakes.

"You said you'd be home by seven. I've been trying to call you," Daniel said irritably.

"I'm sorry. I guess Jake and I lost track of time," Lauren slurred.

"Are you drunk?" Daniel asked incredulously.

"It's ok, man. She just had a few glasses of wine," Jake said casually.

"I didn't ask you, *man*," Daniel addressed Jake icily, then turned back to Lauren and reached out for her arm. "Come on, I'll get you a glass of water."

Lauren jerked away from his reach and gave Jake a big hug. "Jakey, can you pick me up tomorrow morning? My car's still in the school lot, remember?"

"Of course, Doll." Jake kissed Lauren on the top of her head. "I'll be here at 7:15."

"Thanks, sweetie." Lauren blew Jake a kiss as he turned and walked back toward his car. Meanwhile Daniel clucked his tongue in disgust, waiting for her to come inside.

"I take it James is already in bed?" Lauren asked as she clumsily kicked off her shoes.

"Yes, he is. But he was kind of upset that you weren't home in time to tuck him in," Daniel said as he followed her into the kitchen.

"I'm sorry, Daniel, if I actually have a life outside of you. I didn't think you'd mind babysitting him." Lauren swayed a little as she reached for a water glass.

"Of course I don't mind babysitting him. But, what are you trying to prove by going out with that guy?" Daniel was angry now.

"It's none of your business who I go out with," Lauren stated as she filled her cup with water. "I think you made it clear that we're not in a mutually exclusive relationship."

"Look, first of all, you're drunk. And you don't know what you're talking about," Daniel said. "We're going to talk about this. But not until you're sober."

"I'm done talking about this," Lauren said and began walking out of the kitchen. "I've moved on, can't you tell?"

"You know what? I'm going to let myself out. But I'm going to call you tomorrow, when you're in your right mind."

"Don't even bother. I won't answer," she called out childishly as he opened the door.

"Get some sleep," Daniel said firmly as he left and closed the door behind him.

Chapter 27

That was it. Katherine was absolutely resolved to end her relationship with Jonathan. Things had gotten way out of control. She still couldn't believe the conversation they'd had in his truck. She felt so guilty for playing with his emotions. He was serious enough to be considering her for a possible candidate to be his wife. She couldn't even begin to think how he'd react if he found out she was already someone else's wife. She did not want to hurt Jonathan, but she knew that was completely unavoidable at this point.

Then there was the unpleasant matter of trying to repair her marriage. Nathan hadn't spoken one kind word to her in weeks. She didn't even feel physically attracted to him anymore. All of her thoughts were consumed by Jonathan. She couldn't stop reliving their passionate episodes in her head. And it was completely effortless to have a shameless text session with Jonathan right before bed since Nathan didn't even bother to come upstairs at night. He was now sleeping in the guest room every night and had moved his toothbrush and razor into the guest bathroom downstairs.

The affair had even affected her relationship with her children. While she used to interact with them at the park, she would now isolate herself on the bench and use the time to talk to Jonathan. At home, she found herself barely even registering what they were saying to her. The day before she had completely forgotten to toast their waffles. She had set them on the plate still frozen. Keenan didn't care, he dug right in, but Madison let her mom know with a loud complaint. Her mind was constantly wandering off... picturing those green eyes, the way his lips felt on hers.

Stop! Stop thinking about him! She told herself over and over throughout the day. Then she would make it through a few hours of Jonathan-free zone until her phone pinged with a text from him, and then she was back to having her mind completely overtaken again. She craved every word he wrote or spoke to her. It was an addiction she just couldn't tame. But she knew she needed to come down off the cloud.

Nathan and Katherine's anniversary was the day after tomorrow. Even though it was the last thing she wanted to do, she decided she would surprise him with a romantic, candle lit dinner. She was even considering digging out some of her old lingerie. She was so not in the mood for any of it, but she really felt she should give Nathan another chance.

In the meantime, she needed to avoid Jonathan's calls and text messages. She told him she was going to be out of town for a very important client meeting and she needed to devote all of her attention to the assignment. So, she wouldn't be able to talk until the weekend. That would buy her some time. She couldn't deal with breaking Jonathan's heart and trying to woo her estranged husband all at once.

She began to set the plan in motion. She asked Lauren to keep Madison and Keenan for the night. She wrote out the ingredients she would need to pick up at the store for the dinner: lobster, a nice salad with endive, arugula and fresh herbs. Asparagus with hollandaise sauce. Crème brulee for dessert. At the end of the grocery list she added candles and a bottle of champagne. Now she just needed to work on somehow dissolving her anger towards her husband by Thursday.

Lauren's phone rang for the third time during her half hour break. She knew he would just keep calling so she finally answered the phone.

"Daniel, this is not a good time. I'm in the middle of grading spelling tests right now." She rustled the papers on her desk for effect.

"I realize you're busy at work, but you can't just keep ignoring me," Daniel said. "We need to talk about the other night."

"There's nothing to talk about. I told you – I'm moving on," Lauren stated without emotion.

"Quit being ridiculous. Who was that guy anyway?" he asked in annoyance.

"He works at my school," she answered coolly.

"Well, you're not going out with him again," Daniel said firmly.

"You can't tell me what to do. You don't own me."

"Do you realize how childish you're acting?"

"Well, I guess you just bring out the best in me," Lauren taunted him.

"I'm coming over tonight and we are going to talk. Like adults," he told her, ignoring her attempts to rile him.

"I can't tonight. I'm watching Madison and Keenan for Katherine. Then I'm going to bed early."

"Ok, whatever. I'll come over Friday night then. You can't keep avoiding me forever." Daniel sighed loudly.

"Good. I'll need you to watch James for me because I'm going out again Friday night. See you then," she said sarcastically sweet and hung up the phone.

Chapter 28

*K*atherine was in the bath surrounded by a mound of lavender scented bubbles, a mud mask on her face, her hair up in rollers. She carefully shaved her legs, underarms and bikini area. Oddly enough she was feeling a little nervous about the evening. It had been so long since Katherine and Nathan had even come within a few feet of each other. She wasn't even sure if they could have a civil conversation anymore. She didn't want to put a damper on the occasion by attempting to discuss their clearly troubled marriage. She hoped to keep the mood light, and if she could somehow set aside her anger, possibly romantic.

After she toweled off and removed her mud mask, she lightly dusted her face with powder, applied a light blue eyeshadow and some mascara. She took the rollers out of her hair and let the curls tumble loosely around her face. She then put on the cerulean cocktail dress that she knew Nathan loved on her.

It was nearly seven o'clock. She had texted him earlier that day letting him know that she was making his "favorites" for dinner that night and would appreciate it if he could make it on time. She didn't want to give too much away. Deep down she knew he probably didn't remember their anniversary, but she also wanted to give him the chance to prove her wrong. Maybe he would come home with a big bunch of roses and something from the jewelry store and surprise the heck out of her.

Nonetheless, as Katherine sat at the table sipping her second glass of Chardonnay, staring at the candles as the wax slowly tapered closer to the crystal holder and the condensation on the champagne bucket grew, she knew he'd definitely forgotten. She tried Nathan's cell phone, but it just rang and rang, then went to his voicemail. His office phone went unanswered as well. She blew out the candles and cleared the food and champagne off of the table.

After packaging the uneaten dinner and placing it in the refrigerator, she wandered into the living room. She stood, sipping her wine and listening to the quiet ticking of the clock, trying not to let her anger boil over. She tried his cell phone again at 8:40, then at 8:45. Still no answer. She was furious. *Where is he?* She got up, deposited her empty glass in the sink, grabbed her bag and car keys and stormed out of the house.

Katherine pulled into the parking lot of the architecture firm and found a spot right next to Nathan's truck. His vehicle was the only other car in the parking lot. That provided her with a little relief that he probably wasn't with another woman, but she wasn't feeling any less angry.

She threw open the door and called out his name. She rounded the corner where she could see through the glass panes into his office. The lights were on, but he wasn't sitting at his desk. She turned back around toward the bathrooms and knocked loudly before turning the knob. He wasn't there either.

Great. Maybe he left with someone. That's why his truck was still here, but he wasn't. She should have known he was having an affair.

There was no way that his lack of affection for her could only be caused by work stress.

She pulled her phone out of her purse and unsteadily dialed his number again. Surprisingly she heard the faint tone of his phone ringing. She walked back into his office and went to his desk. Sure enough there was his phone, lighting up with her incoming call. But where was he? She picked up his phone and began scrolling through his calls to see if there was evidence of infidelity. However the only recent calls were from her number and Nathan's boss.

She set his phone back down on the desk in frustration. Then as she turned around she saw him. He was asleep on the little couch on the other end of his office. She stormed over.

"Nathan!" Katherine nudged his arm with her knee. "Nathan, wake up!"

He opened his eyes and sat up abruptly, "Katherine? What are you doing here?"

"My question is the same for you." Katherine seethed. "I've been trying to call you all night."

"I fell asleep," Nathan said groggily, rubbing his face.

"Yes I can see that."

"Why are you all dressed up?" Nathan asked, squinting at her.

"I guess I didn't really expect you to remember our anniversary," Katherine spat. "But you could have at least called to say you weren't coming home tonight!"

Nathan ran his hand through his hair and sat up straighter. "Katherine, quit overreacting. I just fell asleep."

"First of all, I am NOT overreacting. It is our anniversary. I cooked a special dinner and I've been sitting at home for hours waiting for you." Katherine turned around and started for the door. She turned around just before walking out. "You know what? Just forget it. I'm done trying. You can bury yourself in your work for all I care."

"Katherine, just calm down." Nathan stood up and started after her. "You're acting crazy."

But Katherine was already down the hall heading toward the front door. She exited the office building and quickly got into her car.

Chapter 29

"*H*ow's my favorite wino?" Jake's deep voice interrupted Lauren's catnap.

She was slouched down on one of the plush chairs in the teacher's lounge with her sunglasses on. She had been up late the night before. Not only because it had taken her an hour to get James, Madison and Keenan settled down after watching three episodes of Ninjago and eating a bowl of chocolate ice cream, but she also just couldn't sleep.

She knew she was acting immaturely with Daniel. She missed him and she really wanted to talk to him. Even so, her pride wouldn't allow it. It felt exactly like seven years ago. She must be a fool to trust him again. What was it Jake had said the other night about men always having a wandering eye? Didn't he say that it was something that probably never changed?

"Lauren? You okay?" Jake asked as he pulled up a chair from one of the dining tables.

Lauren slowly pulled off her sunglasses and sat up straight. "I'm fine," she managed to say. "I was just up late babysitting for my sister-in-law."

Jake plunked himself down in the chair and leveled his gaze at her. "I hate to say it sweetheart, but you're looking a little rough."

"You don't have to tell me. It's not been the best of weeks," Lauren muttered.

"Aw come on. We had a good time the other night didn't we?" Jake teased. He playfully knocked his knee against hers. "Is David still ruffling your feathers?"

"It's Daniel. And I'd really rather not talk about him," Lauren said.

"That's fine. I'm not going to pry. I just wanted to make sure you're ok," Jake said and put his hand on her thigh. "How about we go get a burger tonight? If you feel like talking, then cool. If not we'll just stare at each other and make funny faces."

Lauren laughed and put her hand over Jakes. "That sounds like a great idea."

"Well aren't you two cozy?" Karen said as she entered the lounge and eyed Jake and Lauren with disdain.

"Ok, well... I gotta get back to the gym," Jake said abruptly and stood. "See you ladies later."

"Real classy, Lauren," Karen said as she walked toward the refrigerator.

"What?" Lauren asked while watching Karen take her salad out.

"One guy isn't enough for you?" Karen sneered. "You told me you aren't even interested in Jake."

"I'm not," Lauren said flatly. "I don't know why you're jumping all over me."

"Jake and I went out last weekend. And now you're practically throwing yourself at him."

"First of all I didn't know you two went out. And secondly, you have nothing to worry about. I am not interested in Jake."

"That's not what it looked like to me."

"You can believe what you want. I am so not in the mood for this." Lauren left the lounge in a huff.

What was that all about? she wondered as she walked down the empty hall toward her classroom. Her phone rang and she grabbed it out of her pocket expecting it to be Daniel. She was surprised to see that it was her brother instead.

"Hey, Nathan. What's up?"

"Have you heard from Katherine?" His voice came across the line tense and impatient.

"Well, I saw her this morning when she picked up Keenan and Madison from my house. Why? What's wrong?"

"I just got a message from the school's absent hotline that Madison didn't show up for school today. And I called Keenan's preschool. Same thing there."

"Well, don't panic. Maybe she took them out of school for a day off. It is Friday after all," Lauren said.

"I don't think so. I went home at lunch. Her suitcase is missing," Nathan informed her.

"Seriously? Well, have you tried calling her?" Lauren asked the obvious.

"Of course I have. She's not answering," Nathan grouched. He was silent for a few beats, then added, "We got in a pretty big fight last night."

"Oh," Lauren said with understanding. "Okay. I'll try to get in touch with her and let you know what's going on."

"Thanks sis," Nathan said and ended the call.

"Nathan's calling my phone again," Katherine's mother stated as she leaned over the kitchen counter to peer at her phone screen.

It was the third time he'd called her mom's phone since he'd finally given up trying Katherine's. The first two times Katherine had pushed the Ignore button and sent the calls to voicemail. Now her mother had accepted the call and she held the phone out for Katherine to answer. However Katherine took the phone and immediately hit the End button. Barbara scolded her daughter and after listening to the voicemail he left, she insisted that Katherine call her worried husband back. But Katherine begged her mother to just text him and tell him she was there, but was not ready to talk to him yet.

Barbara reluctantly complied and they waited for a reply text from Nathan. Apparently he was not placated by his mother-in-law's words because less than five minutes later he was calling both Katherine's and Barbara's phones again.

"You need to talk to him. I really don't think he deserves the silent treatment. I'm sure he's just very stressed out because of work."

"Mom, stop taking his side," Katherine said. "I don't care how stressed out he is. It still does not give him the right to completely disregard his wife and children. This has been going on for months now."

"I know, honey. I know it's hard. I remember a time when your father had first started his tax practice. I barely ever saw him. Every night I had to leave a plate in the refrigerator for him to microwave when he got home. I was so exhausted by the time I got you kids bathed and off to bed; I would just fall asleep on the couch. I would only see him in the morning for about ten minutes before he rushed out of the house with a cup of coffee and a piece of toast in his hand." Barbara reached out and placed her hand on her daughter's. "But eventually, things became easier and he hired an assistant and then he had more time to spend with me, you and your sisters. I did my best not to gripe and complain during those times because even though I felt neglected, I knew he was doing it for us."

Katherine stared out of the kitchen window at the oak tree that she used to swing on when she was younger. She knew what her mother was saying made sense, but she couldn't let the frost that had encompassed her heart thaw. She knew Nathan was working hard for her and the children, but she still wouldn't excuse the way he had been treating her. Sure, he came home late and was probably really tired. But so was she. She worked just as hard taking care of the house and the children. He could muster up enough energy for a kind word or two. A kiss good night would be appreciated. Even a "how is your day going?" text every now and then would be nice. But apparently that was too much to ask from him.

As if on cue, Katherine's phone chirped a notification that a text had arrived. She expected it to be Nathan, but instead saw the J next to the sender's mailbox icon.

"Nathan again?" Barbara asked as she stood and cleared their coffee mugs from the table.

"Uh, no. It's just a friend of mine," Katherine said as she clicked open the message.

Hey there! I have the day off tomorrow and was thinking of making a trip to San Antonio :) If you're not too busy, maybe we can get together?

Katherine felt her cheeks flush and was grateful that her mother had her back to her as she rinsed their mugs in the sink. When she had arrived home the night before, still livid from the encounter with Nathan in his office, she had made the decision to leave. She really needed some space from Nathan and she knew that she couldn't handle the anger that would overtake her being under the same roof as him. She had packed up some things for her and the kids and sent her mother a text informing her they would be arriving tomorrow around ten a.m.

Just before she went to sleep she sent Jonathan a text telling him that her client meeting she had told him about was in San Antonio. Then they had chatted back and forth for twenty minutes, before Katherine finally told him she needed to get her beauty rest. She hadn't felt the least bit guilty for flirting with him as she turned off the light.

She hadn't heard Nathan come home, because surprisingly she had fallen asleep so quickly. She had figured she would be up for hours waiting to hear him come into the house and wondering if he was going to come upstairs to apologize. However she knew she was greatly disenchanted to expect that from her callous husband. Her first thought when she woke up was whether he had stayed the night at his office. But when she went downstairs, she saw that the coffee pot was on, still half full, and Nathan's mug in the sink. He must have left before she woke up.

She had hurriedly dressed and put the suitcases into her car and drove over to Lauren's to pick up Keenan and Madison. As they drove away she told them that they were taking a little trip to see Grandma. It was perfect timing too because Katherine's father was in Ireland visiting his brother who was recovering from surgery. Katherine knew her mother didn't like to be alone. She was also a little relieved her father wouldn't be there to drill her about Nathan. Her father thought that Nathan was the greatest guy on earth and Katherine didn't want to have to shatter her dad's good opinion about him.

The children were super excited to miss school and pay a visit to their Grammie. Katherine's parents had made sure to have every form of entertainment at their house to keep their grandchildren happy. A trampoline and playscape in the backyard, a play room upstairs with board games, toys, and a TV and DVD player. And of course tricycles, scooters and a wagon in the garage.

Katherine enjoyed being there as well. Her parents had redecorated her childhood room with soft shades of lavender and pale olive, and updated her canopied twin bed to a queen size sleigh bed. Since they arrived earlier that morning, Katherine had spent an hour trying to fall asleep while the children played in the backyard. Too agitated to rest, she had gone downstairs and joined her mom for coffee.

"Hey, Mom? Would you mind watching the kids tomorrow so that I can get out for a little bit? I really need some time to myself to clear my head." Katherine did not meet her mother's eyes, as if her guilty intentions might be written all over her face.

"Of course, dear. I love spending time with those two little cherubs," Barbara trilled. "Take all the time you need."

"Thanks Mom." She quickly replied to Jonathan:

Would love to see you :)

Chapter 30

*L*auren's plan to go out for hamburgers with Jake had been vetoed. For several reasons: First she was ashamed that she was just using Jake to make Daniel jealous. Regardless of the fact that Jake probably wouldn't even mind – in fact she had the feeling that he rather enjoyed the drama of it all, but she didn't feel right about it. Then there was the situation with Karen. They weren't exactly close, however they were colleagues. She didn't want to upset her if she really was that into Jake. Lastly she felt like her brother needed someone to talk to. So after Daniel arrived at her house to watch James, she gave him a summation of the situation and headed for Nathan's house.

It took Nathan a good five minutes to answer the door. When he saw that it was his sister he opened it and just silently motioned her to come in. Lauren followed him through the foyer into the kitchen, then finally asked, "You're not working late today?"

"No, not today," Nathan said with irritation. Lauren noticed dark circles under his eyes. "I can't really concentrate with all this going on."

"I can imagine." Lauren regarded him with sympathy. "I'm sorry."

"I just don't get it. I'm working my tail off to support her so she can stay at home with the kids. She just doesn't seem to appreciate it." Nathan grabbed a chair out from the table and sat down.

"I don't think that's what it is at all." Lauren sat down across from him. "She misses you and feels like you don't want to spend time with her and the kids."

"I've tried that," Nathan spat out, recalling the hiking disaster a couple weeks ago. "All we do is fight. I can never figure out what the heck she wants from me. The last thing I need right now is more stress."

"She just wants you to love her and show her that you care," Lauren said softly.

"Right now I'm doing that by providing for them. She spends money like crazy, Lauren. I had to take away her credit cards for crying out loud." Nathan shook his head. "She doesn't ever show any appreciation for how hard I'm working."

"I'm sure she appreciates it. She works hard too. I know you're both tired." Lauren felt at a loss for words that would be helpful. She sure didn't know much about marriage herself.

As if reading her mind Nathan changed the subject. "So what's going on with you and Daniel? Last I heard Katherine said he was flirting with some woman while you two were out together?"

"Ugh. Please don't say I told you so." Lauren cringed.

"I won't. It just pisses me off. He needs to man up and think about James."

"Yeah well, according to my friend at work, men never stop having a wandering eye," Lauren said and raised her eyebrows.

Nathan shrugged. "Sure guys like to look at pretty women, but that doesn't mean you do anything about it. I would never cheat on

Katherine."

They sat in silence for a minute, then Nathan asked, "So what are you going to do?"

"I don't know. I've been avoiding him, but I guess I need to swallow my pride and hear what he has to say," Lauren said. Then she asked, "What are *you* going to do?"

"The same thing – talk to her. I guess I'll go to San Antonio tomorrow."

"I think that's a really good idea."

Lauren let herself into her house quietly and set her purse and keys on the table in the front hall. She heard Daniel and James' voices coming from the living room. It sounded as if they were playing Battleship, which was presently James' favorite game. She walked around to the kitchen through the hall instead of going through the living room to give them a little more uninterrupted time.

She filled the kettle with water, put a chamomile tea bag into a mug and sat at the table to wait for the water to boil.

"Hey. I didn't hear you come in," Daniel said as he walked into the kitchen with an empty bowl and cups. "Are you hiding from me?"

Lauren laughed. "No. I just wanted to give you two more time to finish your game."

"Oh, this is our third round. I think James is pretty tired. I just told him to go brush his teeth." Daniel placed the dishes in the sink, then turned around and leaned against the counter. He regarded Lauren silently.

"What?"

"Nothing. I'm just waiting to see if you're going to bite my head off again," Daniel said with a grin.

"No, I wasn't planning to. However, if you'd like, I can try to come up with something."

"No, that's okay. I'm enjoying this moment of peace and quiet."

"Da – ad... I'm ready for bed. Are you coming to read me a story?" James yelled out from his room.

"Yes, I'm coming," Daniel called back, then returned his gaze to Lauren. "Does this mean you're ready to talk to me?"

"I think so." Lauren nodded.

"Ok, I'll meet you in the living room in twenty minutes."

When Daniel joined Lauren in the living room, she had already determined in her mind what she would say to him. So before he even sat down she opened with, "I've been doing a lot of thinking and I'd really like to just keep this about James. That way you're free to date Sarah, or whoever you want to."

"Lauren, it's not like that. I don't want to date anyone else," Daniel said quickly. Then he sat down and let out a frustrated sigh. "Unless you want to. Is that what *you* want?"

Lauren didn't reply right away. She played with the tassel on her tea bag, not meeting his eyes. Finally she said, "No, that's not what I want either. However I definitely don't want to be out with you when you run into your old girlfriends and feel like I've disappeared."

"I didn't mean to ignore you," Daniel said softly. "It's just that I hadn't seen Sarah in a long time. And yes, she was my girlfriend, but there's more to it than that."

"I don't know if I want to hear this," Lauren said, setting her mug on the coffee table.

"It's not that bad. Just hear me out, okay?" Daniel pleaded.

"Sure," Lauren conceded, but crossed her arms over her chest as if the action would soften the blow of what he was about to tell her.

"Something happened and it had a very big impact on my life. I've been meaning to tell you about it for a while now, but I was waiting for the right moment." Daniel shifted on the couch and Lauren could sense that he was a little uneasy. He looked over at the bookcase for a moment, taking in the photos of James as a baby and a toddler, then back at Lauren and continued. "Sarah and I dated about two years ago. We were pretty serious. We were living together and, well... she got pregnant. We had decided to get married after the baby was born because she didn't want to be pregnant for the wedding. But when she was seven months along she went into preterm labor and she lost the baby."

Lauren sucked in a breath and fumbled for something to say, but then Daniel resumed.

"Sarah took it very hard. She became depressed; she was at U.T. at the time working towards her masters and she quit going to her classes. She just sat around the house all day and when I came home she would hardly talk to me. I tried to get her out of the house but eventually she just got angry at me all the time. Finally she moved out and went to live with her parents. She didn't want anything to do with me; she said being around me just reminded her of the baby. I tried to see her, but her parents wouldn't let me in or take my calls. Finally I had no choice but to give up."

This time it was Lauren who shifted on the couch uncomfortably. She wasn't sure if she was expected to offer some type of sympathy for Daniel's ex-girlfriend. She did feel badly for what the woman went through, however she hoped Daniel didn't plan to use the situation as an excuse to keep in close contact with Sarah now that they had been reunited.

"I'm sure that must have been very hard for her. I appreciate you telling me."

"I'm not finished... I was a mess too. I held myself together for her sake, but after she left I fell apart. I couldn't concentrate on work. I lost most of my agents because I just couldn't give them the support they needed. I hardly ever went into the office. I was having trouble sleeping at night. Finally I went to my doctor to get a prescription for a sleeping pill, but instead he gave me the card to a counselor. At first I wasn't going to go, but I realized what did I have to lose? So, I went and the guy turned out to be the pastor of a church. He told me that he and his wife had been through the same thing a few years ago. I saw him once a week for a couple of months and surprisingly it really did help."

"So, you were able to get over her?" Lauren asked not unselfishly.

"It wasn't just about Sarah. I really wanted that baby. Especially after seeing her on the ultrasound screen and feeling her kick in Sarah's stomach. She had already become a part of me. I was angry at God for taking that away. But now with James... I feel like He's given me a second chance. You can't imagine how grateful I am for that." Daniel didn't even bother holding back his tears. He let them stream down his face unashamedly. He wiped them away with the back of his hand and took a minute to compose himself. "Can you understand now why I was so upset when I realized that I had missed out on knowing about James?"

"Yes, I've always been completely understanding about that. And now hearing this I feel even worse than before for keeping him from you," Lauren said, wiping her own tears.

"You don't have to beat yourself up over that anymore. I know you didn't do it maliciously."

"Considering everything, you've really been a lot more patient and kind than what I expected," Lauren admitted.

"Yeah well, that part hasn't exactly been easy. I've had my moments," Daniel said. "But, that pastor also taught me how to have a real relationship with God and about the importance of forgiving one another. How could I not forgive you when I don't even deserve forgiveness from the Creator of the Universe?" Daniel asked.

"So you go to church now?" Lauren asked without disguising her surprise.

"Yeah. I don't go every Sunday, but I try to go at least twice a month. As a matter of fact, I had planned to ask if you and James would go with me sometime soon."

"I... I'm not sure. I'll have to think about it." Lauren was still feeling guarded and she needed time to absorb everything Daniel had told her.

"I understand. No rush. Just let me know," Daniel said gently. "But, I'm really glad we finally had the chance to talk about this."

"Me too," Lauren said sincerely.

"And as far as you and me... We don't have to rush into anything. Let's just take things slow and see what happens." He then added, "I'm not going anywhere and you can trust me. I want to be here for James and for you too, no matter what."

"Thank you. I'm sorry I overreacted," Lauren said sheepishly.

"Yeah... about that," Daniel said with a little smile. "No more assumptions and jealous retaliation."

"Who, me? Jealous?" Lauren attempted to joke, but she knew he was serious and that she needed to work on taming those emotions. "I promise to do my best."

"So no more Jake," Daniel said firmly. "And no more jumping to conclusions every time I talk to someone of the female race."

Lauren smiled. "I said I'd do my best. And yes, no more Jake."

"Alright. Now that we've got that settled... how about if I have James over this weekend? You can have some alone time to think about coming to church with me."

Chapter 31

Katherine sat at one of the small tables at the Alamo Bar and Grill, anxiously stirring her tonic water. She had dressed casually in jeans and a light blue sweater with a colorful scarf loosely tied around her neck. She was grateful she had worn her low heeled boots as she'd had to walk several blocks from the free lot where she parked her car.

Every few minutes she glanced toward the front entrance, checking for Jonathan's arrival. She took a sip of her drink, then resumed taking in the view through the windows at the back of the bar. The river was sparkling as the sun began to make its descent over the famous Riverwalk that stretched through downtown San Antonio. Too bad she couldn't enjoy it because her stomach was in knots and her mind was a non-stop hamster wheel of thoughts about her disaster of a marriage.

Finally, the door opened and in walked Jonathan, looking handsome as ever in jeans, a long sleeve gingham shirt with the sleeves pushed up and western boots. He spotted her immediately and wove his way through the other tables until he was standing in front of her. She stood up and stepped toward him as he held his arms open, his expression warm. As she let him embrace her, she felt the tension leave her shoulders. She had expected him to be upset with her for being so elusive all week. Even though she had used the excuse about her demanding work project, she knew that he must realize making an effort to text him now and then would have been reasonable.

"I've missed you," he said softly into her ear, confirming further that he wasn't at all annoyed with her.

"Me too," Katherine said as she pulled back. "I'm sorry I've been so out of touch lately."

"Kat, I understand. I know I laid some pretty heavy stuff on you the last time we were together." Jonathan sat down and motioned for her to sit as well. "Plus you have your work thing going on."

"Well, thank you for understanding," Katherine said, feeling awkward. She took a long sip of her drink. "I'm really glad we could meet up today."

"So am I. It's been a long week and seeing you is definitely the highlight." Jonathan leaned back in the soft velvet chair. "So, where are you staying?"

Just then, a waitress appeared at their table to ask if she could get them a drink. Katherine was grateful for the interruption so that she could formulate a response. For a moment she forgot that she wasn't supposed to be a stay at home mom, running away from her husband and hiding out at her mother's house. If only she could confide in Jonathan and have him comfort her and tell her everything was going to be okay. What a ridiculous notion.

The waitress disappeared and Jonathan's intense gaze returned to Katherine. She deftly attempted to change the subject, "How was your drive over?"

"It was great," he said easily. "It's nice to get out of Austin."

"Yes, it is," Katherine agreed.

"So are you staying somewhere nearby?" he asked again.

"Yes. I'm, uh, staying at the hotel next door," she said, gesturing to her right, hoping he wouldn't ask her the name because she had no idea.

"Oh, yeah? You got a room with a nice view?" he asked.

"Yes, it's very nice," she replied, peering out at the river.

The waitress appeared then with another drink for her and Jonathan's beer.

"So..." Katherine began, watching as Jonathan tilted the beer to his lips. It took her a moment to erase the image of the last time those lips were on hers. She took a deep breath and tried to ignore the flash of desire. "What went on in your world this week? You said it was a tough one?"

"Nah... it wasn't all that bad. The restaurant was pretty slow and I kept busy with studying. But, it mostly just dragged on because I was missing you. I'm still worrying that I've scared you off for good this time." His gaze became more intense as he waited for her response.

"You haven't scared me off," she said quietly, looking down into her drink.

"Good. I didn't mean to freak you out or anything. I'm not planning on proposing tomorrow, but..." Jonathan set his beer on the table and leaned forward. "You're the most incredible woman I've ever met. Not just because you're beautiful, but because you're smart and kind. And fun to be with. I want to spend more time with you. I think we really have something here. I don't think that you ending up at my table was a coincidence."

"I don't think so either." Katherine said softly. She felt her head spinning as she basked in Jonathan's words.

He leaned in even closer, his knee brushing up against hers. "What would you say about continuing this conversation up in your room?"

Katherine felt her stomach drop at his words. "In my room?"

"I think it would be nice to have some privacy. I feel like I haven't seen you in ages," Jonathan said.

"Well, I suppose..." Katherine felt a little light headed. She wasn't really sure of his intentions for wanting to go up to her room. *Her room that didn't even exist.* What she did know is that she had an overwhelming desire to be in his arms again, without spectators. She also didn't feel as if she owed Nathan any loyalty with the way things stood between them. She thought quickly and came up with a plan.

Walking into the hotel lobby of La Mansion del Rio with Jonathan at her side, Katherine began to rummage through her bag. After a few moments, she turned to him with a frown and said, "I must have accidentally left my key in the room."

"That's no good," Jonathan said with a little laugh. "Well, I'm sure the front desk can give you a new one."

"Oh, right. Of course." Katherine managed a smile and looked apprehensively over at the front desk. "Um... wait here. I'll go see about it and be right back."

As she walked slowly toward the front desk, she contemplated whether Jonathan might be planning to lift his no sex before marriage moratorium. But was she willing to lift her 'no adultery no matter how angry she was at her husband' vow? Her heart began to pound as she approached the desk, her mind racing back and forth with indecision. She could turn around and tell Jonathan that she changed her mind and that she wanted to respect his religious values. Or she could pay for a room, letting lust rule her and risk both of them going straight to...

"How may I assist you, dear?" a middle aged woman with a pleasant smile interrupted her silent moral dilemma.

"I, uh..." Katherine turned around to look at Jonathan and met his irresistible green eyes. His slow, sultry smile completely dissolved her ability to make any sort of proper decisions. "Do you have any rooms with a view available?"

Placing the card into the key reader at the door of room 807, Katherine realized her hand was shaking. She looked over at Jonathan to see if he had noticed, but he just gave her another one of his heart melting grins. The lock clicked and she pushed open the door. Jonathan held it open while she walked in, and then followed her inside. He allowed the door to close with a resounding thud in the awkward silence. They both just stood side by side taking in the surroundings. Jonathan looked at Katherine as if waiting for her to make the first move.

"So, this is it," Katherine said, swiping her arm as if to display the room. She had made sure to ask the desk clerk for a suite, so that they wouldn't be accosted by the sight of the bed when they first walked in. Additionally, she figured Jonathan would be wondering where her belongings were and hoped he would just assume she had them stowed in the bedroom of the suite.

"You sure are tidy," Jonathan commented as he walked over to the window to take in the view. Before she could respond, he continued, "This is great. You can even see the Alamo from here."

Katherine joined him at the window and tried to come up with something to say, besides rattling off some mundane historical fact in reference to the Alamo. But before she could formulate a sentence, Jonathan turned to her and placed both hands gently on her face. He studied her eyes for a moment then placed his lips on hers causing all thoughts to slip from her mind.

Jonathan was leading her to the bedroom. They were still entangled in a heated kiss and Katherine was doing her best to not think about anything except the pleasure of having his hands all over her. Just before they made it to the bed, Jonathan peeled off his shirt. Katherine took in the sight of his tanned, muscular chest and toned abs and felt her legs go weak.

"Umm, Jonathan?" she finally managed to say between kisses. "Are you sure about this?"

"Yes. I'm sure." Jonathan stepped back a little so that he could see her face, but kept his arms around her waist. "I know this is crazy, but I've never felt like this about anyone. I'm falling in love with you Katherine, and I know we have a future together. Otherwise I would have never suggested we come up here." Jonathan looked at her with such passion; all she could manage was to stare back at him, her mind trying desperately to cope with what he had just told her.

But he didn't wait for her to reply. He covered her lips with his once again and smoothly lowered her down onto the plush bed. Katherine did not resist. She let herself be swept away as he continued to kiss her on the mouth, moving down to her neck and collarbone.

Jonathan had just begun untying her scarf when the sound of her cell phone began to chime. She recognized her mother's ring tone and was relieved that she had an excuse to put this heated moment on hold.

"Hold on a sec. I need to get that," she extricated herself from his arms and went to find her purse in the other room.

"Hello?" Katherine tried not to sound breathless as she answered.

"Where are you?" her mother asked irritably.

"I'm just out doing a little shopping." Katherine spoke as quietly as possible and turned away from the other room where Jonathan was now sitting up on the bed.

"Well, I recommend that you come back here as soon as possible."

"Why? What's going on?" Katherine asked with worry, thinking something must have happened to one of the children.

"Nathan's here and he's not happy. He's playing with Madison and Keenan right now. But I can tell he's getting impatient," her mother said in hushed tones.

"Well, tell him he has no right to be impatient," Katherine hissed, cradling the phone against her shoulder and retying her scarf.

"You need to talk to him. The fact that he's here means that he's making an effort. That's what you wanted, isn't it?" Barbara reminded her.

Katherine sighed heavily, wishing now that she hadn't answered her phone.

"Can you please just come home?" her mother pleaded quietly.

"Okay. Okay." Katherine gave in. She looked nervously over at Jonathan. He was watching her, his brow furrowed in concern. "I'll be there as soon as possible."

She took her time putting her phone back into her purse, then turned slowly toward Jonathan. He was now standing and putting his shirt back on, concern still etched on his face.

"That didn't sound good," he said, making his way toward her.

"Yeah," she said, biting her lower lip. "That was my boss. The client isn't happy about something and wants to meet."

"Right now?" Jonathan asked incredulously.

"I know. It's ridiculous." Katherine shook her head, feeling terrible about the lie.

They rode down in the elevator together in complete silence. Katherine felt queasy, wondering if Jonathan was just upset because their moment was interrupted or if he could tell she had concocted a story. She didn't dare try to make eye contact as they exited the elevator and made their way through the lobby.

"I'll call you as soon as I'm done with the meeting, okay?" she said when they reached the front door of the hotel.

"Okay, sure," Jonathan said coolly.

Katherine stood on her toes and gave him an awkward peck on the cheek, then rushed out of the hotel and down the sidewalk.

Chapter 32

*L*auren was nervous about going to church. She wasn't particularly worried about the church part. She was used to going to the Lutheran church her and Nathan had attended with their parents growing up. And she still went with them on Sundays whenever she visited and every Christmas. They had even had James baptized at St. Paul's when he turned two. She enjoyed the comfy feeling she got being in the thirty year old building, the smell of the cedar, the beautiful stained glass windows, the sound of the preacher's voice.

She did not know much about the church Daniel attended – he had told her it was non-denominational, which she presumed meant they accepted people from all backgrounds. So, just how different could it be? Church was church, right? She suspected that the service couldn't deviate too much from what she was used to. All she had to do was sit through the service and listen, and try not to let her mind wander or get too distracted by what everyone was wearing or mentally assessing the women with outdated hairstyles. That part was easy.

Even though she did consider herself a Christian because of her upbringing, she realized after her conversation with Daniel that she hadn't given much thought about God since her last visit to church with her parents three months ago. It was a little intimidating because it seemed as if Daniel was very serious about the whole thing. Daniel had told her that he routinely dedicated time to praying, reading the bible and studying scriptures. She was still trying to wrap her head around seeing him in this new saintly role. Maybe this was a big part of the reason for the positive changes she had seen in him.

Nevertheless, she realized that although they had made huge strides in improving communication between them, their relationship was still far from being defined. She took comfort that he wanted to share his faith with her; that must mean something. But what exactly? Going to church together seemed to be something married couples did, or at least couples that were in a committed relationship. Deep down she knew that was what she really desired, but she was still extremely hesitant. She needed more time to see if Daniel really was sincere about staying faithful to her.

After hearing Daniel's story about Sarah and the loss of their baby, she realized that he must be taking relationships with women more seriously. Although this strengthened her belief that he really had matured in more ways than one, it left her feeling jealous. Why was he able to have a long term relationship with this woman, but not her? He had said that he was going to marry her! When Lauren replayed the conversation in her head later that night, that fact alone had left her heart aching. And of course there was the constant nagging notion that Daniel probably still had feelings for Sarah. The woman was beautiful and now she had her master's degree. Lauren felt at a loss to compete with that.

However she knew that there was one area in which she did not have to compete with Sarah. She and Daniel shared the common bond of James. Not that she would ever use that as a way to entangle

Daniel. She wanted him to be with her because he loved her. And she wanted the best for her son. The important thing was to focus on James right now as he was still navigating the newness of getting to know his father. If in the process it brought her and Daniel closer together, it would be a win-win situation for them all. Mind made up, she reached for her phone and typed in her answer to Daniel's question. *Yes, James and I would both like to come with you to church tomorrow.*

As Katherine pulled into the driveway, she saw that Nathan was sitting on the front porch of her mother's house. He waited until she began walking up the walkway before he stood and studied her with contempt.

"Where were you?" he demanded, his eyebrows knitted together.

"What are you doing here?" Katherine completely ignored his question.

"You can't just take off because I fell asleep at my office."

"You know that's not why I left, Nathan. Don't play games with me." Katherine crossed her arms.

"I'm not the one playing games here. I haven't done anything wrong," he pointed out.

"Oh, you haven't done anything wrong?" Katherine felt her pulse quicken in anger.

"No, I haven't. I'm just working hard to provide for you and the kids. It's not my fault if you're not happy." Nathan took a step back and crossed his arms as well.

"Nathan, this isn't just about not being happy!" Katherine was now shouting. "You don't pay any attention to me! It's like we're not even married. We're just strangers living in the same house, raising two kids together. Of course I'm not happy! That's not at all what marriage is supposed to be."

"Well, I'm sorry that I'm not meeting your ridiculous expectations," Nathan said self-defensively and looked away from her.

"Ridiculous expectations?!" Katherine was so angry now she could feel her face burning. "I don't think it's ridiculous for a man to want to talk to his wife, ask her how her day was, take her out on a date once in a while. What is so ridiculous about that?!"

Nathan remained stoic, his arms still crossed tightly. He continued to keep his gaze from her, focusing on the house across the street. Katherine could tell that the conversation was going nowhere. Nathan was just not going to budge. Her heart sank as she realized that he must truly believe that there wasn't anything wrong with the way he had been treating her. Her anger reached an all time high.

"You know what's ridiculous?" Katherine blurted out, and before she could think, she continued, "It's ridiculous that another man has to fulfill that need for me."

That got his attention. He looked at her with narrowed eyes and said, "What is that supposed to mean?"

Katherine rushed past him and grabbed for the front door handle.

"Wait!" Nathan grabbed her arm. "Where are you going? What the hell did you just say?"

Katherine turned around slowly, her heart pounding, and looking at him with a hardened expression, she said, "I've been seeing someone."

For a few moments Nathan just stood there, still holding on to her arm. Then he let go, backed away a few steps and icily stated back to her, "You've been seeing someone."

Katherine looked away, her eyes filling with tears. She just nodded her head and let the tears roll down her face.

"Are you kidding me? What exactly does that mean? You're having an affair? You're sleeping with another man?" His voice rose in anger at the last question.

Katherine was sobbing now. Wiping the tears with the back of her hand, she shook her head.

"You're serious, aren't you?" Nathan looked at her with disgust.

Katherine was about to try to say that she hadn't slept with him, but Nathan put up his hand and said, "You know what? I don't want to hear it. I don't want to hear anything you have to say."

He turned around and started down the path towards his truck.

Katherine didn't bother to try to stop him. She just went into her mother's house, closed the door, sank down to the floor and continued to sob.

"Are you going to tell me what's going on?" Katherine's mother was asking.

Katherine was sitting at the kitchen table, drinking tea and texting with Jonathan. It was almost eleven o'clock at night. Katherine's mom had not mentioned anything the remainder of the evening as they prepared dinner together, sat down with the children to eat and then watched an episode of Arthur. Katherine had gone to put the children to bed while Barbara cleaned the kitchen. Barbara had then taken a phone call from one of her friends and when she finally hung up, she was determined to get to the bottom of the drama in her daughter's marriage.

"Nothing is going on. It's the same thing I've told you before. Nathan has completely shut me out. All he cares about now is work," Katherine said with annoyance.

"Well, if he didn't care, then why did he drive all the way over here to talk to you?" she asked.

"He just wanted to see the kids. Not me," Katherine said. There was no way she could tell her mother about Jonathan. When her sister's husband had cheated on her with a co-worker from his office, their mom made sure her strong opinion on the matter was heard. Doug ended the affair and he and Evelyn went to counseling. But Barbara still used any chance she got to let everyone know she felt his behavior was inexcusable in both her eyes and God's.

"Who are you texting with this late at night? I'm assuming it's not Nathan?" her mother pried.

"No, it's just a friend. Letting them know I'm going to be out of town for a while longer." She set her phone face down on the table.

"So, what do you plan on doing?"

"I'll probably stay here for a while. That is, if it's okay with you," Katherine said uneasily, not really sure at all what she was doing.

"Well, of course I don't mind. But I don't think it's right. What about the children's schools?"

"They could go to school here. Or I could homeschool them."

Barbara gave her daughter a dubious look.

"Ok, maybe not homeschool. But maybe I could get a job at the elementary here. You know I've wanted to go back to work for a long time."

"Yes, I know. But I think you're jumping ahead here. You shouldn't make any rash decisions right now."

"Honestly, Mom, I think that's a big part of what's gone wrong in our marriage. Nathan practically made me quit my job. He didn't even care that it wasn't what *I* wanted. It's always about what *he* wants."

"Yes, dear, I know that has been hard for you. But I do think it was good for the kids," Barbara said. "And like I said before, marriage requires compromise."

"All I know is I can't go home. I don't want to be anywhere near him," Katherine stated immaturely.

"I really think you need to give Nathan some slack," Barbara said.

"Mother, why are you taking his side?" Katherine asked, feeling hurt that her mom wasn't going to pity her. Even though deep down she knew she didn't deserve it.

"I'm not taking anyone's side. I just know that Nathan's a good man and I know that you two can work this out."

Katherine sighed and picked up her phone as it pinged again with another text from Jonathan, *Kat? You still there?*

Still here. Just getting ready for bed. Give me a sec.

"I really need some time apart from him to figure some stuff out."

"What kind of stuff?" her mom asked.

"I don't know. He's really hurt me these past months. I don't think he loves me anymore," Katherine admitted out loud for the first time.

"Well, do you still love him?"

"I do, but I don't think that I'm *in* love with him," Katherine said sadly.

"Well, then," Barbara let out a slow breath. "Maybe a break would be good for you both."

Katherine yawned and pushed back from the table. "I'm really tired. I'm going up to bed."

"Ok." Her mom yawned as well. "Sleep well, dear."

Katherine hugged her mom and slowly made her way upstairs. Her legs were like lead and she felt as if she hadn't slept in days. When she reached her room, she quickly typed out a text to Jonathan, *I'm back. Sorry.*

It was the third time she had apologized to him. She could tell he was upset with her. When she finally texted him to say that the meeting with her client had taken up the rest of the day, he replied, *I waited for hours to hear from you. Drove back to Austin already.*

She felt awful. She had wanted to get in touch with him, let him know she was done with the client meeting. She wanted to call him and let their conversation drown out the cascade of panic that overtook her every time she thought about what she had done earlier. She still could not believe she told Nathan about Jonathan. The anger and emotions had completely short circuited her judgment at that moment. But now it was too late; the truth was out there. And Nathan had just taken off, once again displaying how little he cared. However much she knew continuing to see Jonathan was wrong, Katherine was just incapable of breaking things off with him. He was her only warm, fuzzy blanket in her world of coldness and discontent.

She waited a few more minutes, then texted again, *Jonathan?*

Still nothing. He must have fallen asleep. She sent, *Good night. Call me tomorrow.* Then she turned off her phone and collapsed on the bed.

Chapter 33

*N*athan was furious. He had already gone through several different emotions since he learned about Katherine's affair. On the drive back from San Antonio it had been complete disbelief. There was no way Katherine would cheat on him. It just wasn't anything he would have ever expected from her. But there was no denying it. She had come right out and said it. Unless she was making it up just to get a rise out of him. But that wasn't like her either. And judging by the way she looked at him when she told him, it was the truth.

From there he moved onto livid anger. He had walked into their house and stood for a moment listening to the deafening silence and then grabbed the first thing he could and threw it across the room. The vase they had received from his aunt as a wedding gift smashed on the tile into a hundred pieces, the scarlet silk calla lilies spewed across the floor as lifeless victims.

Later, after he'd had a couple of beers and cleaned up the mess, he sat in his office staring out the window and jealousy swept over him. Who the hell was this guy? How dare he hit on his wife! If he could just find out where this guy lived! He pictured this faceless man with his hands on Katherine and his blood boiled.

He went up to their bedroom and tore through Katherine's dresser and nightstand drawers. He wasn't sure what he was looking for: a business card, a napkin with a name and number, a photo? He knew it was highly unlikely there was anything in the house that would provide confirmation of her infidelity. The evidence was probably all in her cell phone.

Then finally as he was drifting off to sleep, well after midnight and another beer, he realized he was hurt. It genuinely stung. He had been working so hard to provide for Katherine and the children. Practically killing himself with all the long hours, not to mention the stress. Of course he didn't feel like talking when he got home from work. He was so tired he could barely see straight. He loved Katherine and he was still attracted to her. He had never even thought about being unfaithful to her. But at the end of the day, all he could do was hope to get at least six hours of sleep so that he could get up and do it all over again. *All of it because he loved her.* But she hadn't appreciated it. So she went out and found someone else to hold her and kiss her and who knows what else? He couldn't bear to imagine what all she had done with this jerk.

He tossed and turned all night, only catching glimpses of sleep a few minutes at a time. He dreamed of Katherine laughing and running. She was wearing a white sundress that was sheer and flowing. Her red hair was long and the curls were tumbling around her shoulders. She was looking at him, her eyes pleading with him to follow her. But when he reached for her, she turned away and ran in the other direction. Then a man without a face was next to her, holding her hand and leading her away.

Nathan woke up with a start and sat up. Rubbing his eyes, he looked over at the alarm clock. It was barely six a.m. He laid back down, still exhausted but he couldn't fall back to sleep. Reluctantly, he got up and decided to go for a run.

As he began to jog down their street, Nathan realized he couldn't remember the last time he had exercised. He hadn't even been outside this early in the morning for an extended amount of time. Just from the house to his truck and then from his truck into work. He had to admit it felt really good. The sky was overcast and it was cooler than usual; the damp air washed over his skin. He picked up his pace and tried to put thoughts of Katherine and her boyfriend out of his mind.

As Lauren left Restoration Christian Center, she didn't feel as if she had just attended a church service. It had been more like a rock concert with a mix of motivational speaking and a comedy routine. The sanctuary was enormous with a colossal stage of mahogany spanning the entire front portion of the room. The band consisted of three guitar players, two bass players, a very modern looking drummer, a keyboardist, and three lead singers. This impressive ensemble was backed up with a choir consisting of two dozen men and women dressed in black slacks and black turtlenecks. The praise and worship was spectacular, and the music moved her to tears several times.

After the band and choir left the stage, the pastor's wife took the podium encouraging the women to attend a conference that was coming up in June. She then led the congregation in prayer for the needs of the church and the community and the individuals that had emailed requests earlier in the week.

Then they turned their attention to the large screens on each side of the stage where a professionally choreographed video encouraged high school students to join the youth group. The video was filled with funny quips and outtakes from several of the teenage members of the church.

Finally, the pastor took the stage. He delivered a message of hope and peace using humor and modern day examples that tied into the bible verses he quoted. Lauren found herself completely engaged with no need to scour the pews for something to occupy her mind with. The time passed quickly and when the pastor dismissed the congregation and the band took the stage for one final upbeat song, she felt encouraged and content.

James had thoroughly enjoyed the children's church service that began with thirty minutes in the huge indoor playscape. He had scrambled amongst the slides and tunnels with about fifty other elementary aged children. The play area even had a life sized replica of Noah's ark that the children explored with delight. When Lauren and Daniel picked him up in his classroom, he excitedly showed them the bracelet he had made with silver letters spelling Jesus.

After filing out of the parking lot along with a couple hundred other cars, Daniel suggested they go for lunch at the Little Deli. Once they were seated with their sandwiches, Daniel turned to Lauren and asked, "So, what did you think?"

"I've never experienced a church service like that before. It was so entertaining." Lauren began. After taking a sip of her iced tea she added, "It was also very moving. I absolutely loved the music, and the way the pastor kept my attention." Daniel laughed, "Yeah, I don't think I've ever seen anyone dozing off in one of his services."

"What about you James? What did you learn?" Daniel asked.

James scrunched up his face in thought as he chewed his bite of grilled cheese. "Wellll..... I learned that God loves us and nothing can separate us from His love. Even bad guys and tornadoes."

"Wow. That's pretty awesome." Daniel nodded eagerly and looked over at Lauren with a big smile.

"And they have a really cool playground," James exclaimed.

"Yes, I was impressed with that. When Nathan and I went to Sunday school we just had to sit in our chairs, stay still and be quiet. That was quite a treat," Lauren said.

"It definitely makes going to church more appealing to the little ones," Daniel said.

They ate in silence for a few minutes, then Lauren wiped her mouth with a napkin and said, "I love what the pastor said about all of our past mistakes being erased as if they'd never happened."

"Yes, that's one of the things that really gave me peace," Daniel said.

"I'm sure you realize the mistake I made that has caused me a lot of regret," Lauren said softly to Daniel.

"We've both made mistakes," Daniel agreed gently and reached for her hand. "But obviously God had a plan for us to experience a new beginning. I really do believe that."

Lauren smiled warmly at Daniel. "It seems that way, doesn't it?"

"Mom. Dad." James interrupted their tender moment. "Can we go again?"

"Of course. I mean, that is, if your mom wants to."

Lauren looked at him sincerely and replied, "Yes. Actually, I would like that very much."

Why hadn't he called her back? Katherine had texted Jonathan several times and left him another voicemail, but had still not had any reply from him. He usually responded right away. She hadn't heard anything from him in two days now, since Saturday night, when he had made it clear he was upset about their disrupted moment at the hotel.

She was sitting on the deck in her mother's backyard sipping a cup of English breakfast tea. Her mom and the children had gone shopping. She had slept in later than usual and when she came downstairs she saw her mom's note on the kitchen counter. She was relieved to have some quiet time to herself. She was even more relieved that she wouldn't have to face more of her mother's pressing questions about her failing marriage. At least not for a couple of hours.

After she had set the kettle to boil, she went about the task of calling Keenan and Madison's schools to let them know that the children would be out for a week visiting their grandmother. She felt a little awkward about it, but figured it shouldn't be such a big deal. Keenan was only in preschool and Madison couldn't possibly get behind too much from missing one week of second grade. Besides, they were going to have so much fun with their grandma this week, and she had already asked Rachel, her younger sister, if the children could stay with her one night.

She had put two tea bags in her mug in hopes it would lift some of the brain fog. She'd been up half the night worrying about the conversation she'd had with Nathan two days ago. She was still in utter disbelief that she had told him about Jonathan. What in the world had come over her? She still wasn't sure if it was good or bad to have finally come clean about her affair. She still felt so strange even using that term. But that was what it was. She was having an affair, and now her husband knew.

What was going to happen to her marriage? Would Nathan ever forgive her? Was he going to ask for a divorce? She knew in her heart that was the last thing she wanted. But she was still so angry at Nathan for the months of neglect. There had been little reason before to be hopeful for reconciliation and now it definitely seemed out of the question. But there was one reason that she was glad she had confessed her relationship with Jonathan. She couldn't help but wish that it hurt Nathan as much as he had hurt her.

She didn't want to think about Nathan anymore this morning. She'd already spent enough energy on him last night. The tangled web of thoughts in her fatigued mind had gone nowhere. If he wasn't going to change, then there was no point in them even speaking for now. She wouldn't go back to that lifestyle of being ignored and neglected. She wanted to be loved and cherished. The way Jonathan treated her.

Her phone rang and she quickly reached for it, tipping her mug and splashing tea on the chaise lounge. She cursed under her breath and tried to swipe the milky liquid off the vinyl cushion. She glanced at the caller ID on her phone – Lauren again. She meant to hit the Ignore button, but accidentally hit Accept instead. Sighing loudly, she put the phone to her ear. "Hi, Lauren," she answered numbly.

"Hey. I've been worried about you. What's going on?" Lauren's voice was a little muffled with a lot of background noise.

"Where are you? I can barely hear you," Katherine deflected the question.

"Hold on a sec," Lauren said. "I'm in the hall, just getting back from lunch."

Katherine heard the sound of Lauren closing her classroom door.

"So, how's Daniel?" Katherine asked quickly before Lauren could resume questioning her about her own situation.

"He's great. We're great," Lauren said. "He took us to his church yesterday."

"Church?" Katherine echoed. "Since when does Daniel go to church?"

"Actually he's been going for a while. But, we can talk about that later. I want to know what's going on with you and Nathan. Why did you leave?"

Katherine blew out a breath of frustration and stood up. She began pacing the deck trying to think what to say without giving up too much information. She hoped that she was safe to assume Nathan had not talked to Lauren since Saturday morning and he had not told her about the affair. By the tone of Lauren's voice, she was pretty sure he hadn't.

"I left because he doesn't even want to try to work on our marriage," Katherine stated icily.

"I thought he drove over to your mom's to talk to you," Lauren said in concern.

"He told you that?" Katherine asked nervously. *Uh oh. What else had he told her?*

"Yes, I went to see him after school on Friday. He was really upset and he said he was going to your mom's to talk to you," Lauren explained.

"But you haven't talked to him since?" Katherine winced in anticipation.

"No, I haven't. What happened?" Lauren asked again.

Katherine sat back down, letting out a breath of relief. "Well, did he tell you that he completely disregarded our anniversary?" Katherine asked, but didn't wait for an answer. "I had made that nice dinner for him and sat there waiting like a fool for hours. I had to go track him down at his office - he was asleep on the couch. Did he tell you about that? He didn't even say he was sorry!"

"No. I had no idea. Why didn't you tell me when you picked up the kids Friday morning?"

"Because I just didn't have the strength to get into it. I just needed to get out of town and really think things over."

Lauren said, "I guess he's really worn out from all the stress."

Katherine rolled her eyes. *Another one taking Nathan's side*, she thought.

"Well, I'm tired too," Katherine protested. "But I made an effort. He didn't even remember that it was our anniversary. I told him I made him a special dinner and he didn't even bother to come home."

"I don't think he did it on purpose." Lauren tried to console her.

"It doesn't matter anymore. I'm done trying."

"Well, wait. What happened when he showed up at your mom's? Didn't you guys talk?" Lauren was not going to let her off the hook.

"He didn't want to hear what I had to say," Katherine said half truthfully. "We just fought some more and he left all angry."

"Oh, Katherine. I'm sure you guys will work this out. I know how much he loves you."

Probably not anymore, Katherine thought.

"When are you coming back?"

"Honestly, I don't know," Katherine said impatiently.

"You two just need to sit down and really talk. Come back home. I'll watch the kids for you and the two of you can have as long as you need," Lauren offered.

"I don't think talking is going to fix this," Katherine muttered.

"Oh, come on. It's not even all that bad," Lauren said gently.

Katherine shook her head. *If you only knew.* "Listen, I better go. I didn't charge my phone last night and it's about to turn off."

"Ok, but you'll call me later, right?"

"Yes, I will. Bye."

Katherine set down her phone and began pacing the deck again. She wondered whether Nathan was going to tell Lauren about the affair. They had been very close in the past, but she knew in the last few years they didn't talk as much. But chances were that Nathan might decide to confide in her. If he did, Lauren was definitely not going to be understanding. She might even lose Lauren's friendship over it.

Her phone rang again and once more caused her to jump. Her nerves were so shot; she could practically feel them buzzing inside of her. Still not Jonathan. This time it was her mother.

"Katherine, we're just about to leave Whole Foods. Would you like me to bring you something for lunch?"

"No thanks, Mom. I'm really not very hungry." Katherine slumped back into the lounge chair.

"Honey, you need to eat," her mother said firmly.

"I did. I had a late breakfast," she lied.

"Oh, good. What did you have?"

"Scrambled eggs."

"That's interesting. Because last I checked, I was out of eggs."

Katherine squeezed her eyes shut and put her hand over her head. "Okay, okay. I'll have a chicken salad sandwich."

"That's more like it. I'll get you some of those chocolate muffins you like as well. See you soon."

Chapter 34

$\mathcal{L}$auren once again stood on her brother's porch waiting for him to come to the door. She had called him after school and told him she would bring him dinner. She had an inkling that he probably hadn't been eating very well since Katherine left. After dropping James off with Daniel, she went to the Asian Fusion diner that opened not long ago. The scent of lemongrass and garlic from the bag she was holding was making her mouth water.

Finally after another ring of the doorbell she heard Nathan's footsteps approaching. He opened the door, phone pressed to his ear, a scowl on his face. "I just don't know if I can do that," he was saying. "At the end of the day, I don't have anything left to give."

Lauren followed Nathan into the kitchen where she set the bag on the counter and began taking out the containers of Thai food.

"She's just completely selfish. I don't even know who she is anymore," Nathan said. "Look, Lauren just got here. I gotta get off the phone."

Lauren waited for her brother to finish his call, and then asked, "Mom?"

"Yes," Nathan confirmed.

"Was she helpful?"

"Not really," he muttered.

"Are you hungry?" Lauren asked.

"Starving," he admitted. "Let's eat."

After they finished off the Pad Thai and Lemongrass Chicken, Nathan rinsed the containers and took out the trash. Lauren went to the living room and Queenie plodded along behind her. She sat on the sofa and scratched the old dog on the head and behind her ears. Nathan joined them shortly after and sank into his recliner with a dramatic show.

"So, I'm guessing you don't want to talk about Katherine?" Lauren ventured gingerly.

"Not particularly," he picked up the remote and clicked on the television .

They were both distracted as a sports telecaster's voice filled the room with talk of the Houston Texans' plans for new recruits.

"You know, I would never admit this to anyone else, but I feel so numb inside," Nathan said, surprising Lauren with his honesty.

She let her brother's words sink in for a minute, and then she suggested, "Maybe you could talk to a counselor or something?"

"No way. I'm not going to sit there with someone asking me about my feelings and then expect me to pay them a hundred dollars." Nathan groaned.

"Well, then..." Lauren said, "What are you going to do?"

"I have no idea. All I know is that I need to do something different or I'm going to go insane."

Lauren watched her brother with concern as he irritably began to scroll through the channels on the television. She could see that his shoulders were hunched with tension. Her heart broke for him.

"I have an idea," Lauren said, suddenly inspired. "How would you feel about going to church?"

"Church?" Nathan turned to her, repeating the word with a grimace.

"Yes, church. Daniel invited me to go to his church with him last weekend and it was actually very encouraging. Maybe it would do you some good too."

"Whoa, wait a minute. You're telling me Daniel goes to church? Like, as in every Sunday, not just Christmas and Easter?" Nathan had a look of complete skepticism.

"Yes, he goes to church. I told you, he's changed. In more ways than one."

"Interesting," Nathan murmured absently and continued to stare ahead at the television screen.

"It's not at all like St. Paul's," she told him. "It was really upbeat and the pastor was hilarious. You won't get bored, I promise."

Nathan glanced at his sister again, then back at the television.

"So, will you come with us?" Lauren probed.

"I don't know. Let me think about it." Nathan finally turned to her.

"I'm going to take that as a 'Yes'," Lauren said cheerily. "Daniel and I will pick you up at 10:30 Sunday morning."

Jonathan called her back. Finally. On Wednesday night, at a quarter past nine, as Katherine was just coming downstairs from tucking the children into bed, figuring that by now Jonathan was done with her. Left with the notion that not only had she destroyed her marriage for nothing, but now both of the men that she cared about had completely rejected her. She had been moping around her parent's house the last three days, barely functioning.

She heard her phone ringing, but couldn't remember where she had last put it. By the time she found it laying on the couch underneath the flowered pillow, it had already stopped ringing. Her heart flip-flopped in her chest as she saw the missed call notification with a J beside it.

Quickly she dialed her voicemail and held her breath as she waited for the message to play. *Hey Kat. It's me. Sorry I haven't called you back. I've been busy.* Big sigh. *That's not true. I mean- I have been busy, but that's not why I haven't called. I've been trying to figure things out in my head. I don't know what I was thinking the other night. I shouldn't have gone up to your hotel room with you. I just let myself get carried away. I have incredibly strong feelings for you. But that doesn't excuse my behavior.* Another big sigh. *I don't want to mess this up. I hope you're not mad at me. Please call me.*

Katherine realized she'd been holding her breath. She let it go, breathed in deeply and exhaled with relief. He wasn't mad at her at afterall for spoiling their opportunity to be together. He was upset with himself for letting himself be overtaken with passion. She felt an overwhelming sensation come over her. Jonathan was an amazing guy. He was so unselfish, so genuine, so full of character. Katherine plunked herself down on the couch and sat there in complete astonishment, and a bit of panic. She was falling in love with him.

Without another thought, she hit the call button next to his name and with her heart pounding, she waited for him to answer.

"Hey, Kat." His voice came over the line with tenderness.

"Hi," she said softly.

"You got my message?"

"Yes, I did. It was a sweet message," Katherine said, pausing for a moment. "And of course I'm not mad at you. I think you're incredibly noble."

She heard him breathe out slowly, then he said, "I'm trying. But it's not easy, Kat. Not when I feel the way I do about you."

"I know," Katherine whispered. "I feel the same way."

Silence filled the line for a minute as they both processed their sentiments.

"I really wish I could see you right now. Where are you?" he asked.

"I'm still in San Antonio."

"Dang. I was hoping you were here," he said. "I'd have told you to get your pretty self in your car and drive over here right now."

"Oh, really?" Katherine said in a teasing tone. "What would you have done if I had driven over there?"

"I would take you in my arms and kiss you until we both couldn't stand it anymore," he said huskily.

"That is awfully tempting," Katherine said, twirling a lock of her hair and biting her lower lip. "What if I come over to Austin tomorrow?"

"Well, I guess I could wait that long," he said. "I have class in the morning, but I'm free after eleven. Come to my house and I'll make you lunch."

"That sounds really good," she said. "I'll see you then."

"Okay. Good night, Kat."

"Good night."

"Who was that?" Barbara's voice came from behind her and caused Katherine to jump. She really needed to do something about her nerves.

"Just a friend," Katherine said as casually as possible. Her heart began to pound again as she wondered how much of the conversation her mother had heard. "I'm going to meet them for lunch tomorrow."

"Does this mean you need me to watch Maddie and Keenan again?"

"You don't mind, do you? They're having such a great time."

"Of course they're having a great time. They don't have to go to school and I spoil them," Barbara said with a smile, then she grew serious. "And no, I don't mind watching them. But how long is this going to go on for? Have you even tried to get in touch with Nathan?"

"Mom, I told you. I need time and space. I need to think," Katherine said.

"Okay. Well, what have you been thinking? Are you going to let your marriage fall apart or are you willing to let go of your pride?" Barbara asked with conviction.

"I'm not the only one that's letting it fall apart, Mom," Katherine said. "I don't see *him* putting in any effort to fix things."

"Well, you just need to realize that men see things differently. He doesn't think it's wrong to keep late hours at work – he sees it as his duty to provide for his family. Plus he's probably waiting for you to call him. That's how it is with your father. I always have to be the one to apologize first."

"Ugh. I don't even want to think about him right now. I'm still too angry." Katherine stood up. "I'm going up to bed."

Upstairs, after she had changed into her pajamas, Katherine sat on the bed and tried to suppress her feelings of guilt. She absolutely refused to take the full blame for the wreckage that her marriage had become. They would not even be in this situation had it not been for the way Nathan had treated her the past several months. What did he really expect? For her to be a doormat that he could walk all over? Toiling day and night, taking care of the children, cooking, cleaning, running endless errands.

The more she thought about it, the angrier she became. She poured her love and devotion into her children. At the end of the day, she was completely drained. Not just of energy, but of emotion. Now that Nathan had retreated into his constant state of apathy, he no longer filled her with the love that used to keep her going. No wonder she had found solace in Jonathan's arms. He charged her with an energy that made her feel worthy of something other than just being a mom. He made her feel valued and cherished as a woman. Nathan made her feel dull and old.

She chose to push all thoughts of her husband out of her head and go to sleep with images of Jonathan soothing her depleted heart and mind. She just knew that being with him tomorrow would give her the boost she needed to make it through the rest of the week. As she drifted off, she envisioned Jonathan taking her into his arms and kissing her, overwhelming her with love.

Chapter 35

*J*onathan was in love. For the first time in his life, he truly felt that he had met the woman of his dreams. Kat was everything he had pictured when he began to think about finally settling down. He had spent so many wasted years seeing girls as mere conquests. He hadn't even bothered to try to get to know the girls that he had met in his classes or in bars. He had just spent the night charming them into bed, then quickly forgetting about them the next day.

He had carried on this way for so long that it didn't even occur to him that he might be missing out on something better. When he finally realized what an empty existence he was living, and how many people he had hurt along the way, he was disgusted. Who knows how much longer he would have continued in this lifestyle had it not been for Mark Sheffield, an old high school buddy, showing up at the gym that dreary day last September. The day he hit rock bottom and he realized his life was a complete disaster.

Just a few days before, his life was golden. But he screwed everything up. He'd been hanging out at one of his usual spots, The Pour House. He was with the usual crowd of friends from the restaurant in which he had just been promoted to head chef. After working for only six months as sous chef, he was pleasantly surprised when Keanu, the manager of Bermuda – a Caribbean fusion upscale café, announced that he was extremely pleased with Jonathan's skills. The current head chef had just put in his notice to move to New York, serendipitously leaving the position open for Jonathan to immediately take over. Several of his co-workers insisted on going out to celebrate after work that night. Including Maribella.

Jonathan had been flirting with Maribella since the first day he walked into Bermuda. Maribella was the gem of the restaurant, serving as lead hostess. With her silky long black hair, olive complexion and exotic hazel eyes, she caught the attention of every male in Bermuda, from customers to busboys. She was also Keanu's daughter.

Maribella was gregarious with all of the men that she interacted with. She called them "honey" or "sweetie," flirting openly with them as she tossed her dark hair over her shoulder and laughed heartily. But with Jonathan she was more reserved. She didn't use pet names with him and she always took on a sweet seriousness when he was around. Jonathan had never been sure if this was a good sign or not. But either way he continued to flirt with her whenever he had the chance.

She had shown up unexpectedly that night at the Pour House. She had never gone out with any of the employees of Bermuda before. It was rumored that she was engaged to the owner of Bermuda's son. However, she didn't wear a ring and with the way she flirted, it left the male employees with serious doubts.

Jonathan had been flattered when she strolled into the bar in her red wrap dress that accented every curve, walked right over to him and sat down so close to him she was practically in his lap. Jonathan had looked over at Tony and Dave, the two waiters that constantly told him he didn't stand a chance with Maribella and that he should give up. He gave them both a look full of pride, and mouthed "See? She loves me."

A couple of hours and several drinks later, Jonathan led Maribella out of the bar to his truck and took her home. The next day he woke up with a headache and a note on his nightstand. *Jonathan – I had a great time with you last night. Let's keep this between us. :) xxx M*

Apparently, someone with a nasty case of jealousy did not see fit to keep Jonathan and Maribella's secret. When he came into work the next day, Keanu immediately fired him. Maribella had eyed him with disgust and suspicion as he walked out of the restaurant in shame. Jonathan realized she must have thought he hadn't adhered to her plea to not 'kiss and tell'. However, Jonathan had a feeling that he knew exactly who had spilled the beans.

That night Jonathan went back to the Pour House, where he figured he would find his ex-co-workers. Sure enough Tony would not look him in the eye. When Jonathan confronted him, Tony had said, "You're such a chump. You deserved it." Jonathan punched him in the jaw, sending one of Tony's front teeth flying, and then he was escorted out of the bar into the pouring rain.

For the next few days, Jonathan didn't leave his apartment. He didn't answer any phone calls. Not that many came in. Most of his friends worked at Bermuda, and now he was an outcast. Not only that, but the owner of Bermuda, Antonio, had left him a voicemail, his thickly accented voice seething with anger, that he planned to personally make sure Jonathan would never work in any decent restaurant in Austin again. So, he just watched TV, drank beer, ordered pizza and sulked.

Finally, after five days, when he finally got tired of being with himself, he decided he should at least get to the gym and start working off the beer and the pizza. He was still nursing his wounds – his ego and his bruised fist – as he sat on the bench in front of the free weights. Barely able to press his usual 150 pounds, he didn't really want to be there. But he definitely didn't want to go home and sit around in his apartment either. He was tired of reliving the scenario in his head and ruminating how he had so quickly fallen from grace. He knew that both Antonio and Keanu were very influential with the top restaurants in town and there was no point even trying to charm his way into another kitchen now.

"Big J!" The familiar voice had broken into his depressed thoughts.

He looked up at the guy standing in front of him. He knew the face, but something wasn't quite right.

"It's Brian. Sheffield." Then it dawned on him. He was missing the long dreadlocked hair, messy goatee and bloodshot eyes. The scrawny body that Jonathan remembered was replaced with a well-toned muscular build.

"Are you kidding me, Sheffield??" Jonathan had gotten up and clapped his old friend on the back. "Boy, have you changed!"

"Yeah. It's been awhile, huh?"

"Almost ten years," Jonathan had said. "I still remember you getting hauled out of Prom for smashing the ice sculpture with a hockey stick."

"Yeah," Brian had laughed and rubbed his now clean-shaven chin. "That was pretty hard core. But that's all in the past. I'm a changed man."

"I can see that. You're ripped. And the clean look suits you," Jonathan had been referring to Brian's hair and close shave.

"Ah man, this is nothing. What I'm talking about is an inside job."

"What do you mean?"

Brian had told Jonathan that it wasn't just his physical appearance that had changed. His heart had been completely transformed. He explained how everything had turned around for him when surrendered his life to God. Brian went on, detailing years of partying and causing trouble after graduation, ultimately landing in prison with a felony conviction. He had come to the end of himself, left to sit in shame and regret, with nothing else to do but read the Bible that he picked up in the county jail. By the time he was moved to the state facility to serve out his two year sentence, he had almost read the entire new testament. He then began attending church with the prison ministry that visited every Sunday.

"Man, I traded committing crime to committing my life to Christ. I got out in 18 months and re-entered the world as a new man."

After talking for another half an hour in between lateral raise and shoulder press reps, Brian had invited Jonathan to come to his church with him that weekend. Realizing that he had nothing else going on, Jonathan agreed. During the sermon, Jonathan had felt as if the pastor was talking directly to his heart. He preached about the prodigal son who took off with his inheritance and spent it all on booze and women. Then when he was completely out of money and downtrodden he went back to his father's house to see if he would take him in as a servant, as he believed that he was not worthy of his father's love anymore. However, the father accepted his wayward son back into the family as if he had never left.

Jonathan had never disrespected his own father or spent his inheritance on insubstantial items. He didn't even have an inheritance. But deep down, he knew he had been wrong in the way that he floundered through life: staying out late at the bar, having one night stands, not really focusing on his studies. He felt empty inside and even though most of the time he enjoyed his life, he never really had a true feeling of contentment. He was always looking for something else to make him feel complete. By the end of that church service he knew that he had found what was missing. A relationship with God.

He began attending a weekly bible study with Brian and four other men. Two of the men were married and had been devoted to their walk with God for over a decade. These two men facilitated the study and gave rich examples from their own lives that proved to be encouragement for the younger men. After a couple of months and a handful of talks over coffee with the facilitators, Jonathan knew he wanted what they had. A family of his own. He wanted to be a husband and a father. He wanted to be honorable to God and to respect the woman that would one day be his wife.

And now he had finally met her. Katherine. He believed it must have been fate that she was seated at his table that evening. She was everything he could ever desire in a woman. Beautiful, smart, funny, loving. Katherine was definitely the one he'd been waiting for and he intended to tell her the next chance he got.

He now felt assured that Katherine shared the same depth of feelings for him. They had spent the afternoon together at his house and every moment had been perfect. After his Civil Procedure class, he had picked up a few things at the grocery store to make his favorite pasta dish. Then stopped at the florist and had a custom made bouquet created with fresh daisies, lilies and blue iris.

She had arrived at his house looking gorgeous in a flowery sun dress with gold strappy sandals. Her hair was tied up loosely with a few strands framing her sun kissed face. He had taken her into his arms immediately after opening the door and let his lips linger tenderly on hers until they began to kiss each other passionately. He had kicked the door closed with his foot and backed Katherine up against it as they continued to kiss until they were both breathless.

After gaining their composure, Jonathan had served them lunch on the patio, where they once again sat on the lounge chairs. She had complimented him on the pasta and vegetables – he had perfected his lemon garlic sauce that day. Then they talked comfortably as they sipped sweet iced tea and soaked in the afternoon sun.

When she told him she needed to get back to work, he reluctantly walked her out to her car. He had been tempted to tell her then that he loved her. But he had decided it needed to be declared in a more romantic setting. He didn't see a need to rush it. He would plan a night out for them this coming weekend – maybe even a dinner cruise on Town Lake.

Chapter 36

*N*athan couldn't take it anymore. Lauren had been right about a couple things. The music was very different from what they heard in the church they grew up in, and the pastor was hilarious. He definitely had a gift for public speaking and keeping an audience captivated. But he was not finding the experience inspiring or upbeat as Lauren had promised. It was the topic that the pastor was speaking on that rubbed Nathan the wrong way. Marriage.

For over a half an hour Pastor Rick had been speaking about the sanctity of marriage; the role of the husband was to love his wife, and in turn the role of the wife was to respect her husband. Nathan was feeling nauseous, and beads of sweat were forming on his forehead and neck. He really didn't want to listen to this guy, who seemingly had a perfect life, drone on about his idea of an ideal marriage. He was basically saying that if the husband did everything correctly, the wife will be fulfilled and satisfied. In other words, Nathan wasn't a big enough doormat, so Katherine decided to cheat on him.

He felt bile rising up and quickly got to his feet. Thankfully they had found seats close to the aisle and he was able to make an easy escape. He walked swiftly through the dimly lit sanctuary and pushed through the double doors into the lobby. He continued with his fast pace as his eyes struggled to adjust to the brighter light and his head began to pound.

"Nathan!" He heard his sister cry out just as he was reaching the front of the building. He stopped right in front of the glass doors leading to the parking lot, but didn't turn around.

"Nathan!" Lauren repeated as she came up behind him and put her hand on his shoulder. "Are you ok?"

"I'm fine," he snapped. "I just need some air." He pushed one of the doors open and Lauren followed him.

"Okay. I'll go with you," Lauren said, the warm air a pleasant contrast to the freezing air-conditioned building.

Nathan pulled his sunglasses out of his sports coat pocket and slipped them over his eyes, grateful for some respite from the brightness of the afternoon sun. His headache had intensified and he began to massage his temples.

"This wasn't really the reaction I was expecting," Lauren commented quietly.

"I'm not feeling all that great. Maybe a flu is coming on or something," he said unconvincingly.

"You seemed fine when we picked you up," Lauren said. "If you don't like the church service, then just say so."

"It's not that," Nathan grumbled. "Just go back in. I'll wait out here until it's over."

"Nathan, please talk to me. Tell me what's really going on," she pleaded.

"Nothing else is going on. Just go," he insisted.

"Okay, okay." She held her hands up in surrender and turned to go back inside.

"She cheated on me," he called out as she began pulling on the heavy door. He could not hold it inside any longer.

"What?" Lauren let go of the door handle and spun around.

"She told me when I went to San Antonio."

Lauren didn't believe what she was hearing. Katherine would never do something like that. She let him know her thoughts, "I don't believe it. She would never cheat on you."

"That's what I used to think too."

"Are you sure? I mean, she actually told you this? How do you know she didn't just make it up because she was angry?" Lauren was hopeful that he was somehow wrong.

"I don't think she made it up. I've been thinking about it and I realized there were a lot of nights when she stayed out way later than usual. She said she was having coffee with her friends, but I'm guessing she was really out with... " He didn't know what to call him. "This loser."

Lauren just stood there, too stunned to say anything else for a moment.

"I really can't believe it. I don't even know what to say." She shook her head, still unable to imagine Katherine stooping so low.

The door swung open and Daniel appeared, frowning in concern. "Everything okay out here?"

"Not really," Lauren glanced over at her brother and saw him shake his head.

"Everything's fine," Nathan said loudly.

Daniel glanced at them both in confusion and shrugged. "Okay. Well, service is about to end, so if you want to get going I'll go pick up James from his class."

"That would be great, Daniel. We'll just meet you at the car."

Lauren smiled at him and waited for him to go back inside. "You don't want Daniel to know?"

"Of course not! It's none of his business," Nathan snapped. "Besides, it makes me look like an idiot."

"*You* are not the idiot. She is!" Lauren said in anger. "I understand if you don't want Daniel to know. But it might be good for you to have someone to talk to."

"I really don't want to talk about it, Lauren. I'm dealing with it my own way."

Lauren knew what that meant. He was probably going to brood and suppress his emotions, pretending that he was okay, but all the while just putting on an act for everyone.

Somehow they all managed to get through the drive home. Daniel attempted to make trivial small talk, but Lauren could tell that he felt the tension and knew something was up. Nathan barely grunted out two words and stared out of his window the whole time. Fortunately James, oblivious to the drama of the grown-ups, made up for the gaps in conversation.

Nathan could not have been more relieved when they finally dropped him off. He let himself into the house and slammed the door behind him. Taking in the silence and emptiness of his home that once held evidence of love and family, he broke down and cried.

"What is going on with you?" Daniel finally asked as he came into the kitchen. He had been listening to various crashes and bangs as Lauren prepared lunch. However it didn't sound at all like any cooking was being done, only some sort of vengeance taken out on the pots and pans and cupboards.

"I'm guessing this has to do with your brother. I kind of got the feeling the sermon might have rubbed him the wrong way," Daniel said.

Lauren turned around, her jaw set in anger. She wasn't sure if she should tell Daniel or not, but she knew she couldn't keep it inside any longer. "Katherine cheated on him."

"Oh, man," Daniel said. "He just told you about it at church?"

"Yes. He didn't really want to talk about it, so I don't know any details. But he was positive that she did. He said that Katherine admitted it."

"Wow," Daniel said.

"He didn't want me to tell you, so you can't say anything."

"I won't. I'm sorry, sweetheart," Daniel said, walking over to her and taking her into his arms. "I'm sure he's hurting pretty badly right now."

"Yes, he is," Lauren said. "I just can't believe Katherine would do such a thing. She's supposed to be my best friend. I thought I knew her. I thought she was a good person."

"Have you talked to her at all?"

"Well, yeah, the other day. She keeps trying to make it out to be all Nathan's fault. She said she left because he forgot their anniversary." Lauren was still going over all of their conversations in her head. Trying to remember if Katherine had ever given any indication of her infidelity. But of course she wasn't going to tell her about it. Why would she tell her husband's sister? They were best friends, but Katherine must realize that Lauren's loyalty to her brother came first.

Lauren extracted herself from Daniel's embrace and began to

slam around the kitchen again. She angrily grabbed a carton of eggs from the refrigerator, slamming the door closed. Daniel quickly swooped in, deftly removing the carton from her before the kitchen was redecorated in raw eggs.

"How about you go get changed and relax for a little bit? I'll take care of lunch," he said.

"Thank you," Lauren grumbled and left the kitchen.

She walked through the living room and gave James hair a little tousle as she passed by. He was happily engrossed in an episode of Ninjago. She felt a sad little tug at her heart as she thought about James' pleas to see his cousins the day before. Lauren had told them that she hoped Madison and Keenan would be back soon, but now she was having serious doubts about that.

She went into her closet and slipped out of the dress she had worn to church. She changed into khaki shorts and a light knit sweater, then sat down on her bed. Thinking back to the day she thought she saw Katherine in the café with that young man, she slapped her hand to her head. *I'm such an idiot. Of course that was her. And she just flat out lied to me.* Suddenly, it seemed to Lauren that no one was actually who they presented themselves to be. How was it ever possible to know if you could really trust someone? Lauren suddenly felt very alone in the world.

Chapter 37

I miss you, Kat.
I miss you too.
When can I see you again??
When do you want to see me???
Now!! ;)
Lol. I want to see you too. Hopefully I will be in Austin again this week.
You're still in San Antonio?
Yes.
I could come over there.
That's tempting...

"Who are you texting with?" Barbara asked.

Startled, Katherine jumped up off the bar stool and slipped her phone into her back pocket. She knew her face was turning bright red so she quickly walked away from her mother toward the refrigerator.

"Are you hungry? I'm starved," Katherine said. She opened the fridge door and pretended to study the contents of each shelf.

"What is going on with you?" Barbara asked. "Judging from the smile you had a minute ago, I'm assuming that wasn't Nathan you were texting. And no, I'm not hungry, we just ate breakfast an hour ago."

Katherine closed the door and turned to her mother. She said, "It's just a friend."

"A *male* friend?" Barbara asked.

"He's just a friend, okay?" Katherine said. "Please don't lecture me."

"I am not lecturing you. But I am concerned." Barbara said. "You're not acting like yourself at all."

"I'm fine Mom, really," Katherine insisted.

"When do you plan on talking to your husband?" Barbara asked.

"I don't know. I told you I need more time. Why do you keep pressuring me?"

"Because, you need to stop hiding and address these issues with Nathan."

Katherine rolled her eyes. "I will. When I'm ready."

"Ok. But whoever that is you're texting with... I don't think it's a good idea."

"Mom. Stop worrying. I'm going to go check on the kids."

She left the room before her mother could say anything else. She ran up the stairs two at a time and found Madison and Keenan in the rec room watching TV.

"Hey, you guys wanna go see Aunt Rachel today?" she asked.

"Yes!" the children said in unison, jumping up.

"Is she going to take us out for milkshakes again?" Madison asked.

"Maybe so," Katherine said. "Better go get dressed."

They hurried off to the bedroom and Katherine turned off the television. She was enjoying their leisurely days; letting the kids stay in their pajamas all morning, not having to rush off to school. It was like summer vacation two months early. She was also enjoying her break from the constant rushing around to run errands for Nathan, and washing the extra five loads of laundry that he accumulated each week. The thing that brought her the most relief was not stressing out to plan a dinner that Nathan would approve of, and then have it sit for hours, only to be reheated later in the microwave.

Since she'd been at her mom's house, they had enjoyed many evenings of casual dinners. Pizza, tacos, grilled cheese and soup. One night they just ate popcorn and smoothies for dinner as they watched a movie. Nathan would have balked at this. He always insisted dinner be formal and eaten at the table. Even when he hardly showed up himself anymore.

Katherine felt her phone buzzing in her jeans pocket.

Kat? Did I lose ya??

Sorry. Had to take a call.

It seemed most of everything in her life was a lie these days. Only Nathan finally knew the truth. She knew she couldn't avoid talking to him forever. He had called a couple of times to talk to the children. He had called Barbara's phone, clearly indicating that he was not ready to talk to her either. But her mother was right. She couldn't hide forever.

The problem was that she was completely uncertain of what she really wanted. She didn't want her marriage to end. She definitely didn't want to put her children through the trauma of divorce. But she also did not want to go back to Nathan with the way things had been. That is, if he would even take her back. What if he wouldn't? What then? Jump into a real relationship with Jonathan? Was that even realistic? She would have to come clean to him. But when she did tell him the truth, it was very possible Jonathan would want nothing to do with her. Then she would be alone.

"Mommy! We're ready to go!" Madison called out from the hallway.

"Ok, sweetie! I'll be there in a minute," she called back.

She pulled her phone out and replied to Jonathan, *I might be in Austin later this week. I'll let you know. xo*

Katherine dropped the children off at her sister's house which was only about five miles from their parents'. Rachel had been with the same marketing firm for almost four years now and had the luxury of working from home occasionally. Since she had a light schedule that day she was glad to entertain her niece and nephew for a couple of hours.

After briefly updating her sister that nothing had changed with the Nathan situation, Rachel confided in her about her latest crush at the office. Rachel seemed to be dating a new guy every month. Katherine was so tempted to tell Rachel about Jonathan. She really needed to talk to someone about it. Her mind was a constant hurricane of thoughts. But she knew better. Rachel would tell their mother and that would be a disaster. She kissed Madison and Keenan and told Rachel she'd be back in a few hours.

She got back into her car and drove to the shopping plaza that was just a few more miles up the highway. It was a fairly new development and she'd recalled seeing a sign for Barnes and Noble. She figured she could get a cup of coffee and browse through some romance novels. Now that she had some free time on her hands, she might actually finish a book.

She had always loved going to the Barnes and Noble near her

house before the kids were old enough for school. She would let them play with the train sets in the children's area while she sipped on a latte and read the latest novel by one of her favorite authors. It was great in the winter when it was too cold to go to the park, or on rainy days when she needed to get out of the house for a few hours. She and Nathan had also spent numerous Saturday afternoons in the book store when she was pregnant with Madison. They would sit in the comfy arm chairs and pour over pregnancy and baby name books.

Katherine recalled the day they had decided on Madison's name. She had begun having Braxton Hicks contractions and thought that she was in early labor. Nathan had been so nervous, but incredibly sweet. She had just pointed out the name in *1000 Unique Baby Names*, when a rush of searing pain took her breath away. He had rushed them to the hospital and repeatedly pestered the nurses to get Katherine checked into the labor ward. When they finally settled into a room, she realized she had the accidentally-stolen baby name book tucked into her handbag. After waiting almost an hour to be examined by the obstetrician, she was sent home, being told she was only having "practice" contractions. Nathan went back to the bookstore the following morning while Katherine rested in bed. He returned with the purchased book along with seven pink wooden block letters that spelled Madison.

Katherine smiled at the memory as she made her way over to the café to order a coffee. It seemed that their relationship was so effortless back then. But now after years of dealing with the stress of raising children and the pressures of Nathan's job, it felt like wading through quicksand just to have a conversation. She sat down in one of the arm chairs and sipped the sweet vanilla froth from the top of her cup, suddenly realizing how much she missed Nathan. The old version of him. What ever happened to the sweet, thoughtful, attentive man that she had once known and loved?

Chapter 38

"What are you looking at?"

Jonathan slammed his laptop closed as Sylvia's voice rang out from behind him. He was sitting at a table on the patio of the Starbuck's they had agreed to meet at. They planned to go over the study notes for the upcoming Corporate Finance exam.

"Were those rings?" Sylvia asked in surprise as she flopped her books down on the table.

Dang, Jonathan thought. He hadn't closed the lid fast enough.

"Why in the world are you looking at rings?" Sylvia obviously wasn't going to let this go.

He sighed. "I'm just trying to get an idea of the cost. It's no big deal."

"No big deal? Are you and this girl really that serious?" Sylvia frowned at him.

"Can we just go over the notes?"

"Why won't you talk to me about it?" Sylvia looked hurt. He used to talk to her about everything. Since he'd been dating Katherine, Jonathan had been so distant with her.

"There really isn't anything to tell. I mean, yes, we're getting pretty serious. I'm not planning to propose tomorrow or anything. But I just thought I'd start to plan in case things went in that direction."

Sylvia just looked at him for a minute, keeping her expression stoic.

"What?" Jonathan asked a little wearily.

"Nothing. I'm just a little surprised, that's all. You haven't known her for very long. I mean, what do you really know about her? Besides what she does for a living?"

"We've spent a lot of time together. We've talked a lot. I know her pretty well, actually."

"So, she knows about your faith?" Sylvia asked.

"Yes, of course I told her about that."

"And?"

"And what?" Jonathan was not happy about being cross-examined.

"Does she believe the same way?"

"No, not exactly. But that can change," Jonathan said.

"Come on, Jonny..." Sylvia shook her head. "Didn't you even listen to the lesson we had a few weeks ago on not being unequally yoked?"

Sylvia and Jonathan also attended a bible study together. When Jonathan learned that Sylvia had recently turned her life around and renewed her relationship with God as well, he had invited her to his church. The bible study met on Sunday nights and was geared toward young singles that were newcomers to the church. Just last week, Luke, the singles pastor, had talked to them on the topic of choosing your spouse wisely. He said that one of the most important factors was whether or not the couple both shared the same faith. However, the way Jonathan saw it, he figured once they were committed, he could invite Katherine to church and everything would just flow from there. He wasn't going to sweat it.

"Look, we've talked about it and I'm probably going to invite her to church the next time we get together. Problem solved, "Jonathan said.

"Seriously? Problem solved?" Sylvia stared at him like he'd just announced he was going to jump off a bridge. "You're so naïve, Jonathan. It's not that easy. You barely know her and you're already looking at rings."

"I told you already, I just wanted to get an idea of how much I need to start saving. I'm not buying a ring. Can you just get off my case about it?"

"Okay, okay. I'm just concerned about you. Sorry."

"Can we start studying now?" He opened his notebook.

Sylvia sighed. She opened her notebook as well and scooted her chair a little closer to him. "Shall we start with security regulations?"

They went over their study notes and discussed SEC reporting obligations for a good fifteen minutes, before Sylvia started back in about Katherine. "She doesn't even live here. Have you thought about what happens if she doesn't want to move?"

"Sylvia. Enough." Jonathan closed his notebook abruptly. "I'm going to go get a coffee. Do you want something?"

"Yeah, I guess. Can you get me an iced latte?"

"Sure." Jonathan got up and went into the store. As soon as Sylvia was sure he was occupied at the register, she opened the lid to his laptop and brought up the webpage he'd been looking at. She felt an undeniable ache in her heart as she gazed at the page of beautiful solitaire diamond rings priced in the thousands.

Chapter 39

Fall 1999

Nathan had turned up at Katherine's dorm with a bouquet of mixed flowers, a week later, after Katherine had turned him down at the Paws & Beer event in college. As she had accepted the flowers, putting her nose into them and smelling the sweet scent of roses, lilies and daisies, she noticed he held a leash in his other hand.

"I have a surprise for you," Nathan had said when he noticed her eyebrows knit in confusion. "Come with me."

"What? I don't..." Katherine began to protest, but Nathan took her hand and the warmth and strength of it somehow caused her to forget that she barely knew this man.

"Trust me," Nathan said and led her down the sidewalk to where his car was parked. She gasped in surprise when she recognized the dog sitting in the passenger seat, looking out the open window at her with big brown eyes. Nathan smiled, "I adopted her today."

That night, in a cozy booth at a trendy wine bar, they spent two hours sharing a bottle of Pinot Grigio, a plate of artisanal cheese and their entire life history. Nathan Montgomery was originally from Dallas, where his parents lived and were still married. He had a younger sister, Lauren, who had just graduated from Texas State University and was working on her teacher certification. He played basketball in high school, and with his record 3-point shots, helped their team win the state championship his junior year. He broke his leg in his senior year so he was forced to give up basketball and began drawing instead. He realized that he loved drawing houses in his sophomore year at Southwestern and switched his major from art history to architecture.

Katherine Smith was from San Antonio, where her parents and two older sisters lived. Her oldest sister was happily married and the second oldest was a student at St. Mary's and was a serial dater. Katherine had been on the drill team in high school and still loved to dance. She had always wanted to be a teacher, constantly begging her sisters to play "school" with her when they were little. She loved dogs, chocolate and British romance novels.

Nathan called her first thing the next morning and they made plans to spend the day together. They rented bicycles at the lake and rode around for hours, stopping to feed the ducks the leftovers from the bagels Katherine had brought. She had laughed hysterically when a huge male goose began to chase Nathan around, honking and flapping his wings angrily. After they were exhausted and sunburned, he suggested they eat lunch at the Mexican restaurant that Nathan swore had the strongest margaritas in town.

After two margaritas, enchiladas verde, and another two hours of intense conversation, Nathan drove Katherine back to her dorm. He walked her up to her door and as she began to fumble with her key, he took her by the shoulders and turned her around. Locking his eyes on hers, he gently pushed her up against the door and pressed his mouth against hers, their tequila laced breath mingling together.

During the week, they talked on the phone every night, annoying both of their roommates with their laughter and flirtation. They met at the Brown Fountain and took Queenie on long walks together. The following weekend Nathan took Katherine to a concert in the park and dinner at an upscale Italian restaurant. Afterward, he made his best attempt to entice her to spend the night at his apartment, but Katherine remained resolute. As he slowly grazed her neck with soft, tantalizing kisses, Katherine put her hand on his chest and whispered, "Slow down, Flash".

She kept up her determination for almost two months. He had convinced her to come inside his apartment, but she refused to cross over the bedroom threshold. After a heated make-out session on his couch, she would push him back, catch her breath, and bid him a good night. But on a freezing Saturday in February, after a long day spent working at the animal shelter, Katherine arrived on Nathan's doorstep tired, shivering and crying. The shelter manager had informed her that three of the older dogs were going to have to be euthanized because they hadn't been adopted after the ninety day limit.

Nathan had run her a warm bubble bath in his oversized Jacuzzi tub, and then left her alone to undress and immerse herself in the sudsy water. He returned ten minutes later, tentatively knocking on the door before entering with a bottle of wine and two glasses. He sat perched on the side of the tub while he tried to distract her from the fate of the dogs she had grown to love with talk of his latest project. After the bath water had gone cold, Nathan brought her his white terrycloth robe and turned around while she stood up and put it on.

She came up behind him, wrapped her arms around him, stood on her toes and whispered "I love you" in his ear.

In the morning, after Nathan brought Katherine a steaming mug of coffee, he lay down next to her, and looking up at her with sincerity in his hazel eyes, he told her he wanted to marry her. She looked down at him, giggling, and said, "Whoa, Flash." But he kept a straight face and pulled her down to kiss him, whispering, "And I want us to have at least seven kids."

In the spring, Nathan graduated with his MBA in Architecture and after a few months of interviewing, he accepted a position with a reputable architecture firm in downtown Austin. Nathan asked her to house hunt with him, but Katherine made it quite clear that she wouldn't make it a permanent situation without a proper proposal. So, on a breezy November evening Nathan arranged for a personal boat cruise around Lake Austin in a pontoon. As they ate their dessert with the golden sun setting over the horizon, he presented a one-carat emerald cut diamond set in platinum. She said yes, of course, and they were married at Nathan's parents' Country Club six months later.

After honeymooning in Italy for two weeks, they came home to close on their new home in a quaint suburb ten minutes from downtown Austin. Katherine was beginning her new job as the first grade teacher at a newly opened charter school not far from their neighborhood. One evening as they sat on their sofa, Nathan kneading her feet, he said to Katherine, "So about those seven kids…"

Katherine giggled and swatted his arm, "There's plenty of time for that. Remember my five year plan?"

"Yes, I remember. I was just hoping that we could move the timeline up a little bit," Nathan said hopefully. "And when the time comes, I'd really love it if you stayed home with the baby."

"Well, of course. My school offers a great maternity plan. I'll be home with the baby for at least six weeks."

"No, that's not what I meant. I mean permanently," Nathan said quietly, but Katherine pulled her feet away and sat up in alarm.

"I don't want to give up my job. You know how long I've dreamed of being a teacher," Katherine said.

"Yes, I know. But you'll be doing an even more important job, taking care of our children. And you'll still have an opportunity to teach." Nathan continued, "Sweetie, this is very important to me. I don't want my children brought up by strangers."

"Well, I don't either, but I don't like the idea of just sitting at home all day."

"You won't be. You can still meet your girlfriends for lunch. You'll meet new moms and go on playdates and to baby classes. You'll love it. I promise." Nathan gave her his most irresistible smile and reached out to pull her feet back into his lap. "Besides, by then I'll be making enough money to support us."

"Yes, I know. I just don't want to get stuck in the house all day, baking casseroles." Katherine grimaced. "And I don't want my wardrobe to consist of sweats and mommy jeans."

"You look great in jeans. And what's wrong with casseroles? As a matter of fact I can get my mom to send you some of her recipes," Nathan said and began kneading her feet again.

"That's not funny!" Katherine playfully swatted him.

"I'm not joking. I love casseroles." Nathan had laughed, and then gently placed her feet on the ottoman. He kissed her lovingly and told her, "Trust me. It's all going to be fine."

Chapter 40

"I can't believe you, Katherine. I really can't. You won't even return my calls? You are such a coward. How could you do this to my brother? He didn't do anything wrong. He's been working his butt off for you, and this is how you repay him?" Lauren finished her voicemail to Katherine and angrily punched the end call button, then set her phone down on her desk. The phone immediately began to ring. She picked it up expecting to see Katherine's number, but it was Daniel.

"Hello?" she answered impatiently.

"Lauren, what's wrong?"

"Nothing. I was just leaving Katherine *another* message." Lauren slumped back into her chair. She was on her lunch break, but with her lack of appetite she had only eaten an apple and a handful of walnuts.

"Sweetheart, you've got to just let it go for now. She'll call you back when she's ready. She's probably embarrassed and feeling pretty lousy."

"Well, she *should* feel lousy! And guilty!"

"Have you heard from Nathan since Sunday?" Daniel asked.

"No. He won't return my calls either," Lauren said. "Maybe you should try to talk to him."

"Umm... I don't know if that's the best idea," Daniel said.

"Why not?"

"Well, for one, I don't really know him. Two, I'm not supposed to know about what's going on with them. And three, he probably doesn't even want to talk about it. At least that's the feeling I got the other day."

"Well, I have to do something. I could drive to San Antonio and confront Katherine," Lauren said. "You could come with me."

"Absolutely not," Daniel said firmly. "That's a really bad idea."

"What is your problem? Something needs to be done about this. Katherine needs to be told what a big mistake she's making. And what a big floozy she is."

"It's not your place to judge her, Lauren."

"What? Are you defending her?" Lauren's voice rose.

"No. Don't be ridiculous. I am not defending her. I just don't want you making yourself sick over this."

"Well, it's too late. I already have."

"Look, I know you care about your brother. But really, this is his marriage. You need to let him work this out with Katherine," Daniel said. "To put it nicely, you need to butt out."

"Oh, really? That's your great advice?" Lauren rolled her eyes. "You know what? Just forget I even called!"

Daniel was about to remind her that he had been the one to call her, but she had already hung up the phone.

She started to pace around her classroom, trying to take some deep breaths to calm herself. She was angry at Katherine, not Daniel, but for some reason she'd decided to take it out on him. She knew it didn't require a lesson in psychology to realize that she was reliving the angst of Daniel's tryst with his broker partner, Kelly. Even though Daniel swore nothing romantic happened with her, the fact still remained that when he started hanging out with Kelly, things cooled off real quick between them.

Lauren wanted to be able to completely trust Daniel. She had seen all the positive changes in him, and she really did believe that he cared a lot for her. But every time she thought about Katherine lying and cheating, she couldn't get past the notion that even if you think you really know someone, there were no guarantees that they weren't hiding something.

To top it off, her colleague Karen had continued to give Lauren dirty looks since the conversation in the teacher's lounge last week. Lauren was still trying to wrap her head around what was going on with Karen and Jake. Karen had said that she was seeing someone else, and she had encouraged Lauren to go out with Jake, hadn't she? So, why the sudden change of heart? She shook her head and tried to clear her thoughts. The children were due back to the classroom in a few minutes and she needed to focus on the upcoming lesson on fractions. She took a deep breath and put all of her emotional turmoil on the back burner.

She managed to get through the rest of the day without any further anger rages toward Katherine. And she was grateful that Karen had been out with a substitute, so she didn't have to deal with any awkward moments running into her in the hall. After school, she went by her brother's house to let the dog out as she had promised earlier in the week. She took Queenie and James to the park nearby and let them run around for a half hour while she walked around the track that circled the playground. She could feel the tension and anger ease as she made her way around the gravel track the third time.

She brought a happy and tired Queenie back home and replenished her food and water bowls, then made her way to her own house. She made a simple dinner of pasta and broccoli for her and James, then tried to keep her head in the conversation about the contest James had with his friends to make the coolest sculpture out of the mashed potatoes from their school lunch. She was just finishing clearing off the table when the doorbell rang. James got up quickly and took off like a rocket to the front door.

"It's Dad! Can I open it?" James called out.

"Yes, sweetie." Lauren sighed as she dried her hands on a dish towel. She was feeling a little sheepish about how she yelled at Daniel and hung up on him earlier.

As the day went on she had admitted to herself that the situation with her brother and Katherine had uprooted unresolved feelings about the way things had ended with Daniel all those years ago. She felt as if they had barely skimmed over the 'Kelly issue' before jumping back into a relationship. She was still having doubts whether Daniel was being honest about what really went on with him and his ex-partner. She couldn't help wondering why he had never explained why Kelly left the partnership. She had wanted to ask on several occasions, but the time never seemed right. Things were finally calming down and they were getting closer. Daniel had opened up to her in so many areas of his life. Why couldn't she just let this one part of it go?

No matter how hard she tried to forget about it, the thoughts continued to fester. She knew she wasn't going to be able to really move forward until she knew the absolute truth about what happened with Kelly. But there wasn't really a way to bring it up without causing more tension. She didn't want to risk Daniel knowing that she still didn't completely trust him.

"Hey," Daniel said tentatively as he came into the kitchen.

"Hey," Lauren said. "Listen, I..."

Daniel cut her off. "Wait. Before you say anything, I think I know what's going on."

"What do you mean?" Lauren asked nervously.

"Dad? Aren't you going to come watch TV with me?" James' voice came from the living room.

"We'll talk in a little bit," Daniel said to Lauren and gave her a kiss on the forehead before retreating to the living room.

Lauren finished cleaning up the dinner dishes, then got out a big pot, placed it on the stove and poured some oil into it. Once the oil was hot, she added popcorn kernels. While she waited for the kernels to begin popping, she peeked into the living room and smiled as she gazed at Daniel and James sitting side by side on the sofa. Their matching dark brown heads close together, father and son. She felt tears well up and suddenly she was overcome with a huge wave of gratitude.

She grabbed the oversized blue ceramic bowl and poured the hot popcorn into it, added a few shakes of sea salt, and took it into the living room.

"Yum!" James didn't waste any time digging in.

Daniel laughed as he watched James grab huge handfuls of popcorn with most of it tumbling down to the rug where Burley quickly lapped them up.

"What are we watching?" Lauren asked and grabbed a handful

of popcorn too.

"A documentary on how they make hot air balloons."

"Ah, very interesting," Lauren said.

"Indeed," Daniel said and stood up. He held his hand out to Lauren. "Let's go have a quick talk. James, your mom and I will be back in a few minutes."

"Ok," James mumbled with his mouth full.

Once they were in Lauren's room, Daniel motioned for her to sit down on the bed and he sat next to her. "So."

"So." Lauren shifted and turned to face him. "I'm sorry I yelled at you today."

"It's okay. I know you were just using me as a punching bag," he said good-naturedly. "I understand why you're angry and that you want to support your brother. But holding a grudge against Katherine is only going to hurt you."

"She won't even return my calls. She's such a coward!"

"I know. I get it. But listen." Daniel took her hand in his. "Haven't you ever heard of that saying – Holding onto anger toward someone is like drinking sewer water and expecting them to get sick?"

"What?" Lauren gave him a funny look.

"Okay, maybe that wasn't exactly the right wording. But you get my point. You need to let Katherine figure this out for herself. And letting go of your anger isn't for *her*. It's for *you*. Nothing good can come of it. Trust me, I've been there."

"You mean when you lost the baby?" Lauren asked.

"Yeah, then. And when Sarah refused to talk to me. It made me physically ill sometimes."

Lauren felt her heart ache for Daniel. Once again she realized what a difficult season that must have been for him, and he did make a valid point. She had been hardly able to eat or sleep the past few days and it was catching up to her.

"Ok. I'll try not to spend quite so much time imagining ways to inflict pain on her. But I'm not promising anything."

"Just remember that you're doing this for yourself. Eventually you're going to have to find a way to forgive her, but for now let's just focus on taming the anger a bit. Deal?"

"I'll do my best."

"Hey." Daniel lifted her chin so that she would look at him. "You know I love you."

"You do?" Lauren sat up straight in surprise.

"Yes. Of course I do. I never stopped." He moved his hand to her face.

"I never stopped loving you either," Lauren admitted and let out a muted cry of relief. She put her arms around his neck and he drew her closer to him. They held onto each other for a few minutes, just listening to one another's breath, feeling the walls around their hearts diminish a little more.

Daniel pulled back, kissed her gently and whispered, "We better get back out there before James eats that entire bowl of popcorn by himself."

Chapter 41

*N*athan was beyond tired. The two cups of coffee he'd already guzzled at home had done nothing for him. He was on his third cup, poured from the office's pot of super strong black sludge when his boss walked in and sat down in one of the chairs across from Nathan's desk.

"Bob Johnson called me today. His wife is extremely upset that they won't be in the house by Memorial Day," Doug said with a grimace.

"Yeah, I know. She left me a voicemail and sent two emails over the weekend." Nathan winced as he once again tried to put Mrs. Johnson's shrill voice out of his head, *We absolutely MUST be in the house before Memorial Day weekend. I have been hosting a barbeque at our home for over TWO decades now and I REFUSE to let this year be an exception due to your firm's subpar planning!*

"Well, I don't see there's anything that can be done about it at this point." Doug frowned.

"Actually, I thought of something last night that might work." Nathan had been unable to sleep, as usual. While he was sitting in the kitchen eating a bowl of cereal at 2 a.m., he brainstormed how to get the wayward project back on track. "If we delay the installation of the marble floors until June, we could still have the house ready for final

Restoration Heights

inspection by May 23rd. The kitchen area would be completely accessible and they could still have their barbeque."

"I know Mrs. Johnson isn't going to like that too much. I'm sure she wanted to parade her guests though that grand foyer. Those marble floors are her pride and joy. But looks like it might be our only option." Doug stood up and turned to go. He turned back at the door and said, "You should really try to get some sleep. You look terrible."

Nathan already knew that. He'd been tempted on a couple of occasions to use some of Katherine's eye concealer to cover up some of the dark blotches under his eyes. When he looked at the few things she'd left behind in the bathroom, he felt a wave of mixed emotions. He missed her – the way she would chat non-stop while they were getting ready for bed or in the morning as she brushed out her hair and applied her make-up. Even though he hardly ever really listened to what she was saying, just having her there and the sound of her voice had been soothing.

But those thoughts quickly turned to anger as he envisioned her with this other man. Talking to him sweetly, whispering in his ear, laughing at what a sucker Nathan was for not realizing how she had betrayed him. When he walked into their closet and looked at the clothes she'd left behind, he wanted to yank them all off the hangers and throw them out. How dare she enjoy all the nice things he bought for her while she was running around with someone else?

He had to put her out of his mind. That was the only way he could cope. If he just didn't think about her, he felt a sliver of his sanity return. Instead, he pulled up the pictures of Madison and Keenan on his phone. He could feel his shoulders relax a little as he focused his attention on their sweet faces. He realized how much he missed them running up to him, grabbing him around his legs, begging him to play with them. The fact that he didn't want to face Katherine shouldn't keep him from seeing his children. He banged out a text to her.

I want to see Maddi and Keenan.

Nathan's text appeared on her phone and made Katherine nauseous. It was Thursday afternoon and she had just returned to her mother's house with the children. They had gone grocery shopping for a few items, and then she treated them to an ice cream cone at the trendy malt shop that just opened in the strip center. It seemed she was doing a lot of "guilt treating" lately. Surprisingly, she hadn't heard one peep from Nathan about the extra money spent.

She had been surprised that neither of the children had asked to see their father in the two weeks they had spent at Grandma's house. She knew some of it was because they were so distracted with all the fun things to do. But perhaps it was mostly that they had grown used to him being so absent. However, when she read a bedtime story to them the night before, Madison had declared that she missed her daddy and asked when they were going home. Katherine had kept her answer vague, but comforting, letting her children know that they would see him soon and she was sure he missed them too.

She didn't want to deny them a visit with their father no matter how awkward it might be to see Nathan. She was so angry that he hadn't contacted her at all since she told him about the affair. Did he not care at all? Was he glad to have her out of his life for good? If that were the case, then so be it. She would just have to accept it and move on.

If she took the children to hang out with Nathan on Saturday it would be a perfect opportunity to visit Jonathan as well. There was no point in denying the strength of her feelings for Jonathan anymore. Who knows? She might even confess the truth to him about her failed marriage. She'd eventually have to tell him about her children as well. She suddenly started to feel as if her relationship with Jonathan could really go somewhere, and it was a liberating notion. She sent Nathan a text saying that she would bring the children to the house at 3:00pm on Saturday.

Chapter 42

Daniel and Lauren were just getting into the car with James to head out to the park.

"Dad, did you pack my baseball and glove? Because I want to practice catching again. I'm ready to try some pop flies." James bounced up and down in the backseat.

"Yep! I got it all. Baseball, bat, glove, soccer ball, frisbee. Anything else?" Daniel asked, looking at Lauren who was putting on her seatbelt.

"I think you've covered all the bases. Pun intended." She gave him a sideways smile.

"Oh, you are just so clever," Daniel teased her.

"I know. And you are just so handsome," Lauren said in gushy tones and touched his face.

"Why thank you. You're looking pretty good yourself," Daniel said and leaned over to kiss her.

"Gross!" James yelled from the back and covered his eyes. "Can't you wait 'til I'm not looking to do that?"

They both laughed and Lauren said, "Sorry, James, but you're just going to have to get used to it. Your dad and I are in looooove."

"Double gross! Can we go to the park now?"

"Okay, okay. We'll save all of our love bird stuff for when you're not looking,"

Daniel laughed and put the keys in the ignition.

"Thank goodness." James sat back in his seat crossing his arms.

"Wait!" Lauren grabbed Daniel's arm. "I forgot my sunglasses."

"I'll get them. Where are they?"

"On the desk, next to my computer."

"Be right back." Daniel grabbed the keys, hopped out of the car and ran up to the front door.

He let himself in and walked through the entry hall to the small study where Lauren had a computer desk, bookshelf and a set of pale-yellow velvet Parsons chairs. He saw her sunglasses sitting in front of the keyboard. When he reached for them, his hand bumped the mouse. The computer screen saver with the montage of photos faded away and the monitor lit up with a web page. Out of curiosity, Daniel glanced at it. PeopleCheck.com

Daniel grabbed the sunglasses and was about to turn to go, but something drew him back to the computer screen. He looked more closely and saw the name at the top of the webpage. Kelly Evans.

Seeing Nathan was a lot harder than she had expected. Not only did he still have the same angry expression as the last time she saw him, but he also looked truly awful. He had dark circles under his eyes, and he had lost weight. He had more than a couple of weeks' worth of stubble on his face and was in need of a haircut. The two of them barely made eye contact as they stood awkwardly on the front porch.

After giving their father a hug, the children ran inside, excited to be home again. Katherine was grateful to have the distraction of

Queenie, who came out to greet her. The old dog circled around her while Katherine scratched behind her soft ears.

They exchanged the least amount of words possible, only reiterating the time Katherine was expected to be back to pick them up: 6:00pm. That would give her three hours to spend with Jonathan, then pick up the children and get back on the road to San Antonio, arriving before bedtime.

Katherine was surprised at how unsettled she felt as she drove the familiar route to Jonathan's house. She had not expected to feel anything but contempt for her husband, but after seeing how haggard he looked she couldn't deny that she was responsible for his downtrodden countenance. She had imagined him working his usual long hours, barely even noticing that they were not there. Perhaps he was even glad for the solitude. No one to nag him about coming home late or being on his computer past midnight. But it was clear that he had not been enjoying himself the past two weeks. He looked downright miserable.

As she approached Jonathan's house, she did her best to clear her head and convince herself to redirect her focus. She wanted to let go of everything negative and just enjoy the next few hours with Jonathan. Afterall, it was Nathan's lack of care and concern for their marriage that was to blame for the current circumstances.

Jonathan was sitting on the front porch when she pulled into his driveway. He immediately stood up and walked over to her car. When she got out, Jonathan took her into his arms and lifted her up. She laughed and clutched him tightly around his shoulders. Once he set her back down they kissed each other hungrily.

"Okay, we'd better get inside before the neighbors break out their binoculars." Jonathan laughed and grabbed her hand to lead her up the short gravel path. "How was the drive?"

"It was fine. I listened to the playlist you sent me the whole time. I love the old songs. I didn't know you were so sentimental."

"Yeah, I wasn't sure if I should keep the Chicago in there or not. A little cheesy, but it's definitely a classic."

"I loved it. All of it." Katherine followed him inside and set her purse down on the little table in the foyer.

"I'm glad. I think of you when I listen to those songs. It helps me get through the time that we're apart." Jonathan took her into his arms and they kissed again. After they were both breathless, Jonathan pulled back. "Are you hungry?"

"Not really," Katherine admitted.

"Do you want to go swimming? The water's still a little cold, but the sun's out, so it shouldn't be too bad."

"Sounds refreshing, but I didn't bring a suit," Katherine said.

"You don't need a suit." Jonathan gave her a mischievous look and Katherine's eyes widened. "I'm just teasing you. You can borrow a t-shirt and a pair of my boxers."

"Hmmm... it's tempting, but I don't know..." Katherine peered out the back windows at the sparkling pool. It did look very inviting.

"I'll tell you what... You can just sit on the side and put your feet in. If you change your mind, then great. If not, I might just have to pull you in." Jonathan laughed.

"You wouldn't dare!" Katherine crossed her arms.

"You'll just have to see." He winked at her and motioned her to follow him into his bedroom which was right off the entrance hall.

She walked into his room and peered around while he

rummaged through his dresser drawers. His bed was made, but the pale blue comforter was slightly rumpled as if he'd possibly been taking a nap before she arrived. She wasn't quite sure why, but it made her feel uneasy. It was such an odd feeling of intimacy to be in his bedroom. She looked at the various trinkets on the nightstands and dressers. A docking station with compartments for coins and business cards, an oversized beer stein with a Longhorns symbol filled with beer caps, a Corporate Finance Law book, crumpled receipts, a framed picture of a middle aged couple - presumably his parents. She suddenly felt as if she didn't really know this man, but she was just acting out a part, like they were in a movie. Her mind went to Nathan and the familiarity of their life together, their home, their bedroom. She felt a little dizzy and steadied herself with the dresser.

"Are you okay?" Jonathan turned to her and ran his hand over her arm.

"I'm fine." Katherine fanned her face with her hand. "Why don't you go ahead? I'll get changed and meet you out there."

"Okay. Don't keep me waiting too long." Jonathan smiled and handed her a grey t-shirt and plaid boxer shorts. He walked out of the room whistling, completely unaware of her internal angst.

As Katherine began to change, the impression of feeling like an imposter intensified. His clothes felt so foreign to her. She'd worn Nathan's t-shirts and boxers plenty of times, but it always felt familiar and safe. Jonathan's were a bit larger and smelled different. It was like the feeling she got when she drove someone else's car. She looked in the mirror and began fussing with her hair, trying to distract herself, in hopes that the anxiety would dissipate. But it didn't, and the image of Nathan from earlier appeared in her mind. He was so gaunt and unkempt, his eyes were so empty.

"Pull yourself together," she told her reflection harshly. "Your husband doesn't care about you, remember?"

Katherine tied Jonathan's large t-shirt into a knot at her waist so that her belly button was showing and strolled out of his room, determined to direct her attention to the man that really did care about her.

Chapter 43

"What's wrong?" Lauren asked him again.

Ever since Daniel had returned to the car with her sunglasses his mood had gone downhill. Lauren didn't understand what could have possibly changed his tune. They had been having such a great morning so far. They'd actually been getting along great for days since their conversation the other night when they had declared their love for one another. Everything seemed to finally be going in the right direction. She'd even managed to stay somewhat levelheaded when thoughts of Katherine came her way.

"Nothing's wrong," Daniel answered grumpily, even though he was clearly upset. He had tried to keep up a cheerful attitude when he was playing catch with James, but Lauren could tell he was faking it. Now that James had taken off to explore the playscape, Daniel sat on the bench, frown on his face, his arms crossed. Clearly something was bothering him, but he wasn't about to let Lauren in on it.

"Maybe we should just go home." Lauren tried to get a reaction from him.

"That's probably a good idea," Daniel mumbled.

Great, Lauren thought. Not exactly the reaction she had hoped for. She got up from the bench and strolled over to the playscape. Perhaps Daniel just needed some alone time. They had been spending an awful lot of time together. Against her better judgment, she had let him sleep over twice that week. Both mornings they had tried to make it look like he just arrived there from his own apartment when James woke up. Lauren felt a little guilty about it, but it felt so good to fall asleep knowing that Daniel was just down the hall in the guest room.

"Hey sweetie."

"Hi, Mom. What's wrong with Dad?" James asked as he came around the corner of the curly slide. So, he had noticed, too.

"I'm not sure. Maybe he's tired." Lauren shaded her eyes with her hand and turned back to look at Daniel who was still looking miserable. "I think we're going to get going soon."

"Can we still go get some frozen yogurt?"

"I don't know. Why don't you ask your dad when we get in the car, okay?" Lauren said, but somehow she already knew the answer.

The ride back to the house was unbearable. James was pouting in the back because Daniel said that he needed to go home to review a lease agreement for one of his agents. Even though Lauren assured him she would still take him for the frozen yogurt, James was not happy. Plus, Daniel continued to give Lauren the cold shoulder. She didn't bother trying to get anything out of him during the drive. She didn't want to discuss it in front of James anyway- whatever it was.

Daniel pulled into the driveway and put his car into park. At first Lauren thought he wasn't even going to get out of the car. She glanced over and saw the way he was clenching his jaw and gripping the steering wheel. *What in the world got him so angry?* She got out of the car and opened the back door for James, who looked at her then glanced back at his father as if waiting for him to change his mind.

"Come on, James. Let's go," Lauren said impatiently. James

heaved a dramatic sigh and slowly climbed out.

Finally, Daniel opened his door and stood up. "Come give me a hug, James."

James ran to his side and wrapped his arms around Daniel's waist. Daniel leaned down and hugged him back. "Cheer up. We'll spend some more time together tomorrow night, okay?"

"Okay," James said sulkily.

"James, go wait on the front porch for me. I'll just be a minute," Lauren said. Once he was out of earshot, she turned to Daniel. "You need to tell me what's really going on."

Daniel looked away and jiggled the keys in his hands.

"Tell me what happened! Everything was fine before we left here. What is going on with you?" Lauren tried not to raise her voice, but she wanted him to know how frustrated she was with his strange behavior.

Daniel turned as if he was going to just get back in his car, but then turned back around. "You're the one who needs to tell me what's going on, Lauren. Why are you hunting down my ex-partner?"

Lauren's heart began to race. *How did he know that?*

"You know what? Never mind. You don't need to tell me. I already know the answer." Daniel got into his car and slammed the door. He backed out of the driveway quickly and took off down the street.

Lauren made her way to the front door, trying to make sense of what had just happened. Her legs felt like jelly and her hand shook as she unlocked the front door.

"Why's Dad so mad?" James asked as they walked in.

"I'm not sure, James. Can you let Burley in? I need to check on something," Lauren said, her voice shaking.

Her whole body trembling, she quickly made her way to her office and jiggled the mouse so that the monitor came to life. She held onto the desk as a wave of nausea came over her. She saw the webpage with the background search on Kelly. Daniel must have seen it when he came in to get her sunglasses.

She had been unable to sleep the night before. Her curiosity about the woman that ended her and Daniel's relationship years ago was something she just couldn't let go. So, she had gotten up in the middle of the night and ordered a background check. However, when she crawled back into bed, she immediately felt the shame of betraying Daniel. As she tossed and turned once again, she had decided she would cancel the search first thing the next morning.

Right after breakfast she had gone over to the computer and logged onto the website. But she had been in the middle of the transaction when James had knocked over one of the houseplants in the living room while he was practicing some ninja warrior moves. She had gotten distracted with the clean-up and then the rush of getting ready to leave the house for the park. She had completely forgotten that she left the webpage open.

How could I have been so stupid? She put her hands over her face. No wonder Daniel was so upset. She realized she'd ruined everything. How could she ever fix this? Lauren slumped into the chair and sobbed.

Chapter 44

"I've really missed you guys," Nathan said for the third time as he hugged both Madison and Keenan.

"I know, Daddy," Madison said. "You already said that."

"I know, sweetie. I'm just really, really happy to spend some time with you."

"Do you miss Mommy too?" Madison asked innocently.

"Umm... sure, of course," Nathan frowned and rubbed at the thick stubble on his chin.

"Then why can't we come home?" Madison asked.

Nathan was surprised by the question, and he fumbled for a way to answer his daughter. "Well, of course I want you to come home. But Mommy and I have some things we need to figure out."

"What kind of things?"

"Well... grown up things. It's stuff that you don't need to be worried about, okay?" he said gently.

"You mean because you fight too much, right?"

"Yes, that's part of it." Nathan was not prepared to have this conversation.

"Are you mad at Mommy?" Madison pressed on and Nathan hesitated to answer.

"Daddy, can we go to the park?" Keenan chimed in.

Nathan sighed with relief. The park he could handle. "Yes, that's a great idea! Let's go to the park."

Nathan peered into the rearview mirror and smiled. He loved the sight of his children side by side in the back seat of his truck. He had missed them so much, his heart ached at the thought of them leaving in a matter of hours. The empty, quiet house had become tortuous for him. He used to get a little annoyed at how noisy they were when he was trying to concentrate on work. But lately he felt like he couldn't work at home because of the eeriness of the silence.

He wanted more than anything for them to come back home. But there was no way that would be happening anytime soon. Not with what Katherine had done. Even if she did end the affair, he didn't think he could forgive her. Seeing her earlier had completely turned his stomach sour. He figured she was still hanging out with this guy, whoever he was. She was probably with him right now. But he didn't want to think about it. He turned on the radio in an attempt to drown out his thoughts.

They arrived at the park and Nathan pulled into a spot right in front. The children quickly scrambled out of the truck and raced each other to the playscape. He grabbed his phone and got out, making his way slowly to the benches that encircled the playscape area. Madison came running back just as he sat down, begging him to play with her, but he told her that he needed to check his email. "I'll just be a few minutes, then I'll come play, okay?"

"Okay, Daddy," Madison said with a note of doubt in her tone and skipped back toward the playscape.

He was scrolling through his email when an incoming call with Mrs. Johnson's number appeared on his screen. He grimaced and answered with a wary hello.

"I'm calling about the plan you presented to my husband regarding Memorial Day. I really don't believe that is the best solution. I am not pleased at all that my guests will have to enter my home through the back door. Not to mention that the marble floors were to be the pièce de résistance." Mrs. Johnson's stern, clipped tone came over the phone and Nathan stood and began to pace in front of the benches.

"I'm sorry, Mrs. Johnson, but that really is your best option right now," Nathan said as calmly as possible, trying to ignore the clenching sensation in his gut.

"There must be some way you can get your crew to finish the floors before Memorial Day. Pay them overtime," she insisted.

"If we do the marble floors, we won't be able to finish the plumbing in time for inspection. Without that, you won't be able to have a party at all," Nathan reminded her.

"I'm aware of that, dear. However, I do not see why both of these things cannot be accomplished at the same time."

"We've already been over this in detail with your husband. There really is no other option." Nathan continued to walk back and forth trying to displace the adrenaline that had begun to course through his body.

"Maddie! Mommy said we're not supposed to climb up there, remember?" Nathan became aware of Keenan's voice in the distance. He once again tried to calm Mrs. Johnson with the fact that she could always show off the marble floors at a future party. But she was only becoming increasingly aggravated. He pinched the bridge of his nose with his eyes closed as he tried to ward off the throbbing pain in his head.

"Daddy! Come quick!" Keenan yelled again.

"Hold on a sec, son!" Nathan said as he covered the phone with his other hand. Then he continued to try to placate his angry client. "Mrs. Johnson, I assure you that there is no other way around this. We've gone over this several times with our team and this is the best solution."

Nathan was about to tell her he needed to go when he heard Madison scream. He whipped his head around to see her lying on the ground under the playscape. Keenan was running toward him, calling his name and pointing toward Madison. Nathan dropped his phone and ran toward his daughter.

Katherine was sipping her second glass of chardonnay. Her guard had come down and she once again allowed herself to be consumed with Jonathan's affection. They were floating side by side on an oversized inflatable that had two cup holders in between them. Jonathan had just paddled them over to the side of the pool where the bottle of wine sat in an ice bucket. He refilled both of their plastic wine glasses, then pushed off the side of the pool with his feet, sending them floating back into the deep end.

"Mmmmm... this is so nice," Katherine said, her eyes closed.

"We should do this every weekend." Jonathan grabbed her hand and brought it up to his lips.

"I'm definitely up for that." Katherine lifted the corner of her sunglasses and peered sideways at him.

"Spend the night with me," Jonathan continued to kiss her hand.

"Jonathan. I can't. I have to go get my..." Katherine was feeling so relaxed from the wine and the sun, she almost said she had to get her kids. She cleared her throat, removed her hand from his and took a long sip of her wine.

"You have to go get your what?" Jonathan asked.

"My, um... sister. I'm taking her to the airport tonight." Katherine quickly improvised.

"I'll go with you," Jonathan said. "Then we'll come back here."

"That's crazy. We'd be in the car for three hours."

"So? We'd be together. I want to spend time with you. We barely see each other as it is. Plus, I'd love to meet your sister." Jonathan seemed to be getting a little annoyed at her resistance to his idea.

"Well, let me think about it," Katherine said and pushed herself off the raft into the pool. "I need to get some water. I'll be right back."

Katherine made her way out of the pool, grabbed a towel and let herself into the house through the door that led to Jonathan's bedroom. She was passing by the dresser where her phone sat and noticed that it was blinking. She picked it up and swiped the screen saver. She had multiple texts from Nathan and five missed calls from him. Her heart rate picked up a little. She quickly scrolled through the texts.

Call me ASAP
Madison is hurt
On the way to ER
Where are you???
Answer your phone!!!

Katherine's heart began to pound. She quickly changed out of Jonathan's shorts and t-shirt and put her clothes back on. She looked around frantically for something that she could scribble a note out on for Jonathan. There was a little sticky notepad on his dresser but no pen. She scrounged through her purse until she found one, then wrote: I had to go. I'll explain later. Kat

At a stop light she listened to Nathan's voicemail. "Katherine! Why the hell won't you answer your phone?! I'm taking Maddie to the ER. She fell at the playground. Call me back!!"

Katherine's eyes filled with tears. The person behind her honked their horn loudly to let her know the light had turned green. She wiped her eyes with the back of her hand and drove forward. Picking up speed, she headed toward the hospital.

Chapter 45

Lauren had tried to call Daniel several times. The phone rang and went to voicemail each time. She barely managed to make James a turkey sandwich for dinner, and she let him eat in the living room with the TV on. Something that she rarely allowed, but she didn't want James asking her any more questions about why his dad wasn't coming over for dinner. She didn't bother making herself anything to eat as her stomach was in knots.

Her phone rang and she rushed back to the kitchen to get it, hoping and praying it was Daniel. It wasn't.

"Lauren! I'm at the ER with Maddie. She got hurt at the park," Nathan's voice came over the line.

"Oh my gosh! What happened? Is she okay?"

"We're waiting for the doctor right now. I can't get a hold of Katherine. Have you heard from her?" Nathan asked.

"No. I haven't talked to her at all lately," Lauren said. "Not since..."

"I need to go with Maddie into the exam room soon. Can you please try and reach her?"

"Yes, of course. Do you want me to come up there?" Lauren asked.

"Yeah, you probably should. If I can't get a hold of Katherine, I'll need you to take Keenan to your house."

"Ok. I'll try calling her and then head over there," Lauren said and ended the call. She tried Katherine's cell number and got no answer. She left a message telling her what Nathan had said and that she was heading up to the hospital too.

Katherine parked her car in the closest space available and ran up to the double glass doors of the ER. She rushed to the triage station and began asking the nurse questions about how to find her daughter. Before the nurse could answer she heard Keenan's little voice cry out. She whipped around to see Keenan and Nathan in the waiting area.

She made her way toward them and Keenan ran up to her, throwing his arms around her legs. "Maddie got hurt, Mommy."

"I know. I know, baby." Katherine couldn't stop the tears from flowing. She looked at Nathan and asked, "What happened? Where is she?"

"She was playing at the park and she fell," Nathan choked out. "The doctor just took her to get a CAT scan."

"What? A CAT scan? How serious is it?" Katherine started to panic.

"I don't know, Katherine. That's what they're trying to figure out," Nathan said, not bothering to hide his irritation.

"Well, how did this happen?" Katherine demanded to know.

Before he could answer her, Lauren and James came through the doors and rushed over to them. Katherine and Lauren eyed each other but neither spoke to one another.

"How's Maddie? Is she with the doctor?" Lauren asked Nathan.

"Yes, they took her in for a CAT scan a few minutes ago," he repeated the information to his sister.

Lauren gave her brother a hug, while James handed Keenan one of the Matchbox cars he had brought with him. The two boys started running their miniature cars along the lime green plastic seats that lined the wall in the waiting area.

"You still haven't told me what happened," Katherine snapped at Nathan after he pulled away from his sister's hug. "How did she fall? Weren't you watching her?"

"Of course I was watching her!" Nathan snapped back.

"Well, then how did she fall?" Katherine demanded.

"I told her, Mommy. I told her that we weren't allowed to climb up on top," Keenan chimed in.

Katherine looked over at her son. "Do you mean on top of the roof part?"

"Yes, she went up there and I told her not to, but she didn't listen to me," Keenan said, always the rule follower.

"Is that what happened? She was up on that roof? Why'd you let her go up there? I never let them go up there!" Katherine yelled at Nathan.

"Come on, guys. This isn't the time to be arguing," Lauren said, and Katherine glared at her.

"Can you please just stay out of this?" Katherine said angrily.

"You have no right to talk to me like that!" Lauren said, her voice rising.

"Knock it off, both of you!" Nathan stood in between the two women. "This isn't helping."

"Mr. and Mrs. Montgomery?" a male voice interrupted the tense conversation.

Katherine and Nathan turned to see a young doctor standing behind them. He told them, "We've completed the scan on your daughter and she's in an examination room now if you'd like to come with me."

"I'll take Keenan home with me. Call me as soon as you know something," Lauren said and gave her brother another quick hug.

Nathan and Katherine followed the doctor silently down the stark white corridor to a room at the end. Madison lay motionless in the narrow bed, hooked up to an IV line and blood pressure monitor.

"Oh, Maddie," Katherine sobbed as she made her way to her daughter's side. She knelt by the bed and then turned to the doctor. "Can you please tell me what's going on? All my husband has told me is that she fell."

"It appears she has suffered a concussion from the fall. The scan will determine the grade of concussion and we should have those results shortly. The good news is that she has no broken bones. Just some minor scrapes and bruising."

"Is she asleep?" Katherine looked at her daughter then back to the doctor, her face etched with concern.

"She could be, or she might be in a mild coma from the shock of the fall. We won't know for sure until we have a look at the scan."

"A coma??" Katherine stood up, the panic rising.

"When you say 'mild', what does that mean?" Nathan asked.

"It's possible that she will wake up within the next twelve hours. However, if she goes past that point with no signs of waking, that's when we need to be concerned and run more tests."

"So, what now? We just wait?" Katherine asked, her hand at her throat.

"I'm afraid that's all we can do for now. I'll be back as soon as possible with the results." The doctor placed Madison's chart in the holder on the door and walked out of the room.

"How could you let this happen?!" Katherine yelled at her husband. "You weren't watching her!"

"Katherine, stop! This doesn't help Maddie," Nathan said, trying to keep his voice down.

"You can't even tell me what happened! Where did she fall from?" Katherine demanded once again.

"The playscape," Nathan said impatiently.

"I know that, but from *where* on the playscape? Was she up on that rooftop?"

"Katherine! Keep your voice down!" Nathan said through gritted teeth.

"You can't tell me because you don't know! Is that it?" Katherine came closer to him.

Nathan blew out an exasperated breath and ran his hand through his already tousled hair. "Please just calm down."

"Nathan, answer me!" Katherine pounded her fists on his chest and began to sob. Through the tears, she choked out, "You were on your phone, weren't you?"

"You have no right to judge me, Katherine. You didn't even answer my calls. I know you were with *that guy*. You make me sick." Nathan pushed his wife away and sank into one of the chairs. He put his head in his hands. His shoulders began to shake, and Katherine knew he was crying too.

She shook her head in anger and went back to where Madison lay. She gently sat on the side of the bed, putting Maddie's small hand into her own. She looked down at her child's sweet face, taking deep breaths to ward off the panic and calm her racing heart. She leaned over and kissed her daughter's forehead and let the tears stream down her face.

As soon as Lauren got James and Keenan settled into bed, she called her parents and told them what had happened. Her father said that they would drive down first thing in the morning. Then she once again tried to call Daniel. He still did not answer. She left him a message telling him about Maddie and prayed he would actually listen to it. She was about to drift off to sleep when her buzzing phone startled her. She leaned over and grabbed it off the bedside table and breathed a sigh of relief when she saw Daniel's name on the screen.

"Hey," she said sleepily.

"I got your message about Maddie. Have you heard any news yet?"

"The last text I got from Nathan said that the scan showed she had a mild concussion, but still hasn't woken up," Lauren explained. "He said that the doctors expect her to wake up within 12 hours. But if she doesn't, they'll have to run more tests."

"Oh, man. I'm sorry. Please tell your brother I'm going to be praying for him," Daniel said.

"Okay, I will." Lauren waited to see if he was going to say anything about what had happened between them earlier that day. But the silence went on and became awkward. "Well, I guess I better get some sleep. I'll probably head up to the hospital tomorrow morning."

"Right," Daniel said. Then he added, "I'll come and watch James.

Just call me when you're ready to go."

"I have Keenan too," Lauren told him.

"That's fine," Daniel said. Once again silence filled the phone line.

"Okay, well, I'll talk to you tomorrow then," Lauren said and tried to keep her voice from shaking with emotion.

"Okay. Good night." Daniel ended the call.

Lauren tossed and turned most of the night. She finally fell into a deep sleep around three in the morning, only to be startled awake when she heard Keenan crying. She sat up and rubbed her eyes, then noticed it was still dark outside.

James came into the room, leading his cousin by the hand. Both boys crawled up into the bed with Lauren. She let them both cuddle up next to her, one boy on each side and they all fell back to sleep.

Chapter 46

Someone was knocking at the door. But Lauren was too tired to open her eyes. She felt so cozy in between her son and nephew, who were both still sound asleep. Burley started to bark, so she reluctantly and slowly crawled out of the bed. She grabbed her robe and put it on as she walked to the front door. Burley met her there, wagging her tail enthusiastically.

Daniel stood on the other side of the door looking serious and all business. It reminded her of the first night he had shown up at her house after running into him at the park. Her heart sank as she realized he wasn't going to grab her and hug her. He just gave a slight nod and asked if the boys were up.

"They're still asleep. Come in," she said. "Would you mind brewing some coffee? I didn't get much sleep last night."

"Sure," Daniel said as he patted Burley's head.

"Thanks. I'm going to go get dressed." Lauren headed back to her room where she still found the boys sleeping away. She was glad they were resting and hoped that Keenan would be comfortable with Daniel. She knew he must still be confused and upset about his sister.

Lauren washed her face and brushed her hair, then dressed in jeans and a pale-yellow blouse. She didn't bother with make-up. She had second guessed the decision for a moment, but then realized that not only had Daniel seen her plenty of times without make-up, but it was clear he didn't care what she looked like at the moment. Every time she thought about how badly she'd messed things up with him, she wanted to burst into tears. But now wasn't the time for dwelling on that situation. She needed to focus on doing whatever was needed to help Nathan and her niece.

She dreaded seeing Katherine again. It took all of her strength not to cause a scene and tell Katherine off in the hospital waiting room. She had wanted to say all of the things that had gone through her mind in the past couple of weeks. Like what a fake Katherine was, and how disgusting it was for her to run around with some other guy. How she was making a fool of Nathan while he worked his butt off for her. But she held her tongue because she knew that it wouldn't do any good.

James began to stir in the bed and he sat up. Lauren put her finger over her lips and pointed to Keenan who was still asleep. James looked at his younger cousin and gave him a little pat on the head. Lauren smiled at the sweet gesture, then whispered, "Your dad's here. He's going to stay with you and Keenan while I go to the hospital. Okay?"

"Okay, Mommy," James whispered back and scrambled out of bed to find his dad.

Lauren followed him out into the kitchen where the smell of coffee filled the air. She gratefully poured some into a ceramic to-go cup while Daniel and James talked quietly. She didn't have an appetite, but she knew she needed to keep her strength up, so she grabbed a protein bar and an apple.

"Try to keep Keenan busy. Hopefully the two of you can keep his mind off his sister," she said.

"We can handle that. Right, buddy?" Daniel said and ruffled James' hair.

"Yep! I have lots of stuff we can do!" James declared.

"Okay, then. I guess I'll just check on you guys a little later," Lauren said. She looked at Daniel, hoping for any sign of tenderness in his eyes.

"Sounds good. Let us know if there's an update on Madison," Daniel said, but his expression remained stoic.

"I will," Lauren said and waited once more to see if Daniel might walk her to the door. However it was clear he was staying put, so she turned to leave.

She stopped by The Bagelry and picked up an onion bagel with cream cheese and a large coffee for Nathan. He had texted her earlier letting her know that Katherine had gone home to shower, so there was no need to get something for her as well. Lauren was guiltily relieved that she would not have to see Katherine first thing this morning. She didn't have anything positive to say to her, no matter how badly her heart hurt for Madison.

"How are you doing?" Lauren asked her brother as she handed him the coffee and paper bag that held the warm bagel.

"Thanks," he said and took a grateful sip of coffee. He shrugged, and his bloodshot eyes darted to Maddie's bed. She was still asleep, her tiny body hooked up to all kinds of monitors. "I'm okay. I just wish she'd wake up."

"I know. Me too." Lauren sat on one of the chairs near Madison's bed. "Did you sleep at all?"

"Not really," Nathan admitted. "I don't know who I'm more

upset with: myself or Katherine."

"You can't blame yourself, Nathan."

"Yeah, I can. I wasn't watching her. I was on the phone with Mrs. Johnson. I should have just let her leave a message." Nathan sank into the other chair and put his head in his hands. "Everything's so messed up right now."

Lauren's eyes filled with tears. She didn't know what to say. She realized there was nothing she could say or do to make things better. "Mom and Dad should be here soon. Have you heard from them?"

"Yeah, Mom texted a while ago and said they were about an hour away."

"Eat your bagel. You need to keep strong for Maddie," Lauren said and picked up the bag from the table, handing it to him again.

Nathan nodded solemnly and dug into the bag. He ate a few bites, then said, "What's up with Daniel?"

"What do you mean?" Lauren asked.

"Are things going okay with him?"

"Oh, yeah, it's fine." Lauren didn't want to admit that things were a mess. Not only did it seem trivial compared to what was going on with Maddie, but she didn't want to give her brother any further reason to dislike Daniel.

"You don't sound very convincing."

"I'm just tired. And worried about Maddie." Lauren quickly changed the subject. "Did you and Katherine talk about anything last night?"

"No. Not unless you count arguing." Nathan shook his head. "I don't see the point in talking to her. She made her decision. I'm done."

"Done? As in 'divorce' done?" Lauren asked with surprise.

"I don't know," Nathan said in frustration. "I just don't see how we can get past this. I won't forgive her."

"Yeah, I understand." Lauren blew out a breath.

Nathan finished his bagel, wadded up the bag and tossed it into the trash can. He stood up and began pacing the room.

"Why don't you go outside and take a little walk around? Get some air." Lauren suggested. "I'll text you if the doctors come in or anything."

Nathan looked at his sister for a minute, feeling inner conflict about leaving Madison.

"Don't worry. I'll sit and talk to her. I heard the doctor say that she can hear us and it might help wake her up."

"Okay. I could use some fresh air. I won't be gone long," he said, grabbed his phone off the table and strode out the door into the corridor.

Katherine had taken a quick shower and picked out some clean clothes from her closet. It felt so odd to be back in their house. It didn't feel like it was hers anymore. Not only was it a mess and didn't smell too great, but it also just seemed different. She felt like an intruder, like she didn't belong here anymore.

She dressed in jeans and a sweatshirt, then dried her hair a little bit. Her cosmetic bag was at her mother's house, but she wasn't worried about it. Her only concern right now was her daughter. Every time she thought about how careless Nathan had been, she saw red. It was so typical of him – paying more attention to work than his children. And he *knew* that she didn't like them climbing up on top of that roof. But most of all, she was angry at herself. She felt ashamed that she had been lounging around the pool with Jonathan as if she had no responsibilities.

Before heading downstairs, she went into Madison's room. She grabbed some of her stuffed animals from her bed, making sure to include "Blinkie", her bear that the dog had chewed the eyes off. Maddie had cried and cried, declaring that she hated Queenie. Katherine smiled when she recalled how Nathan had stepped in to handle the situation, as Katherine had been busy with Keenan who had a stomach bug at the time. He had hot glued the half-eaten eyes back on and told his daughter that it now looked as if the bear was blinking.

She sighed and went to the dresser for a pair of pajamas for her daughter. She picked up the picture on the dresser – one of her favorites of Madison. She was four years old and was atop an American Paint horse. They had been at the rodeo and it was during a phase where Madison was obsessed with horses. She had the biggest smile on her face, in her little blue western dress and boots, her hair a mess of strawberry curls.

Katherine wiped the tears from her eyes and grabbed the pajamas. As she was walking out of the room, she heard her phone ringing in her purse. She ran down the hall to make sure she didn't miss the call. It could be an update on Madison, hopefully good news. But it was Jonathan calling again. She pressed the Ignore button. She didn't want any more calls coming in from him. Especially when she was at the hospital and Nathan was around to glance at her caller ID. She pulled up Jonathan's contact and pressed the Block option.

Chapter 47

Jonathan pulled out his phone again to check if he had any new texts. Nothing. He felt like throwing the phone over the balcony. He was sitting at a table on the patio of The Oasis, a renowned Tex-Mex restaurant with multiple layers of decks overlooking Lake Travis. He was supposed to be enjoying the sunset and the company of his friends, but he was in a horrible mood and he wasn't hiding it.

"What's wrong?" Sylvia asked him, even though she already pretty much figured it out. Katherine was giving him the silent treatment again. It happened at least once or twice a week. Sylvia could always tell if Jonathan's mysterious girlfriend was showering him with attention or MIA. It was usually the latter, and Jonathan was no fun to be around when that was the case.

Jonathan ignored Sylvia's question and abruptly pushed his chair back from the table. He stood up and stalked inside the restaurant. Sylvia craned her neck and followed him with her eyes. He was at the bar. Apparently he couldn't wait for their server to come around and refresh his beer. She decided to follow him inside. Things must be pretty bad. He'd been in moods before, but this one topped them all.

"I think it will help if you talk about it," Sylvia said as she came up beside him at the bar.

Jonathan looked at Sylvia for a few moments. He turned his attention back to the bartender who had just delivered a bottle of Shiner. He took a long drink of the beer, then looked at Sylvia again. She expected him to say something flippant or that she should mind her own business, but he surprised her.

"I don't know what the hell is going on," he said. "One minute everything is perfect, then she just disappears. The last I heard from her, she texted that there was a family emergency, but couldn't say what it was. She won't answer my calls, and now it's going straight to voicemail. I'm worried and I'm pissed off at her at the same time."

"Well, this is pretty typical for her, though. She's been like this from the beginning," Sylvia pointed out.

"Not like this. I mean, she was at my house and we were having a great time. Then she just left without even telling me." Jonathan was still angry when he recalled the events of yesterday. He waited in the pool for at least twenty minutes, expecting her to return. He finally went inside, looked around for her, then went out to the front to see that her car was gone. He had been shocked when he realized that she'd taken off without saying a word to him. If there was an emergency, he could have gone with her and supported her. The worst part was that she wouldn't return any of his calls. "I just don't get why she won't talk to me about it. I thought we were getting really close."

"Maybe *you* were. It doesn't seem like it on her side." Sylvia had done her best to bite her tongue when it came to Katherine, but she didn't feel like being nice anymore. "She treats you like crap, Jonathan."

"Look, I know you don't like her. Maybe she's got some issues, but you don't know her like I do. She's a good person."

"Okay, okay." Sylvia put her hands up in surrender. "I'll give her the benefit of the doubt, for your sake. But it just really pisses me off that she's always making you miserable. I don't like seeing you like this. I care about you." Sylvia put her hand on his arm and Jonathan turned to look at her.

"Thanks, Sylvia. I'm sorry – I don't mean to take it out on you."

"I know. It's okay. You can vent at me anytime. But how about we go back outside and try to enjoy the evening? If you want to talk about it later, I'm all ears."

Jonathan finished off his beer and placed some cash on the bar. "I'm not going to promise anything, but I'll do my best."

"That's fine. Let's just get through dinner, then maybe the two of us can go have a coffee and talk some more." Sylvia looped her hand through his arm and they walked back to the table together.

Chapter 48

Things weren't looking good for Madison. She had passed the twenty-four hour mark and had still not woken up. The doctors said that all of her vital signs were normal and that was a positive sign, but the concern was that she hadn't roused or shown any sign of waking.

The doctor had sat down with Katherine and Nathan, explaining the severity of Madison's condition. Katherine had tried to focus on what he was telling them, but her mind felt fuzzy and her eyes glazed over. She could barely concentrate as he went on about the Glasgow scale and how Madison's score was at a 13, which meant that although the coma was considered mild, there was still concern about the length of time she'd been asleep. He encouraged them to continue to talk to her as much as possible.

The doctor left the room and once again, Katherine felt the overwhelming need to place blame on Nathan. She spewed the same accusations as she did the night before, going on about how he never paid attention to his family. His head was always at work. How careless he had been to not watch her at the playground. She tried hard to keep her voice down, but it was impossible as her emotions took over and she began to sob uncontrollably.

Nathan had heard enough. He got up in her face and began to whisper menacingly through gritted teeth. It wasn't his fault Maddie fell. It could have happened regardless of him being on the phone or not. If anyone was to blame, it was Katherine- taking off and leaving her children to go fool around with another man. He was disgusted with her behavior and deeply offended that she'd broken her wedding vows.

It was then that Lauren walked into the room. Neither Katherine nor Nathan even noticed her standing in the doorway. Lauren watched the two of them for a moment, as Nathan continued to berate his wife for her infidelity. Katherine had turned away from him, but Nathan grabbed her by the wrist, spinning her back to face him. Katherine put her hands on Nathan's chest and shoved him away from her.

"Stop it!" Lauren yelled out. Both Katherine and Nathan turned toward her, faces red with anger. "Just stop. This isn't helping Madison."

"Oh, great. Now you're here to gang up on me?" Katherine said.

"What are you talking about? I'm not ganging up on you," Lauren replied angrily. "And you have zero reason to be mad at me. I'm not the one who messed up."

"Exactly. You just think it's your place to judge me?" Katherine took a step toward Lauren. "I thought you were my friend. How many times did you sympathize with me about Nathan working late and blowing off his family?"

"Katherine, I tried to call you. You wouldn't return my calls. That's not much of a friend if you ask me." Lauren crossed her arms.

"Right. Because I knew there was no point. You were going to take your brother's side no matter what. That's why I couldn't talk to you about it. Nobody cared about how *I* felt. How I was alone practically all the time, trying to take care of the kids by myself. Feeling like all I was to anyone was a cook and a maid. Feeling like my husband didn't love me anymore," Katherine said as tears began to stream down her face. She wiped at them angrily and walked out of the room.

Lauren turned to Nathan, "You guys need to stop fighting in front of Madison. She can hear you, you know."

"Yeah, I know. But you have no idea how hard this is. Everything is so freaking messed up!" Nathan whisper-yelled at her.

"I realize that, Nathan. I know it's hard. But, you and Katherine need to be here for Maddie, together."

"Are you kidding me? I can't even stand to be in the same room as Katherine right now!"

"I understand. And I don't blame you one bit. But you've got to pull it together for Madison's sake," Lauren said sternly.

"I can't. I just can't right now!" With that, Nathan strode out of the room as well.

Lauren watched him leave with disbelief, then looked over at her niece, still lying as still as two days ago. She walked over to the bed and put her little hand into both of hers. "Oh, Maddie. Please wake up. We really need you to wake up."

She remained for a few minutes, holding her hand, just watching Madison breathe in and out. She looked so peaceful even though the world around her was in such chaos. That thought reminded her of something the pastor at Daniel's church had said last Sunday. That even in the midst of a raging storm, God could bring perfect peace if you remained in faith. She whispered, "Please, God. We need your peace. Please help us. I don't know what to do."

Lauren held on to Madison's hand a few minutes longer. Then she placed it gently back under the covers and adjusted her teddy bear so that he wouldn't fall off the bed. She walked over to the window and looked out at the dark sky. Her parents were at her house now watching James and Keenan. They had already spent a couple hours at the hospital, trying to comfort Nathan, talking to Madison and taking turns reading books to her as the doctor had suggested. Daniel had gone back to work today and Lauren had not heard from him all day except one text asking for an update on Madison.

Daniel had still barely said anything to Lauren since the day he found out about her background check on Kelly. They'd only discussed Madison's condition and the logistics of him watching James while she was at the hospital. Lauren knew now wasn't the time to bring any of it up anyway, but she hoped that he would eventually be willing to talk to her about it. However, she was terrified that things might really be over between them. Just when everything was going so perfectly. She had almost had it all, but she'd ruined it.

Tears filled her eyes once again as she thought of a future with Daniel just being James' dad. Passing James off between each other on the weekends. Awkward conversations that only consisted of two parents making decisions for their son. She now saw little hope of James having his mother and father living under the same roof. The chance to give James a real family had slipped right through her fingers.

"Hey," Nathan said quietly as he came back into the room.

Lauren wiped her eyes before turning to face him, "Hey."

"I'm sorry I lost my temper earlier. I just needed to vent."

"I know. It's okay."

"Can you do me a favor?" Nathan asked.

"Sure. Anything," Lauren said.

"Can you call Daniel? Can you ask him to come here and pray for us?"

Chapter 49

Lauren sat in the living room in her favorite armchair, legs pulled up, her hands wrapped around a warm cup of tea. She stared out at the backyard through the foggy windows. It had been raining non-stop for days. Puddles were forming in the flower beds and the sandbox. Even Burley looked depressed as she lay on the floor in front of the window, her head resting on her paws, ears pressed down.

Lauren's parents were at the kitchen table playing a board game with James and Keenan. Everyone was getting cabin fever, from either being cooped up in the house or at the hospital. They were all still taking turns relieving Nathan and Katherine so that they could go catch a few hours of sleep at home in an actual bed. Of course, the estranged couple never went to their house together. They took turns, swapping out staying at the hospital with Madison. They were still not speaking to each other, but at least they had stopped arguing.

It was still the same situation with her and Daniel as well. They only spoke when he came over to spend time with James, and Daniel continued to be cold and distant. Lauren had tried to give Daniel a chance to talk to her in private. She'd walked outside with him when he left for the night, but he just said good night and quickly walked to his car. It was almost too much to bear.

She had finally confided in her mom about what she had done.

She had felt embarrassed when she confessed her internet search on Kelly. As she told her mom the story, she realized how stupid it all sounded. What had she hoped to gain from the information anyway? It wasn't going to provide her with any clues about what took place between Kelly and Daniel all those years ago. The bottom line was that Lauren had let her jealousy get the best of her judgment.

Her mom had encouraged her to let Daniel have more time. She assured her that he would come around when he was ready to talk to Lauren about it. Besides, right now there was just too much going on with Madison. Daniel had been to the hospital several times to pray with Nathan. This was the only thing that comforted her right now. From what Nathan had told her, Lauren could tell that the two men had begun to forge a friendship. Daniel was genuinely gaining Nathan's trust and Lauren was pleased that her brother was leaning on Daniel's strong faith. Nathan told her that Daniel had brought his Bible with him last night and encouraged him with several scriptures.

It shall come to pass that whoever calls on the name of the Lord shall be saved. The words from Romans comforted Lauren as well. Nathan had texted that one along with another from Proverbs: *Trust in the Lord with all your heart, and lean not on your own understanding; In all your ways acknowledge Him and He will make your paths straight.*

As she read them once more before going to bed, she felt a peace wash over her like never before. She wanted so badly to be able to share the feeling with Daniel. Instead, she whispered a request to God. She vowed to be patient and asked Him to give her the strength to wait and give Daniel time. Then she also pleaded that the Lord would help Daniel to forgive her.

As she was about to drift off to sleep, still feeling that uncommon peace, she realized that she had some forgiving to do herself. Even though she still didn't condone what her best friend had done, Lauren finally let the anger go. She whispered before she dozed off, "I forgive you, Katherine."

Katherine was in the chapel at the hospital. Daniel had come into Maddie's room several days in a row now to pray with Nathan. Each time she had excused herself, so that the two men could have some solitude. The evening before, she had gone out to her car to charge her phone and listen to the radio. She'd had to run with her sweatshirt hoodie covering her head to dodge the rain that had been continuing for days now. After about thirty minutes, when she came back, the men were still deep in conversation, so she retreated back out of the room. It was raining too hard to take a walk around the parking lot, and the cafeteria was closed, so she just began to wander around the corridors. It was then when she came upon the chapel.

At first she didn't know if she should go in. She felt like she didn't deserve to talk to God, but as she peered into the dimly lit room, there was an elderly woman in there that gave her such a warm smile, she found herself being drawn in. When she sat down in one of the pews and began to sob, the older woman came and sat next to her, putting a hand on her heaving shoulder. When Katherine calmed down, the woman asked if she needed someone to talk to. Katherine let it all out.

The kind woman patiently and intently listened to the entire tale, from Nathan's neglect, to her affair, then to Maddie's condition. She gave Katherine a packet of tissues from her bag as the tears flowed non-stop. When she was finally done talking and sobbing, the woman asked Katherine if she believed that God could forgive her. Katherine just shook her head and began to cry again. Then the woman retrieved the Bible from the table at the altar and brought it back to the pew. She rustled through the thin golden-edged pages until she came to the place she was looking for. Placing the heavy Bible in Katherine's lap, she pointed to the page where she wanted Katherine to begin reading and silently exited the chapel.

Katherine had mulled over those verses all night. She had actually slept – not just the one or two hours that came in snatches the previous nights, when she would constantly wake and peer over to check on her daughter. She slept seven hours straight, waking a little before 6 a.m. Now she was back in the chapel, the Bible in her lap, opened to the page in Psalms the woman had shown her.

The Lord is compassionate and merciful, slow to get angry and filled with unfailing love.
He will not constantly accuse us, nor remain angry forever.
He does not punish us for all our sins; He does not deal harshly with us, as we deserve.
For His unfailing love toward those who fear Him is as great as the height of the heavens above the earth.
He has removed our sins as far from us as the east is from the west.

Once again, the tears flowed. However, this time Katherine cried with relief. She finally felt a surge of hope flood into her situation. If the God of the universe could forgive her, she knew that she had to forgive Nathan. And if she did, then maybe, just maybe Nathan would forgive her too.

Before leaving the pew, Katherine prayed once again for Maddie, begging God to help her wake up and come back to them. She remained in the darkened chapel a while longer, just soaking in the peace that filled the room. She had been in overdrive since the accident; her heart seemed to be constantly racing and her already rattled nerves were like sparks firing chaotically. But now she felt the tension leave her muscles, her heartbeat was steady and slow. Her stomach no longer retched and churned. Her mind wasn't torturing her with awful guilt-ridden thoughts.

Katherine left the chapel feeling refreshed and ready to take on the day. She still had the heaviness of not knowing when her daughter would wake up. But she now felt confident that Madison was going to be okay; it was just a matter of time. She didn't quite know why, but she had the impression that God just wanted her to trust Him. It occurred to her that most of her life she had only given God a few thoughts here and there. Christmas, Easter, her wedding, the children's baptisms. Only on special occasions or holidays- a handful of times a year. But in the past two months, God had clearly been a dominant theme in her life. She couldn't ignore that tremendous impression of serendipity.

When she returned to Maddie's room, she saw that Nathan was awake. He was standing at the window with his back turned to her. She took in the sight of him, his much too long hair a mess, his clothes hanging off of him, and her heart completely broke. She walked tentatively toward him. He heard her and glanced behind him, but then quickly went back to staring out at the busy highway, flooded with rain and rush hour traffic. She wanted to go to him and put her arms around him, but she was too afraid. She didn't want to feel the sting of rejection.

Katherine turned to leave the room. Maybe she should just go get them both a coffee. As much as she longed for a physical connection with her husband, she had seen the way Nathan looked at her the past few days. She felt his hatred and disgust penetrate her soul. It was unbearable, but she knew she deserved it. She'd been a complete fool. She wouldn't be surprised at all if he asked for a divorce once Maddie pulled through.

But when she got into the corridor, something stopped her. It was almost as if an invisible force halted her steps. She needed to at least try to make things right. She turned around and strode back into the room. She walked straight over to Nathan and very gently put her hand on his shoulder. Just as she expected, he shrugged it off. She stood next to him, looking straight ahead and whispered, "I'm sorry."

Nathan continued to ignore her. He kept his eyes on the colorful collage of cars zipping along the slick overpass down below. She inched her body as close to him as possible, and he moved away from her. She wasn't going to give up. Tears began to flood her eyes and she let them fall unashamedly. She turned toward him, grabbed onto his shirt, put her face into his shoulder and sobbed, "Nathan, I'm sorry. I'm so sorry."

Katherine continued to cry into his shoulder for a few minutes. Nathan remained tense, but at least he didn't push her away. When she was about to pull away to go in search of a tissue, she felt his arm come around her waist. She remained still, not wanting to mess up the moment, waiting to see if Nathan would pull her into his arms. But, instead, she heard him say, "Did you hear that?"

"Hear what?" Katherine looked up at him.

He gently pulled away from her and started towards Madison, "I thought I heard Maddie say something. Look, she's moving. Quick, Katherine, call for a nurse."

Lauren sighed once again and took a sip of her tea. It was now cold and bitter tasting. She set it on the end table and stood up. The dog seemed to sense her uneasiness and got up to nudge her with his big head. She scratched him around his ears and he leaned his big body into her legs.

"You probably need to go out, don't you?" she asked and peered back outside at the unrelenting rain.

Lauren opened the back door for Burley and stepped outside onto the patio. Even though she was tired of being stuck indoors, the rain seemed to suit her mood. She felt as if God was cleansing her soul as the rain poured down onto the earth, washing the landscape of impurities. With each passing day that Daniel gave her the silent treatment she had a greater awareness of her own flaws. It wasn't his fault that she held onto her insecurities. It was time to let them go.

Lauren knew in her heart that Daniel had a solid character foundation. He always had. His confidence and drive were some of his best qualities, yet they had intimidated her. She now realized it wasn't just the women that he gave his attention to that she was jealous of. She was also jealous of him. He always seemed to know exactly who he was, what he wanted and how to get it. She wanted that. She needed to feel that she was good enough.

"Hey, sweetie," her mother's voice broke into her revelation. "Daniel's on the phone for you."

"Thanks." Lauren took her cell phone from her mom and said

hello.

"Hey. Would you be okay with James spending the night at my place tonight?" Daniel got right to business, as usual.

"Sure. I don't see why not." Lauren was grateful for Daniel's offer, as James had been whining non-stop about his father spending the night with them. Unfortunately she had seen her parents exchange a look when James brought up the fact that Daniel had spent the night at their house numerous times already. Lauren knew her parents wouldn't say anything to her, but she could tell they didn't approve. Of course, they were probably right. The only thing accomplished by their innocent sleepovers was drawing them that much closer, making their current separation so much more painful. "Will you be picking him up right after work?"

"Yeah, it'll be early. Today's been pretty slow."

"Okay." Lauren sighed and closed her eyes. She couldn't stand the distance between them a moment longer. "Do you think you'll be ready to talk about us soon?"

Daniel sighed as well. Then the silence lingered for a minute. "I don't know Lauren. I'm really tired of being on trial for a crime I didn't commit. I don't deserve that."

"I know you don't. I've realized some things and I really want to tell you about it," Lauren pleaded.

Another long silence, then Daniel said, "I do want to talk. But before we do, I want you to read a book I have."

"Okay." Lauren agreed easily.

"Don't get mad, but my Pastor gave it to me to give to Sarah. She never wanted to read it, but I held onto it."

This time it was Lauren's turn to go silent. She squeezed her eyes shut and took a deep breath. Why was it so hard for her to not be jealous?

"Lauren?" Daniel said, his irritation obvious. "This is the kind of stuff I don't want to deal with. You can't hold my past against me. Just like I don't hold the fact that you kept James from me against you."

Lauren began to panic. "I know. I know. I'm sorry. I want to read the book. I want to change, Daniel. I want what you have. With God."

"Then this book will be more perfect for you than I thought. I'll bring it tonight."

"Ok. Thank you." Lauren ended the call with Daniel and remained outside for a few more minutes, feeling frustration rise within her. Why was this so hard? She wanted so badly to feel the security that would never give cause to doubt any of Daniel's intentions. But she had so quickly defaulted to the old green-eyed monster the second Sarah's name was mentioned. She was extremely curious what this book was about and hoped like crazy that it would help her.

"Lauren, come quick." Her mother was back at the door beckoning her to come inside.

"What is it? What's wrong?" Lauren felt panic rise for the second time. But then she saw that her mother was smiling.

"It's Madison. She woke up!"

Chapter 50

*T*hree weeks later...

Jonathan needed a break from studying. He had been up since 7 a.m. going over the notes for his Business Law II final. It was the only thing keeping him from getting stuck in his head, going over and over what happened with Katherine. He'd long given up on calling and texting her. It was clear she wasn't going to respond. A couple of weeks ago he had considered trying to call her office to see if she was okay. But he couldn't find a listing for the name of the company she worked for. He was beginning to wonder how much of what Katherine had told him was even true.

Some days it almost felt like it was all a dream. But he knew that the feelings he'd experienced were very real. However small the amount of time he'd spent with Katherine, he couldn't deny that there had been a genuine connection between them. He had never met a woman that he wanted to spend more than one night with, let alone the rest of his life. Although he was still shocked at her sudden exit, he had slowly let go of the anger that had plagued him over the past few weeks.

He had done everything he could to distract himself so that he didn't have endless hours to think about her. He dedicated more time to studying. He took on more shifts at the restaurant. He spent more time with Sylvia. He opened his Bible and began reading more often.

It was just a little after 10am. He had spent most of the past three hours making great headway on memorizing everything he needed to know about bailments, risk bearing, and copyrights. He had only taken a few breaks to stretch, refill his coffee mug, and watch a little bit of TV. He was famished, and since he hadn't been to the store in the last two days there wasn't much to eat. He was really craving a breakfast burrito.

He changed into a pair of jeans and a t-shirt, splashed some water on his face and brushed his teeth. He grabbed his keys, phone, and wallet. Walking out to his car, he felt the sun hit his face like a hot campfire. It was approaching the end of May and the temperatures were already in the 90's so early in the day. Summer was definitely around the corner. He got into his car and cranked up the air conditioning. He put on his sunglasses, then pulled out of the driveway and headed out of his neighborhood toward Mopac. It was just a few miles up the highway until he reached his exit. When he had turned down 5th Street he heard his phone ping with an incoming text. At the stoplight he picked up his phone and saw that it was from Sylvia.

Meet up for coffee later? I'll quiz you ☺

He quickly tapped in a reply: *Sounds good*

The downtown Whole Foods parking lot was already packed. He circled around the main lot in front just in case someone was leaving, then drove down into the recesses of the parking garage. He found a spot not far from the underground entrance and parked. He strode up to the glass enclosure and pulled open the door, holding it open for two young ladies coming up behind him. He smiled at them as they walked past and he realized he actually felt pretty good today.

Still smiling, he lightly hopped onto the escalator and waited for it to transport him to the top and into the bright and noisy world of healthy food. He stepped off and glanced around. The hot food bars were at the other end of the store, but since he was already near the produce section, he thought he might grab some fruit for later. That's when he saw her. She was in the produce area near the summer fruit, pushing a half-loaded cart and glancing down at a piece of paper. She looked beautiful, as always, in jeans and a light blue short-sleeved blouse. Her red hair was pulled into a ponytail, her bangs lightly framing her face. He just watched her for a moment as his heart picked up speed. For a split second he debated whether he should just keep on walking and pretend he never saw her. But he knew he couldn't. He had to talk to her; he had to know what had happened.

As Katherine began picking through the organic plums, trying to find the ones with the perfect amount of softness, he walked up to her. He didn't say anything, just stood next to her silently. She finally looked up at him and when she recognized him, the color drained from her face and her eyes widened. It was clearly not a look of pleasant surprise.

"Hi Kat," Jonathan said as calmly as possible.

Katherine continued to just stare at him. She had dropped the plum that she'd been holding. He waited another moment for her to say something, but a little girl with curly red hair came up behind her and began to tug on her arm.

"Mommy! Are you almost done?" the little girl asked and then gave Jonathan a suspicious glance.

Mommy? Jonathan returned his gaze to Katherine, then back to the girl who was an exact replica of her. *What in the world?*

"Daddy said to tell you he's going to the meat counter," she said and took off running toward the back of the store.

Jonathan looked back at Katherine, and then followed her gaze in the direction where the little girl had gone. The child had stopped in front of a guy who looked to be about 30-something, with another child at his side, a young boy about the age of four, with the same shade of red hair. Jonathan caught the other man's eye and saw a frown cross his brow as he looked at Jonathan, then back to Katherine. It was then that Jonathan noticed the gleaming diamond ring on her left hand.

"I have to go. I'm so sorry," Katherine managed to whisper, those familiar blue eyes pleading with him- an unspoken message of angst and shame. She turned on her heel, hastily pushing the cart away from him, leaving her bag of plums behind.

Jonathan watched her continue to push the cart toward the man and the two children and suddenly he felt like the biggest fool in the world.

"Who was that guy at Whole Foods?" Nathan asked her as they were getting into bed.

Katherine knew the question was coming. She could tell by how quiet Nathan had been the rest of the day. Even though things were still extremely strained between them, they had made great strides in talking civilly to one another. They had already had two counseling sessions with one of the pastors at Daniel's church and their third session was scheduled for tomorrow.

"That was him, wasn't it?" Nathan asked, trying his best not to sound hostile.

"Yes." Katherine saw no point in lying anymore. She was done with that.

"How did he know you were at Whole Foods? I thought you said you weren't talking to him anymore." Nathan's tone grew angry.

"I swear I haven't talked to him at all, Nathan. He just happened to be there." Katherine was still shocked over the random meeting.

"Do you really expect me to believe that?" Nathan asked.

"I swear to you, Nathan. It was a total coincidence. You have to trust me."

"That's the problem. I don't think that I can anymore."

The silence filled the room. The sound of the ceiling fan above them whirring around became ridiculously overt. Katherine toyed with the frayed edges of the comforter. Nathan remained motionless, staring ahead at the wall, his expression as cold as the Arctic.

"I still don't get it." Nathan finally broke the silence but continued to look straight ahead.

Katherine began to cry. "I know. I don't either. I was just so hurt. I thought you didn't care about me anymore."

"It's still a lame excuse."

"I just wanted so badly to feel loved again. That feeling we had when we first started dating." Katherine reached over for a tissue from her nightstand. "I can't say that I never meant to hurt you. Because that's not true. I did want to hurt you. I wanted you to hurt as much as I did. All those months you ignored me and made me feel like I didn't matter to you anymore."

Nathan fell silent again. Katherine's sobs grew louder. She covered her face with her hands and cried until her head ached. When she finally looked up to grab another tissue, she glanced over at Nathan. His face was still set in anger, but she was surprised when she noticed the unmistakable dampness of tears as well.

"I'm sorry, Katherine," he croaked out. "I had no idea you were hurting that bad."

"I tried talking to you, but you just didn't want to listen to me."

"I know. I know." Nathan sighed and looked at her. "But I still think you could've tried harder. You didn't have to..."

"I'm sorry. I don't expect you to forgive me. But I really am sorry. I wish I could go back in time and take it back, but I can't." Katherine turned toward her husband and tentatively put her hand on his arm. She expected him to pull away from her as he'd done in the past couple of weeks when she'd tried to initiate any sort of physical closeness. Each time she had gotten closer than a few inches to him, he'd backed away, putting up the invisible barrier that had come to define their marriage. The other day when they'd been tucking the children in, Katherine had put her hand on his shoulder, but Nathan had quickly shrugged it off as if her touch burned him. But tonight, he didn't jerk back or brush her hand away.

Katherine continued to look at her husband until he raised his eyes to make contact with hers. She saw the raw pain there and it broke her heart. She did her best to quench the fear of possible rejection, and she leaned in toward him, putting her arms around his neck and letting her head rest on his chest. Once again she braced herself for the impending brush-off, but he surprised her. He wrapped his arms around her waist and held onto her with a fierceness that told her everything was going to be okay.

Chapter 51

"Only one more week until summer!" Lauren heard one of her students exclaim as the class filed out into the hallway for dismissal. Lauren smiled as she watched some of the boys do a fist in the air with a "Yes!" proclamation.

Her students joined the rest of the stream of excited children making their way toward the front entrance. This Friday had been even more charged than usual, as everyone was not only excited for the weekend, but for the upcoming summer break as well. Lauren knew that next week was going to be crazy, the children's heads already in summer mode. Not much schoolwork would be happening. She already had plenty of games and fun activities planned to try to keep them somewhat under control.

She began to gather her belongings to take home for the weekend. The first thing she grabbed was the book that Daniel had given to her almost a month ago. She took it out from the top drawer of her desk and placed it in her tote bag. The book was precious to her. Not only because Daniel gave it to her, but because of the dramatic changes the message had already brought out in her. The title was *You Are Significant*.

The author had taught her that she was loved by her Heavenly Father no matter what. It didn't matter what career she had, if she was extremely successful, if she knew how to cook a gourmet meal, or if she knew the best parenting techniques. God loved her just the way she was. One of her favorite chapters was the one that spoke about feeling significant because of who she was in God's eyes, not in the eyes of a romantic partner. She knew this chapter was the main reason Daniel gave her the book. It had definitely built her self-esteem as she read through the scriptures that pointed to how much God lavishes His children with love and tender kindness.

"Hi Mom!" James burst into the room, a huge smile on his face.

"Hi sweetie. How was your day?"

"It was awesome! I got to paint another picture. This one will be a surprise for Dad, though," he said, his voice becoming a little serious. "Is that okay? I don't want your feelings to be hurt."

"Of course it's okay," Lauren said and gave him a hug. "Your dad will love getting a surprise from you."

"Okay, good. Because it's kinda scary, so you wouldn't have liked it anyway."

Lauren laughed at her son's comment. "It's pretty scary, huh?"

"Yeah, it's got a giant spider in it."

"You're right. That one is better for your dad." Lauren laughed again. "Here, can you help me with that bag?"

"Sure." James picked up the tote bag and they made their way out of her classroom.

Just as Lauren was closing her door, she saw Karen coming out of her classroom as well. Lauren cringed. She had still been avoiding her colleague as best she could since the day Karen let her have it about Jake.

"Hey Lauren." Karen walked over to them and stood right in

front of their path. There was no avoiding her now. "Do you have a second?"

"Actually, we really need to get going," Lauren said, not meeting the other woman's eyes.

Karen put her hand on Lauren's arm and said, "I just wanted to apologize for the way I got on your case."

"It's fine, Karen. Don't worry about it," Lauren shrugged.

"No, it's not. I thought you were going after Jake, and when he started ignoring me, well, I was jealous. But I shouldn't have taken it out on you," Karen said and shook her head. "You actually did me a favor, though. I realized what a player he is, and I finally moved on."

"I'm sorry." Lauren gave her a sympathetic look.

"No need to be sorry. I met someone online and he's great." Karen smiled and held out her hand. "So, we're good?"

"Yes, we're good," Lauren said and pulled her into a quick hug. "You can tell me all about your new guy at lunch next week."

"You betcha!" Karen said with a wink. She waved and sauntered back into her classroom.

"Jeesh! You grown-ups and all your love problems!" James declared. "I sure am glad I don't have to worry about all that."

Lauren tousled his hair and laughed. "Just wait. You'll be there soon enough."

"I hope not!" James said, walking along happily, swinging the bag.

Lauren's cell phone rang and she smiled recognizing Daniel's ringtone.

"Hey, how's my favorite teacher?" Daniel's voice came over the line. It sounded like he was in a great mood.

"I'm fantastic. We were just leaving. How was your day?"

"No complaints. Glad it's over. I'm looking forward to tonight." Daniel's tone was mischievous. "You'll be ready on time? I'm going to pick you up right at 7."

"Don't worry. I'll be ready," Lauren said. "Are you sure you won't tell me where we're going?"

"Quit trying to ruin the surprise. Trust me, you're going to love it."

"I trust you," she said sincerely.

"Okay, then I'll see you soon."

Once Lauren ended the call, James asked excitedly, "Was that Dad?"

"Yep."

"I know where he's taking you!" James said in a sing-song tone. "But I promised not to tell, so I won't."

"Good. I want to be surprised," Lauren said.

"Oh, you're going to be very surprised," James said, nodding his head dramatically.

As they walked out into the bright sunlight, Lauren smiled once again. She had a feeling she knew what the surprise was. Daniel had taken James on a "mystery mission" last weekend. Even though James promised not to say anything about the trip to the jewelry store with his dad, he couldn't resist giving his mom a little hint about the store being very sparkly. Daniel knew he ran the risk of the surprise being foiled by having James along to pick out the ring, but he didn't mind. He knew either way, Lauren would be extremely happy.

Chapter 52

One Year Later

Even though it was barely the beginning of March, signs of Spring were evident in the botanical gardens in South Austin. Brilliant roses in pink, red, and yellow hues were budding on the bushes that lined the winding path. Puffy white clouds dotted the azure sky, floating methodically over the sun, casting shadows across the lawn. The path led to a gazebo in the center of two ponds, lined with fairy shrub roses.

Katherine stood in front of the gazebo, holding a bouquet of lilies, tulips, and chrysanthemums. She looked at the people sitting apprehensively in the white, tulle-covered chairs lined in neat rows before them. Friends and family - her parents, Nathan and Lauren's mom, and Daniel's parents in the front row. She glanced over at Daniel, standing on the other side of the entrance to the gazebo, looking serious and a little nervous. Next to him stood Nathan, looking a little nervous as well, as they both peered down the aisle, the strains of Handel playing in the distance. Nathan glanced over and met Katherine's gaze. His look became tender and he smiled at her, then winked. She smiled back, feeling a warmth come over her.

Finally, Lauren appeared, looking beautiful in a silk sleeveless wedding gown with a scooped neckline and sequins on the embroidered bodice. She made her way down the aisle, her arm hooked through her father's. Mr. Montgomery had a smile on his face, his eyes beaming with pride. Katherine could see the moment Lauren's eyes met Daniel's as she grew closer to the gazebo. She saw tenderness, love, and appreciation in her best friend's gaze as she looked at Daniel, taking in the sight of him, so handsome in his light grey tuxedo.

Her father kissed her on the cheek then placed Lauren's hand into Daniel's, giving his soon-to-be son-in-law an approving nod. Pastor Sam, from Restoration Christian Center, began with reading from the book of Song of Solomon. "My beloved speaks and says to me: Arise, my love, my fair one, and come away; for now the winter is past, the rain is over and gone. The flowers appear on the earth; the time of singing has come, and the voice of the turtledove is heard in our land."

Lauren beamed at Daniel as she recognized the scripture that he had read to her a couple of weeks ago. He had told her it was how it felt when he had been reunited with her last Spring: As if a long barren winter had finally come to an end and everything was blossoming with the excitement of their new future together. It seemed as if everything was falling into place. Lauren's faith was growing every day; she went to church with Daniel on Sundays and a women's bible study on Tuesday night. She was still learning so much, but she felt secure knowing that no matter what, God would always love her. And James was over the moon about having both of his parents under the same roof. Even though he continually groaned about them kissing in front of him, he loved seeing his parents together and in love.

Daniel and Lauren shared their first kiss as husband and wife, then turned toward their friends and family and began to stroll down the aisle. Katherine hooked her arm through Nathan's and began to walk slowly down the aisle as well. Little Madison jumped up from her seat and followed behind her parents, throwing the remaining rose petals from her basket. James and Keenan joined the parade too, trying to catch the petals in the air.

The reception was held in the main ballroom. The guests sat at round tables covered in lavender linen, bouquets of white and lilac flowers in the center, surrounded by tiny tea light candles. Daniel stood up and began to clink his crystal champagne flute and the room fell to a hush.

"Nine years ago, I met a woman who immediately captured my attention. She was young and a little naïve, but intelligent, kind and warm. I knew right away that she had a big heart. I was young too, ready to take on the world and so focused on my career that I lost sight of how much she meant to me. I messed up and I lost her. But God had another plan for us. He brought us together again seven years later. Thankfully, I did a lot of growing up during our years apart. And I owe almost all of that to the Lord, who taught me how to be a real man. How to love myself so that I could give my whole heart to the woman that would become my wife. And not only did I reconnect with the love of my life, but I found out I had a son. At first I was shocked, but then I was amazed. Nothing could have prepared me for the way this young boy would change my life. Things were a little rocky in the beginning, but once Lauren finally decided to behave herself, things started to turn around." Daniel winked at Lauren and everyone laughed. "But seriously, I have seen the most amazing changes in her over the course of the past year. She's still the most beautiful lady in the world, but now she's confident and so full of love and joy, and I couldn't be more proud to call her my wife."

As everyone lifted their glasses in a toast and some dried a tear, the happy couple exchanged a tender kiss. After the wedding cake had been cut and enjoyed by all, Daniel and Lauren opened the dance floor with a slow waltz to John Legend's 'All of Me.' After Lauren danced with her father, the D.J. put on 'Marry You' by Bruno Mars and everyone danced until their feet ached. Including Nathan.

"Well, I guess your happily ever after came true," Katherine said to Lauren. They were in the bridal room of the Barton Creek Country Club. Lauren was changing out of her wedding gown into her send-off outfit - a chartreuse dress with a jewel neckline, cap sleeves, and a knee length flare skirt.

"I wouldn't have believed it if anyone would have suggested it a year ago," Lauren admitted as she slipped her feet back into the white satin wedge heels.

"I remember you telling me you wanted to take James and run away so that Daniel could never find you."

Lauren laughed. She was now so grateful that she'd run into Daniel at the park that day. She realized that it was Divine timing and there was no way she could deny that God definitely had a plan for them. "Daniel's right. I've grown up a lot since then."

"Yeah, me too," Katherine said wistfully, thinking about the events of the past year. She and Nathan had come a long way. They were still meeting with a couple's counselor from the church once a month. Their relationship wasn't the same as it had been. Although they still had issues to work through, many things were better; they were definitely doing a better job at communicating.

Nathan had finally completed the Johnson's house and he had agreed to make it a priority to come home in time for dinner at least three nights a week. He also agreed to reserve Sundays for church and family time. He was helping with the bedtime routine again and Madison and Keenan loved having their daddy spend more time with them.

In one of their counseling sessions Katherine had shared that she'd like to resume teaching again and Nathan was on board with that as well. Katherine applied at the elementary school where Madison attended and landed a position as a fifth grade English and Language Arts teacher. Keenan had begun kindergarten in the fall, so they were all at the same school together. Madison had completely recovered from her fall with no signs whatsoever of brain trauma. They all knew that it had been a miracle.

Katherine's faith had grown as well. She loved attending church services every week and she had begun volunteering in the children's ministry once a month. She would never forget Jonathan and the way his faith had opened her heart to search for something more. She had asked God and Nathan for forgiveness for the affair, and she had even forgiven herself. The hardest part was not being able to ask Jonathan for forgiveness.

She genuinely missed his friendship and she worried about him often; whether he was heart-broken, or angry and bitter toward her. She wondered if he had moved on and found someone else to love. But, she knew she needed to let it go. She had promised Nathan that she would delete his number from her phone and never contact him again

But God gave her a chance for closure one rainy day in February. Katherine still couldn't believe it happened on the exact anniversary of the date she had first sat at Jonathan's table at Tiramisu. She had been at the mall shopping for a gift for her mother's upcoming birthday.

She was walking down the main hallway of the mall, heading toward her mom's favorite cooking store. She was enjoying the leisurely walk, peering into the different stores, watching the other shoppers milling about. As she passed the jewelry store, she felt a sudden urge to go browse the watches. She thought that maybe she could begin getting ideas for a gift for Nathan for their upcoming anniversary.

She entered the store, glancing at some of the sparkling diamond and emerald earrings in the case, thinking to herself that it would be nice if Nathan surprised her with something special this year as well. As she was about to walk toward the sales clerk, she noticed that he was already occupied with a couple. A striking couple; a tall, well-built man with sandy brown hair and a woman with long, dark hair. Katherine turned her attention back towards the rows of two-toned Bulova watches, but she felt something stir in her. As she looked at the couple again, she suddenly realized that it was Jonathan. She was startled and was about to make a quick exit, but the dark-haired woman standing next to him turned around and she saw that it was Sylvia. The two women locked eyes for a moment, then Katherine turned on her heel and made haste back into the mall.

Katherine was walking briskly and had almost made it to the cooking store when she felt a tap on her shoulder. She jumped and turned around, expecting to see Jonathan, but it was Sylvia.

"Hey," Sylvia said, nervously looking over her shoulder back toward the jewelry store.

"Hi, Sylvia." Katherine nervously shifted from one foot to the other, readjusting her purse strap, glancing toward the jewelry store as well. "It's nice to see you again."

"Jonathan doesn't know I saw you. I told him that I saw someone from high school, and I wanted to run and say hi really quick."

Katherine just nodded her head and waited, curious why Sylvia chose to chase her down. "I know things didn't end very well for you and Jonathan. But I thought you should know that he and I are getting engaged. We're actually looking at rings right now."

Katherine did her best to hide her surprise. She knew that she didn't do a very good job when Sylvia said, "I know, it's fast. But after you broke his heart, I was there for him. As a friend at first. I mean we already had a connection, but I think when he met you it became kind of muddled for him. He really needed to know that he could trust again. I helped him sort through his feelings and he slowly recognized that it was possible to love again. It helped a lot that we both shared the same faith."

Katherine was taken aback at how much Sylvia's words stung. She had the feeling that she was competing with Sylvia back then, but now she realized just how right she'd been. Jonathan and Sylvia already had a history. They shared friendship, their law courses and the common bond of a relationship with Jesus. She knew that Jonathan's faith meant a lot to him. It made perfect sense that he'd end up with Sylvia, but it still hurt a little.

"I just wish I could tell Jonathan how sorry I am. I really did care